The 90s Club & the Whispering Statue

Eileen Haavik McIntire

Amanita Books
Imprint of Summit Crossroads Press
Columbia, Maryland

The 90s Club & the Whispering Statue

LCCN: 20139097430

ISBN 978-0-9834049-7-2

Editors: Holly Berardi, Susan Branting

Cover Design: Six Penny Graphics

Publisher's Cataloging-in-Publication

McIntire, Eileen Haavik.
    The 90s club and the Whispering Statue / Eileen Haavik
McIntire.
      p. cm.
      ISBN 978-0-9834049-7-2

    1. Older people--Fiction. 2. Retirement communities
--Fiction. 3. Crime--Fiction. 4. Detective and mystery
stories.   I. Title. II. Title: Nineties club and the
whispering statue.

PS3613.C5422012   813'.6

Acknowledgments

At 95, singer and dancer Kitty Carlisle took her one-woman cabaret show to Olney Theater Center outside Washington, D.C., and brought the house down. Who says you have to be young to make an impact?

Despite the growing number of productive, active elderly people, most of us resist the idea of growing old because we are besieged by the common stereotypes of aging—weakness, infirmity, loss of faculties, etc. As we age, we risk accepting these stereotypes as models and conforming to them because they provide an excuse for avoiding exercise and good health habits. Nancy and her friends in the 90s Club set a different example.

Nancy is based on a woman I met some years ago at a pool party. She was slim and attractive, and the only one in the pool swimming laps. She was 91 years old.

Another influence was a grandmotherly private investigator who spoke at a meeting I attended. She had been an investigative reporter for the *Miami Herald* before becoming a private eye.

She looked like a matronly housewife, and I'm sure could act most dithery. She used that image in her work. She sometimes tracked down suspects by walking door to door in a neighborhood, carrying a leash, and asking if anyone had seen her lost dog. People were always willing to help, sometimes inviting her in for a cup of coffee and a chat. She learned a lot about the neighborhood—and often found the culprit—that way.

Nancy and the 90s Club live at upscale Whisperwood Retirement Village in central West Virginia. Like many such retirement communities, Whisperwood resembles a cruise ship, offering services and amenities such as a gym, pool, tennis court, dining room, and pub in a setting that is safe and secure—most of the time (see *The 90s Club and the Hidden Staircase*).

But facilities for the elderly take many forms. In this mystery novel, the 90s Club travels to a retirement cooperative in Fort Lauderdale. It is similar to a place I once knew as I scraped together a living by cleaning apartments while living on a boat.

I am blessed with supportive and loving family and friends. Many thanks to my husband Roger McIntire who always encourages me and provides welcome comments on the characters and plot. Frank Hazzard, Deputy Chief/Shift Commander, Baltimore City Fire Department, provided details about the protocol for responding to a 911 medical emergency. I also owe many thanks to my fellow writers in the White Oak Writers, the Columbia Fiction Critique group, and the Maryland Writers' Association. Mary Doyle, Gary McCann, Susan M. Branting and Holly Berardi contributed hours of editing.

This is a work of fiction and any resemblance to a particular place or person is entirely coincidental. Any mistakes are entirely my own.

Eileen Haavik McIntire

Chapter 1

Jessica sat cross-legged on top of the trawler cabin, eyes closed, listening to the frogs and fish splashes in Fort Lauderdale's New River. The trawler was tied between a houseboat and a small powerboat at a dock that ran alongside the river. Secure in this serenity, Jessica relaxed, tossed her long, blonde hair, and leaned back on her elbows.

She was glad the trip down the waterway was over. It took longer than she'd expected, considering she could have driven from Annapolis to Fort Lauderdale in two days. She'd felt bored most of the time and tense when she was left to steer the boat, keeping it in the channel and avoiding crab pots that could snarl the propellers. Tomorrow she'd be back home, seeking another adventure.

The boat rocked, and Jessica looked up as the boat's captain, Ray Slocum, tossed a couple of cushions on the cabin top and sat down next to her. The white T-shirts and navy shorts they wore were the uniform for this boat's crew. She offered him the tube of sunscreen she was using, but he shook his head. She frowned at his deeply tanned face. He was only ten years older than her twenty-two years, but with that kind of sun damage, he'd age fast.

"How's Brian?" she asked, knowing he'd just called his ex-wife to chat with their five-year-old son. Touching how close he was to the boy. She'd heard a lot about him on this trip.

"He drew a picture of a boat to give me when I get home." Ray grinned. "What a kid."

"Cool." She glanced at him, thinking of his patience and kindness. He was a lively companion, and she'd enjoyed trekking into the waterway towns with him, but there was no chemistry at all between them.

She looked back at the shallow inlet separating this property from the neighbor's. The dense mangroves on each side of the river made it seem jungle-like, unpopulated, and remote. From her perch, Jessica could see over the mangroves to the next dock and also part of the house behind it. That house was a fresh-painted pink and seemed larger and in better condition than the decrepit dwelling housing the old codger who rented them this dock space. His place was concrete block painted a faded green and stained with black streaks of mildew. The green matched the patches of lawn that spread from the dock to the house.

She sighed, wishing they'd stayed at one of the fancy marinas on the waterway, but Ray liked to save money. Staying here had its drawbacks, though. This narrow stretch of river amplified the rumble and growl of boat traffic and the stink of diesel from the next dock. She glanced at Ray, who enjoyed listening to the boats and speculating about them.

He sat up to watch a low-lying motorboat ease out of the inlet and turn down towards a bend in the river. "Cigarette boat," he said. "The kind drug-runners use. I'd sure like to get my hands on one. Make it to the Bahamas in an hour, I'd bet."

"Really?" With more interest, Jessica studied the expensive-looking speed boats that came and went. They seemed to be all deck. Not much space for passengers. "Why cigarette boat?"

"Built to smuggle cigarettes into Canada to avoid taxes. Smugglers like 'em 'cause they're fast, low, and hard to detect by radar."

"Cool. I'd think, like, the police would be interested in that place," Jessica said, nodding toward the inlet and the pink house on the other side.

Ray leaned back against the cushion and yawned. "Those boats are pretty common down here." He studied the other dock. "Anyway, there's a dive boat there too. It's probably just another place that rents dock space."

Jessica dug the binoculars out of a cubby hole, and they traded them back and forth as they watched the boats at the other dock come and go, steered by dark young men wearing wrap-around sunglasses, white T-shirts, and trim bathing suits or cut-off jeans. An assortment of cars, partly hidden by the mangroves, also came and went. The gas and diesel fumes drifting their way were giving Jessica a headache.

"Should we alert the police?" she asked irritably. Wasn't anyone else annoyed by the noise?

Ray shook his head. "Stay out of it. You don't want to get mixed up in that."

She trained the binoculars on the house. This time a group of men came into view. One of them wore a police uniform. "Something's going on over there," she said.

An older man wearing a guayabera and smoking a cigar, looked directly at her, then motioned to the man in jeans and T-shirt at his side and nodded her way. The man in jeans held a rifle. Jessica gripped the binoculars. A rifle? The man raised it and pointed it at her. Jessica gasped and slid off the cabin top into the cockpit. She reached up and tugged at Ray's arm as she kept her head down.

"What?" asked Ray, yawning as he sat up.

She pulled at him. "Get down!" she whispered. "He saw us."

Ray looked over at the other house. Jessica heard the shot and watched in horror as a round red hole burst between Ray's eyes.

***

Come to Fort Lauderdale!

Whether it's excitement you seek or relaxation on the beach, Fort Lauderdale offers you the vacation of your dreams. Its world-famous five-star beach, rich cultural history, scenic waterways, and international business center—all contribute to a vibrant and diverse community. Come to Fort Lauderdale for the good life!

"The Beaches at Fort Lauderdale" Newsletter

Chapter 2

The shrill ring of the phone jarred Nancy awake in her chair. The book she'd been reading fell to the floor. She glanced at the old clock on the credenza. Ten p.m. Too late for a social call. Had a friend died? Alone at ninety years old, she couldn't think of any emergency someone would call her about. Certainly no one here at Whisperwood Retirement Village would phone her at such an hour. She pulled the thick wool robe around her and picked up the phone.

"Nancy? Nancy, is that you?" A male voice sounded breathless and urgent.

Nancy tried to identify it. "This is Nancy Dickenson."

"Thank God."

Nancy heard a huge sigh.

"Sorry. Ou-ou-out of breath. R-R-Ran home after it happened."

That stuttering—he sounded terrified. Who was he? Why was he calling her? Surely he didn't want her help. She'd retired from the private investigation business thirty years ago.

"Nancy, this is P-P-Peter Stamboul."

Peter Stamboul. Of course. At once a flood of warm memories rushed through her thoughts.

"Sorry. J-J-Just a minute. Gotta sit down."

Nancy waited, thinking of the last time she'd seen Peter. At Bill's funeral, was it four years ago? He'd been such a support, taking over all the little things that needed to be done and helping her get through those dark days.

"Remember me? I need your help."

"Of course I do, Peter." At one time, she'd thought she was in love with him, but nothing came of that. She had wondered why, but she'd married her high school sweetheart after all. Then he died. Peter lived abroad at the time, and she met Bill. How sad that she hadn't seen Peter since Bill passed away. Her own grief had swallowed her, and she'd let old friendships lapse. Sadness dropped onto her shoulders. Nancy shook herself awake from such sentimental memories. Peter was in trouble. "What's wrong?"

"Just a minute."

Nancy heard him catch his breath. "I'm a little better now. Gotta get my head together. You know I retired and moved to Fort Lauderdale? Needed the sunshine."

Nancy glanced at her own dark windows. The bleakness of the West Virginia winter was closing in on Whisperwood, adding to the depression that she fought every day. Thank goodness she was so busy and had so many friends at Whisperwood that most of the time she could smile and laugh along with everyone else.

After another long pause, Peter said, "Sorry. Had to calm down. I need your help."

"Of course." Nancy sat up. *He was afraid.* "What can I do?"

"I live in a retirement condo near downtown Fort Lauderdale." She heard the tremor in his voice. "Someone here is trying to k-k-kill me."

Nancy gripped the phone. "All right," she said as she pushed herself out of the armchair, stretched her legs to get the kinks out, and stepped over to the desk. "Tell me what's been happening." She sat down, picked up a pen, and opened a notebook.

"I didn't believe it at first," said Peter. "Little accidents kept happening to me. A flowerpot fell off a wall and almost hit me in the head, then a car tried to run me down at a crosswalk." Nancy heard him take another deep breath.

"Those could have been coincidences, Peter," she said. "Really just accidents."

"Sure. But tonight I got s-s-shot at."

"Someone shot at you?"

"Can't believe it myself. Just walking my dogs. A car drove up beside me and stopped. Some man I never saw before aimed a gun at me and shot it. He almost got me, Nancy. The dogs jumped toward the car barking. Rattled him, I think. He barely missed me then the car sped off." He paused. "That's three, Nancy. That was deliberate. No mistake."

"Three incidents. Any one of them could have killed you." Nancy kept her voice slow and calm to give Peter more time to collect himself.

"I ran home and called the police, then I called you." He hesitated as if afraid of the next thought. "What's the fourth one going to be? Will that one hit the bull's eye?" His laugh sounded grim. "Me, I mean."

"I see." Nancy scribbled notes on the pad. "Could it have been a random drive-by?"

"Could have been, but I don't think so."

"What did the police do?"

Anger crept into his voice. "They're sending around someone to fill out a report. Fat lot of good that'll do. I need you, Nancy. You're not going to treat me like a crazy old fart." He stopped. Nancy heard him take a few breaths. He was still trying to calm down. "I need you to help me find out who is trying to kill me."

Nancy's ears buzzed with the effort to reject his words. She was ninety years old. Retired. Last summer she almost lost what remained of her life to murderers here at Whisperwood. Could she track down another murderer? At her age? Even for Peter? Nancy pursed her lips. Peter was imaginative, but he wouldn't make up a story like this. She wanted to help him, but. . . . "No evidence? No witnesses?"

"Of course not. No one saw anything. No one ever sees anything." The anger had taken over. "Nancy, those frickin' idiots patronized me. Called me an old man." He paused. "Which I am not."

Nancy recognized the feeling. He was every bit as old as she was. The 90s Club, that's what they were, but they were not to be discounted. No indeed.

"Asked me what meds I was taking." His voice rose. "That's why I need you, Nancy. "It's too easy to dismiss all these attempts as accidents or. . .or fantasies."

Nancy tapped the pen on her cheek. What could she do that the police couldn't? That is, if he needed police help at all. She thought of Beth Ann Crowley, who had lived here at Whisperwood on the second floor. Beth Ann started insisting that someone was out to kill her. Her family soon moved her to the Assisted Living Unit and psychiatric care.

Peter sounded sane and frightened. "Any family or friends down there who could vouch for you?" she asked.

"A lot of acquaintances," Peter said, "but you know my family has scattered. No close relatives here or anywhere."

Nancy chewed her lip. Yes, she understood what that was like. She still had her close friend Louise, but most of her other friends and family were gone, dwindled over the years. And, like Peter, she had no children to come to the rescue.

This is Peter, and he thinks his life is in danger. I may be the only support he has. Even if he's just imagining all this, he needs my help. Am I up to providing it? Would I be useful? Self-doubt filled her thoughts.

Almost everyone in the outside world, even here at Whisperwood, would say she couldn't do anything helpful for Peter, and they'd use the most hurtful words, "You are too old." If someone was actually trying to kill Peter, it was dangerous stuff. If she tried to help and failed, they might both lose their lives. Her stomach hurt at the decision ahead of her.

She perused her calendar. She was so busy here. The bridge tournament was coming up, and her partner was counting on her. And Louise's surprise birthday celebration. And she'd volunteered to help at the crafts fair. She'd disappoint a lot of people. On the other hand, she knew how easy it was for the young and the authorities to dismiss an older person's fears and concerns. Every day despite the attitudes and examples around her, she fought the pervasive invitation to play the "getting old" game. She looked down at her trim, athletic figure. *I'm not to be discounted.*

"Who do you think is after you?" she asked.

Peter hesitated. "I don't know. You were always the pro. You pick up on things that I miss."

"Used to be a pro. Thirty years ago." Nancy caught a glimpse of her white curly hair and *experienced* face in the mirror. She looked ninety, all right, even if she found that hard to believe. She sat up straighter.

His voice dropped to a whisper. "Something funny's going on here, Nancy. I'll pay for your airline tickets. You're a puzzle solver, and this is a big one. Can you come right away?"

She tapped the pen on the desk. She'd miss the bridge tournament, but Louise's party was four weeks away. She would be back before then. May Brooks could handle the planning and the invitations just fine—prefer it, probably. Nancy heard sleet outside pattering against her windows. Fort Lauderdale. Warm, sunny days. "I'm not sure how helpful I'll be. . ."

"At least you'll listen to me. You'll know I'm not lying or gaga."

Nancy took a deep breath, feeling as if she were being pushed toward a precipice yet unable to stop herself. "All right," she said slowly, perusing her calendar. "I can come down day after tomorrow and stay for maybe three weeks." She gazed at the blackness outside her windows. "We'll have to work fast."

Relief flooded Peter's voice. "You can't come too soon, I'll meet you at the airport. We can catch up on old times. We've never worked together, but I've always wanted to see you detect."

"Wait a minute. The first thing you have to do is get away from there. Leave. Find someplace safe." Nancy's voice was stern. "And don't tell anyone where you're going."

"I'm not going to let them run me out of my home."

"Yes, you are. Immediately." Nancy waited for Peter's reply. He could be as stubborn as a lid on a frozen honey jar. "I mean it, Peter. You're not safe there. And another thing, I'd like to bring my friend Louise." Louise was a good back-up and support. They worked well together. And she was feisty. She'd enjoy the challenge.

"Sure. Sure. Plenty of room." He hesitated, then added, "It might be better if you didn't use your real name."

"Hardly anyone recognizes me anymore," Nancy said, but she remembered her arrival at Whisperwood. People she'd never met before had known of her career as a private detective. It worried them. "I'll just use the name Davis, Nancy Davis. Used it before. Not a problem."

"Good. Don't want to tip anyone off and maybe make you a target too."

Yes. Despite the danger, she had to help Peter. Her life had again become precious to her, but in this case, she could use age as a defense. "Don't worry," she told Peter. "Louise and I will act our most doddering."

"I would have protection for us." He hesitated. "Do you like dogs?"

"Dogs?"

"I have two. Little guys. They won't be any trouble, Nancy. And they're great watchdogs. Around my apartment, that is. Not too good outside."

Nancy glanced at her bedroom where she could see her huge, fawn-colored cat Malone glaring at her from the pillows. He had a difficult personality, not at all cuddly. Might be nice to be around normal pets for a change. "I like dogs," she said.

"Good. You'll get a kick out of my two guys."

"You'll have to tell me everything you know about what's been happening."

"Of course."

"And get out of there."

Nancy hung up the phone, knowing she had a recalcitrant client. Peter wouldn't leave his apartment until he was carried out. Nancy felt her stomach turn. The enormity of what she had just done hit her. What had she gotten herself into?

***

Luxury Retirement Condos for Rent and Sale
Make your Florida dream come true. Riverside Acres on Fort Lauderdale's scenic New River offers a beautifully landscaped gated community for your retirement years. Minutes away from broad sandy beaches on the Atlantic Ocean, world-famous Las Olas Boulevard, and award-winning museums. Luxury condos available now!

Magazine Ad for Riverside Acres

Chapter 3

Nancy called her friend Louise the next morning. Louise chuckled as she heard Nancy explain the Florida invitation, but then Nancy told her about the threats to Peter's life.

"What do you think, Nancy?" Louise asked. "Is he on the level or is he a nut case? How long have you known him?"

Nancy hesitated. "A long time, Louise, but I haven't seen him since Bill died."

"Hmmm."

"I've got to help him," said Nancy. "Whatever the case." That's what a friend did. She hoped she was still up to doing a good job. The thought she might fail scared her. She felt her stomach twinge.

"Of course," Louise said enthusiastically. "I'm always willing to help. Might even be dangerous." She chuckled.

Nancy heard the glee. She felt a surge of relief. She could always count on Louise.

"It's another case for the 90s Club," Louise added.

Nancy smiled. She, Louise, and their friend, George Burroughs, had formed the 90s Club at Whisperwood last year when they had all turned ninety. Their efforts through the club had saved Whisperwood last summer but almost cost them their lives. Nancy shivered, remembering the terror and the friends who'd been murdered. She never wanted to go through that again. With a sigh, she thought of Peter. Unless necessary.

"A bunch of people here are planning a surprise birthday party for me in four weeks," Louise added.

Nancy laughed. "You know about that? Can't keep a secret from you, can we?"

"Not when people like that dumb-ass Margie O'Shaughnessy call up and apologize for not being able to come," snorted Louise.

Nancy flicked a cat hair off her khaki slacks. Didn't people here know what "surprise" meant? "We'll be back in plenty of time for your party. I don't want to leave Whisperwood right now either, but Peter sounded terrified. He wants us down there as soon as we can get there."

"I'm thrilled to get such an invitation, even if it might be dangerous," said Louise, then paused. "Shit, especially if it might be dangerous. This place is hell to live in right now with all the renovations. I'll be glad to get outta here. I'll look through my closet and be packed in no time."

Nancy hung up the phone and went online to make airline reservations. After a few more calls, canceling appointments and other obligations, she called Fitz, her neighbor down the hall. "Can you take Malone while I'm out of town?" she asked. She saw the cat prick up his ears when he heard his name. He narrowed his eyes suspiciously at Nancy.

Fitz laughed. "If he'll take me, luv. He's choosy, don't you know, but he saved our lives, so I'll be glad to keep him out of a boarding cattery. Feed him mackerel, too."

"He loves mackerel." Nancy smiled at Malone and threw him an air kiss. He turned his back and began licking under his tail.

"Just let me know when to pick him up. He'll be company, Nancy," Fitz said. "Maybe I can teach him some manners." He laughed and Nancy did too, but did Fitz really know what he was in for? Dear Fitz. He was such a support.

Once those chores were done, Nancy walked over to her own closet. She was sorting through her slacks and polo shirts when she bent her head to the front door and listened. Did she hear a knock? The sound could have been part of all the hammering going on in the basement.

Malone lifted his furry head, sniffed the air, and stalked into the bedroom, pausing at the door to look back at Nancy. The hammering made him edgy too, and he was inclined to hide when visitors dropped by. For that, Nancy was grateful. She eyed his erect body and upright tail. What a character.

The hammering stopped, and she heard a soft knock, so soft she wasn't sure it was at her door, but only a few people lived down her end of the hall since the renovations had begun.

She walked to the door, paused to run a hand through her wavy hair, smooth her khaki slacks, and pull down her black turtleneck. She heard the knock again and opened the door.

Outside stood a timorous, large-eyed woman Nancy sometimes met in the halls and dining room. Amelia Cantwell. Nancy's eyes flicked from the woman's wiry gray hair, tightly curled in an old woman's permanent, to the mousy brown dress she wore as if to melt into her surroundings.

Nancy smiled and said, "Hello, Amelia. I wasn't sure I heard the knock. Won't you come in?"

The woman answered the smile. "Thank you, Nancy. She walked in, examining Nancy with a question in her eyes. "I'm surprised you remember my name. We've only eaten dinner together a few times."

"Of course I remember you." Nancy gestured to the sofa, moved the piles of paper heaped on it, and hurriedly transferred an armload of magazines to the table. She watched Amelia glance around the apartment, doubt growing on her face as she saw the stacks of newspapers, magazines, and papers, the dust, and the vase of dead flowers Nancy had forgotten to throw away. Nancy shrugged. She'd never learned to pay attention to such things.

She walked toward the kitchen. "Tea? Coffee?"

"No, thank you. I don't want to be any trouble." Amelia sat tentatively on the edge of the sofa and folded her hands on top of the black purse that rested in her lap.

"No trouble," Nancy said. "I always find tea relaxing, don't you?"

"Yes, all right." Amelia's voice quavered.

Nancy dropped teabags in two cups filled with water, heated them in the microwave, and served them on a tray with the sugar bowl. Nancy smiled at Amelia. "Now, what can I do for you?"

Amelia picked up a cup with trembling hands. Nancy watched the tea splash from side to side in the cup. What could have upset Amelia so much?

Amelia set the cup back down on the tray and twisted her hands in her lap. "It's about my granddaughter, Jessica. I have no idea what to do, and you used to be a detective. . . ." She hesitated and glanced down at her hands. "I'm so embarrassed to be coming to you like this, but I ran into Louise in the hall, and she told me about your trip. I came right over to talk to you."

Nancy gazed at Amelia with growing interest. Where could this be heading?

"We all know about your career as a private investigator. You saved our lives and our retirement village for us last summer."

"It was the 90s Club, you know," Nancy said, "not just me."

Amelia took a deep breath and then cleared her throat as if hesitant to begin. Her eyes darted around the room.

"Tell me what's wrong," Nancy said.

Amelia's body tensed, and she learned toward Nancy. "Louise

told me that you two are going to Fort Lauderdale for a couple of weeks."

Nancy nodded. "That's right. I need to get away from the hammering and all the chaos here." That was the story they had agreed upon and what Peter was telling everyone at his condo.

"I am terribly worried about Jessica." Tears sprang into Amelia's eyes. "She's impulsive, you know. Just out of college."

Nancy remembered meeting Jessica several times in the dining room. Blonde, blue-eyed, attractive young woman. They had even shared the same table once. Jessica's intelligence and open curiosity had caught Nancy's attention.

She was working in Washington, D.C." Amelia took a breath. "Temporary work until she found a good job, but she met a young man there through a friend. I hope it wasn't an online dating service." Her mouth twisted in distaste. "We don't know a thing about him."

"I can see why you're worried. She's quite young."

Amelia pulled a tissue from a box on the end table and dabbed at her eyes. "This man convinced her to quit her job and take off on a boat. The two of them. Can you imagine?"

Nancy smiled. Yes, she could imagine. It's just the kind of adventure that would have appealed to her in her youth, but of course, not alone with a young man, let alone a stranger. "And they headed for Fort Lauderdale?"

"The last I heard from her, she had reached Fort Lauderdale. That was a week ago. I tried calling her cell phone and left messages, but she hasn't called back. I'm worried sick."

"Have you contacted the police?"

"We did, and they contacted the Coast Guard. They traced the boat to Fort Lauderdale but haven't located where it went from there. We're all terribly worried, but we're hoping she's just having fun and forgot to call us."

"What about her friends? Has anyone contacted them?"

"Yes, of course. Her mother talked with Jessica's roommates in Washington and her friends at home. One of them knew the boat captain. She'd gone to school with him. They were long-time friends." Amelia dabbed at her eyes with the tissue. "She said he was a nice man."

"So he has a boat and went to Florida. What's the name of the boat?" Nancy asked. "What kind of boat?"

Amelia reached into her purse and brought out a slip of paper. "The name is the *Bonny Scot*," her voice quavered. "Jessica said it was a trawler, whatever that is."

"Sturdy powerboat. Maybe a fishing boat. Not a sailboat." Nancy took the paper. "And the man's name?"

"Ray Slocum." Amelia fluttered her hands. "And it's not his. He takes boats up and down the coast for the owners, who want their boat to be in Florida in the winter and up north someplace in the summer. That's his job." Again Amelia's eyes teared up. She straightened her back as if it hurt. "I hate to come to you with such a problem."

Nancy frowned. She could see how upset Amelia was. "I understand why you're worried."

"Since you'll be in Fort Lauderdale anyway," Amelia said, "maybe you could watch for her." She fumbled in the purse and pulled out several snapshots. "I've got some recent pictures. Her full name is Jessica Amelia Cantwell." She shuffled through the photos, a fond smile on her face, before she handed them to Nancy.

Nancy studied the eager young face, smiling and pretty. A young girl who should have a long life ahead of her. "Does she have a driver's license? Passport?"

"Driver's license, yes." Amelia tapped her lips. "She must have a passport. She went to Europe the summer after she graduated."

"What type of work would she look for?"

Amelia shrugged. "She was some kind of administrative assistant in D.C. All kinds of computer skills. I'm hoping she'll come right back home. I don't know what she'll do in Fort Lauderdale." She shook her head. "Waitress maybe? She did that in college. "

Nancy flipped through the snapshots. "I'll be happy to do what I can," she said, "but as a friend. I'm not a detective any more. Probably she is just having a good time and hasn't thought about how worried you must be."

"She's usually so thoughtful." Amelia seemed to shrivel as Nancy watched. "I'd appreciate it if you'd just check around for her. That's all I ask. I hate to impose, and I can pay you for your trouble."

"May I keep these photos for the time being?"

Amelia stood, relief on her face. "That's why I brought them. Maybe they'll help."

Nancy saw Amelia to the door and watched her totter down the hall with one hand on the rail. It was January, so Jessica wouldn't get caught up in spring break shenanigans, if kids still went to Fort Lauderdale for spring break. She'd heard they went to Cancun now. Probably Jessica was waitressing or had some kind of temp job. Even so, Fort Lauderdale was just a short and tempting jaunt across the Gulf Stream to the Bahamas.

Maybe Jessica was simply having a good time, but Nancy had read a lot of articles about drug trafficking and piracy in the Bahamas, the Caribbean, and South Florida. A lot could happen to a young girl alone in a strange town. Rape, assault, murder, slavery, drugs—a hundred possibilities flooded her mind, none of them good. Amelia feared the worst, and, years of detective work behind her, so did Nancy.

She gazed out the kitchen window as she washed the tea cups. Peter and Amelia both asked for her help. A year ago she was so depressed and alone she would have refused. But now, with the 90s Club as backup, she felt faint stirrings of excitement countering the fear of failure. Travel and two puzzles to solve. This was going to be interesting.

***

Boaters Beware

Thieves target boaters living in the Sunshine State more than anywhere else in the U.S., reports the National Insurance Crime Board. The NICB recommends that boaters lock and secure their boat to the dock with a steel cable, remove expensive equipment when not in use, chain and lock detachable motors to the boat, never leave title or registration papers in the craft, and install an ignition system kill switch to prevent thieves from starting the engine when the boat is docked.

Notice Approved by Riverside Acres Management

Chapter 4

"How will you start looking for that girl?" Louise asked Nancy as they pulled their suitcases through the Fort Lauderdale airport. Louise carried a cane and wore a khaki vest of multiple pockets that flapped as she walked—she refused to carry a purse. The back was emblazoned with faded environmental slogans from *Save the Whales* to *Give a Hoot, Don't Pollute*. Her hair hung down in a single braid that swung behind her as she walked.

"One step at a time," Nancy said, pushing aside the fear and doubt to marvel at her escape from the drab winter scenery around Whisperwood. Back in West Virginia, snow and ice covered the ground, but here she was, stepping out of an air-conditioned terminal into a blistering afternoon sun. Despite her light cotton slacks and white polo shirt, the heat and humidity almost knocked her to the pavement. She stopped to fish sunglasses out of her purse.

"Peter said he'd pick us up, but our plane is so early. . ."

They stood at the curb. Nancy pulled out her cell phone and tapped his number. She hoped he'd listened to her and moved away from his apartment. "Peter? We've arrived." She listened, frowning, to Peter's weak and garbled voice. She glanced at Louise.

"What is it?" Louise asked as Nancy put the phone away.

Nancy turned to Louise. "Something's wrong. Peter sounded sick. We need a cab."

A taxi rolled up, and they slid onto the backseat as the driver threw their bags into the trunk. Nancy dug through her purse, found a note with Peter's address, and gave it to the driver.

Nancy stared out the window as the cab sped along. Despite her advice, Peter had stayed in his apartment, and now what had happened to him? From what he said, it was most likely a stomach ache, but maybe he was downplaying how bad it was. Naturally he wouldn't want to drive to the airport feeling sick, but why was he sick? What had happened? Was she already too late? Defeated before she'd even started?

"I hope he's all right," Nancy said. "I hope he was just imagining those threats—and just ate something that disagreed with him. Whatever is going on, I'm looking forward to seeing him again, catching up on old times." She hoped a miracle had wiped away Peter's fears and all was well except for a simple stomach ache.

Louise glanced at the cab driver and spoke softly as she stared out the window. "Could have been fluke accidents. Except for the shot, of course." Louise looked at Nancy. "Maybe an unrelated incident."

"Whatever it is, I hope we can provide whatever help he needs," Nancy said. "He's not one for sitting still, and from what he told me about his life at Riverside Acres. . . ." She smiled at Louise as she quoted the slogan, "'Luxury apartments for the 55 plus,' he keeps busy."

Louise sat back and stretched her arms. "Didn't take me long to decide to come with you." She smiled. "Danger or no danger."

Nancy followed the cab's route on a map of Fort Lauderdale, hoping to orient herself. They drove toward the tall buildings of downtown, then took a couple of turns that led them down Las Olas Boulevard, which appeared to be a street of pricey shops and restaurants. They turned right onto a tree-shaded street that wound along a river. The cab cruised down a couple of blocks, slowed, entered a private drive, and approached a gate and guard house.

Louise nudged Nancy and nodded at the sign on a pillar beside the gate. "Riverside Acres" was spelled out in large, gothic letters. The cab driver stopped at the guard house and looked back at Nancy. "Who we gonna see here?" He nodded at the gate guard.

"Peter Stamboul."

The guard called Peter before admitting them, then they rode down a curving driveway lined with tall and stately royal palms on a lawn so exuberant and green it would seem artificial in West Virginia. The cab halted in front of a three-story, peach-colored building. Hibiscus shrubs sporting large red flowers flanked the entranceway.

"Nice landscaping," said Louise, studying the shrubs along the building. "Don't know Florida plants. I hope they're all native species."

Nancy glanced at her. Louise the Activist was already looking for another environmental battle.

Nancy's eyes swept across the building. An open but covered walkway with a waist-high balustrade on the outside edge ran the length of each story in front of the apartments. Potted plants hung from the outside of the balustrade at frequent intervals. Did one of those planters fall on Peter? They looked very heavy. Lethal, in fact.

She put that idea out of her mind. Just a few hours ago, she had left grim and institutional Whisperwood with its six stories and all-white façade in winter-bleak West Virginia. The bright colors now around her lifted her heart. Would she ever want to go back to Whisperwood after this?

Louise and Nancy trundled their suitcases up the elevator to the third floor and then down the open walkway to Peter's apartment, No. 311. Nancy looked over the balustrade down to the lawn below before ringing the doorbell. Then she heard dogs barking as if this was their best amusement of the day. Watchdogs indeed. For a moment, misgivings surfaced. What if someone was trying to kill Peter? What if she failed? A twinge of fear raced down her back. She ignored it. She was here now. The only way to go was forward.

Perhaps the dogs were calling for help. The door opened, and a short, gaunt man peered out at them. He held his stomach and his eyes looked bleary, but when he saw Nancy, he pulled her in with a hug. "Thank goodness you're here," he said.

Nancy could feel his shivering. He seemed to be hanging on to her, and his heart was racing. His blue-and-pink flowered Hawaiian shirt hung limply on his body and his white slacks were wrinkled as if they'd lain in the bottom of his closet. A gold ring hung from his left ear.

Louise followed them into the apartment.

Behind Peter, two furry brown faces dripping slobber eyed Nancy and Louise and growled. He turned to the dogs. "Hush, hush. These are friends." The knee-high dogs slunk to the floor and whined but watched Nancy and Louise with wary dark eyes.

Nancy had never seen dogs that ugly. She frowned at the slobber dripping from their mouths under the snub noses. Surely they weren't bred that way. She glanced at Peter.

"What are they?" asked Louise, reaching down to let them sniff her hand.

Peter shook his head. "They're muts, rescues. Maybe part Pekingese. I'd guess part Newfoundland because of the slobber. Not the size, though." He managed a weak laugh. "No one else would take them, but they're nice dogs. You'll like them."

He bent over and clutched his stomach and gasped before turning and staggering down the hall. Nancy heard a door slam and then the sound of retching.

She stared after him. "What on earth…?" Did he need help?

Should she check on him? She glanced at Louise who gazed down the hall toward the bathroom.

Peter emerged, leaning against the door. "Call an ambulance, Nancy."

"You watch him. I'll call," Louise snapped and stepped to the phone, but shied away as a string of small, white, Christmas tree bulbs switched on when she crossed the living room. She halted with a start, and her eyes traveled the length of the cord. She took another look at the lights, picked up the phone, and dialed 9-1-1.

Nancy rushed to Peter's side and helped him to the sofa. She sat beside him, patting his hand. She felt his forehead for fever. It was beaded in sweat but didn't seem hot. "What can I do to help?"

He groaned but managed a weak smile. "I look at you and see halos. You're an angel, Nancy," he gasped. "I need a doctor. I think…I think I've been poisoned."

"Poisoned!" Nancy's eyes examined him swiftly from head to toe. Was this another attempt to kill him? Upset stomach. Vomiting. Racing heart. Could be poison.

Peter suddenly bent over, clutching his stomach. "Are they coming?"

Louise flung down the phone. "They're on their way." She leaned on her cane as she tottered to the door.

"I tell you, someone is after me. I need you. . ." Again he gasped.

"Another accident?" Nancy asked. It could simply be a case of food poisoning. But then the other attempts had seemed like accidents, too. Except for the gunshot, of course. If he was poisoned, the doctors would find out. She could feel Peter's fear and fought her own. She had to be strong for Peter.

Peter groaned again, clutching his stomach as he leaned over and threw up on the floor. The dogs crept forward to sniff the vomit. Nancy squeezed Peter's hand before herding the dogs into a bedroom and closing the door on their sad little faces.

"I'm so sorry," said Peter. "Couldn't help it. I feel terrible."

"That's all right," soothed Nancy. "We'll take care of it." He looked terrible too, but Nancy could think of nothing she could do to help.

"I'll go down and direct the paramedics," Louise said. She stepped out the door.

Peter sank back against the cushions. "Oscar and Rupert," he said, his voice slurred. "Take good care of them, Nancy."

He spoke with difficulty, but reached into his pocket and pulled out a ring of keys. "House and car."

She pocketed them. His eyes seemed yellowish, almost green. That was a sign of something but what? Whatever it was lurked in the back of her mind.

She took his hand. "You're going to be fine." She watched his haggard face and wished the ambulance would hurry. He needed to be in a hospital. She hoped he'd get there in time.

Several minutes later, she heard the ambulance swing into the drive, then, faintly from the entrance, Louise's excited voice directing the paramedics. Nancy squeezed Peter's hand and ran to the door, beckoning the paramedics toward her as they trotted from the elevator. Louise tottered along behind them.

"What's the problem here?" asked one.

Nancy motioned to Peter on the couch. The other paramedic was already checking Peter's pulse and body signs. In a few minutes, they had assessed the situation, helped Peter onto a gurney, strapped him in, and were out the door.

"Wait!" called out Nancy. "What hospital?"

"Broward General," one of the paramedics yelled back to her.

Nancy sank down on the couch. She needed to pull herself together. She took several deep breaths to calm her trembling hands. Poor Peter. Thank goodness they had arrived in time to help, but he looked terrible.

"You all right?" asked Louise, sitting down next to her.

"In a minute. Call for a cab, Louise." Nancy pushed herself off the couch and stumbled into the kitchen. She found a clean, empty jar and used a spoon to scrape the vomit off the floor and shake it into the jar. She tucked the jar into her purse. The doctors might need to analyze it. She cleaned up the mess and then reassured the dogs as she released them from the bedroom.

Nancy and Louise sat in the hospital waiting room for hours. As Nancy paced the hall to quell the anxiety and pass the time, she stopped at the visitors' desk. A motherly woman put down the phone and smiled at Nancy. A tag on her blouse said, "Volunteer." Nancy leaned toward her. "I'd like to visit Jessica Cantwell. Can you tell me what room she's in?"

The woman typed the name on her computer and studied the screen. "No Jessica Cantwell is staying here." She looked up at Nancy. "Did I spell it correctly? What section would she be in?"

Nancy thanked her and returned to the waiting room. Finally, a woman in a white jacket holding a clipboard walked out from behind the closed doors, peered down at the clipboard through her bifocals and called out Nancy's name. Nancy walked to the doctor, fear and hope in her heart.

"I'm Dr. Elise Meadows. I've been attending Mr. Stamboul. He's stable right now and resting," the doctor said. "We need to monitor his heart rate and keep him under observation until tomorrow. Are you family?"

Stable and resting. Thank God. Nancy shook her head. "Long-time friend."

"Does he have family here I can contact?"

"What's wrong with him, doctor?" Nancy said. "We're his friends, staying at his apartment, but we just arrived and found him so sick we called the ambulance."

The doctor studied Nancy as she talked. "He ingested a significant amount of digitalis, a medication prescribed for heart patients, but I checked with his doctor whose records show no heart concerns and no digitalis prescription. Could he have taken it by mistake? Or borrowed someone's prescription?"

An overdose of digitalis? "I don't think so," said Nancy. But did she really know? She hadn't seen Peter for years. What had happened to him in those years? The old Peter wouldn't have done anything so stupid. Was this another attack on his life?

Nancy gave her the jar. "This is what he threw up," she said. "In case you want to test it to confirm your diagnosis."

The doctor held up the jar and studied the contents. "I'll ask the nurse to take it to the lab." She looked at Nancy over her reading glasses. "He insists he was poisoned."

"Some strange accidents have happened to him lately," Nancy replied. "I think you should take him seriously."

The doctor studied Nancy for a moment. "I see. I'll have to notify the police."

Nancy nodded. "He has filed a report but not about this."

The doctor pursed her lips. "He is elderly, though. Perhaps there is some dementia."

Nancy refused to let the doctor take that path. "Peter is perfectly all right mentally, and he is not paranoid." She hoped.

"Whew," said Louise as they walked out of the hospital. "What a welcome."

Nancy hailed a cab, and they returned to Peter's apartment. The dogs barked and danced around them in excitement.

"It's not too late," Nancy said. "These dogs and I need a walk.

We're pretty wound up."

"You go ahead. My knees have had it for today." Louise bent down to pet one of the dogs. "I guess we're friends now, but I've never seen dogs this homely." She brought up a hand wet with slobber. "He needs a bib."

Nancy pet the other one, who licked her leg. "There, there, you little darling, everything's all right now." In the living room, Nancy pulled a tissue out of a box on the coffee table and wiped her leg. She looked up at Louise. "They both need bibs."

"Towels too. Hope they're housebroken." Tense and worried about Peter, Nancy leashed the dogs and headed out the door with them. Apparently Peter had been poisoned, and the police would be brought into the case. They might be able to track down the poisoner who had to have perpetrated the other attempts and then Peter could relax. She didn't think Peter's problem would be solved that easily. She remembered how terrified he was when he'd called her, then thought of his haggard face when they arrived.

She returned to the apartment and unleashed the dogs. She brought out the sheets from Peter's bed and threw them in the washer. Then she pulled a clean towel out of the linen closet, returned to the living room, and spread the towel out on the plush white sofa. She saw Louise's questioning look. "Protect it from the dogs." She sat down, and they jumped up beside her.

"Peter was always unique in his furnishings," Nancy said, casting her eyes around the living room. A thick oriental carpet with a blue, red, and yellow flowered design covered most of the tiled floor, and the couch was placed in front of a deep purple wall, but the other walls were white. The armchairs were a lighter shade of purple. A large potted palm stood in a corner, adding a tropical flair to this exotic room.

Louise rose stiffly from the armchair. "Now, you gotta see

this," she said. Leaning on her cane, she stepped forward on the rug, stopping as a chain of Christmas tree lights, blue this time, switched on across a side wall.

Nancy laughed. "Look at this." She moved to the other armchair. The lamp next to the couch turned on. "And this." She tilted a large planter in a corner of the room. The small ficus tree it contained lit up with a string of red lights. "I forgot to warn you. Peter's an electrical engineer. Lights are his hobby."

She walked over to a light switch. "I'm sure there's a switch somewhere that will turn all the extra decorative lights off." She tested several switches before finding the right one. "There. We don't need those little surprises as we walk around this place." She sat down on the couch.

"I thought he hadn't taken down his Christmas decorations. Gave me a start when I first walked in." Louise pushed the dogs aside and sat down between them with a sigh. "All this running around has exhausted me."

"Me, too." Nancy said. She wiped the chin of one dog while Louise fondled the ears of the other.

"So which one is this?" Louise asked.

Nancy peered at the tag on the dog between them. "This one's Rupert. You've got Oscar."

Louise scratched behind Oscar's ears. "What do we do next?" she asked.

"Let's wait and see what the doctor has to say." Nancy walked into the kitchen. "Peter seems to be right, someone is after him."

"I still think it looked like plain ol' food poisoning to me," said Louise.

"The doctor says it was digitalis." Nancy glanced inside the refrigerator. "Don't see anything unusual here." Eggs. Yogurt. Jam. Butter. Oranges and lemons. No leftovers that could have gone bad.

Not too much of anything. Maybe Peter ate out a lot and if he did, the opportunities for poison increased.

"Another case for the 90s Club." Louise stretched and yawned. "Shit. I was planning to spend my time at the beach."

"Of course, you could, if you wanted to." Nancy couldn't keep the disappointment out of her voice. She hoped Louise would want to go with her as they searched for the answers to Peter's problem and Jessica's disappearance, if indeed she had disappeared.

Louise flicked her braid. "You gotta be kidding."

Nancy smiled. "It will probably be tedious, and I thought Peter was. . .well, elaborating on what were really just unfortunate accidents, but he sounded afraid and that's why I came."

Louise straightened her back with a grimace. "I'm counting on excitement, but I came for the warm weather." Louise walked over to her suitcase. She'd dropped it at the door when they arrived. "So we're sharing the second bedroom?"

Nancy nodded. "I think so, and I'll fix up Peter's bed for him, but this place is too dangerous. I'm taking him out of town whether he likes it or not."

***

Take Care in the Kitchen

Fort Lauderdale's many picnic areas are an attractive place for families and friends to gather. But be careful about the food you bring. Make sure it's properly refrigerated and kept cold until it's served. Don't leave it out more than an hour or two. Food poisoning can kill.

Riverside Acres Health Team

Chapter 5

The next morning Nancy and Louise found Peter still hooked up to the heart monitor. He looked so frail and shrunken that Nancy's heart swelled. She sat beside his bed and held his hand, saddened at his wan face. His eyes fluttered. Nancy's pity grew as she saw how valiantly he tried to smile.

"Don't try to talk," she said. "We're here. We'll take care of everything, and the dogs are fine."

He nodded and squeezed her hand. "I have…" he stopped. His voice sank to a whisper. "Nancy. . . I told you. Someone is trying to kill me."

"I know," Nancy said. She leaned forward to hear him.

He paused and took a breath. Nancy waited, sorry for this poor man. He had been such an athlete, so strong, still strong when she'd last seen him. He'd played tennis then against a much younger friend—and won.

"A police detective came by earlier and took a report." Peter closed his eyes and took a breath as if to gather strength. "I got the feeling he was just going through the motions. Made a big point of my age and the possibility of mistake," Peter whispered. "So I'm relying on you. Find out who did this," he added, "but be careful."

Nancy squeezed his hand, which lay in hers like a dead herring. "I understand." Then she added, covering up a tremor of fear and uncertainty, "You can trust us." Seeing how weak he was, she held her questions for now.

"One more thing." Peter tried to sit up but sank back. "In my desk drawer," he whispered, "on the left, there's a bug detector. Use it, Nancy. I found one bug in the lamp last week."

"A bug!" Louise frowned at Nancy.

Nancy raised an eyebrow. All the attempts on his life could possibly have been accidents, but a wiretap was unmistakable.

Dr. Meadows arrived. Nancy and Louise excused themselves from the room, but they waited outside the door and pounced on her when she emerged.

"Did you check his medicine cabinet for digitalis?" the doctor asked.

"I did check but didn't find any," said Nancy. "Nothing like that in the kitchen, either."

"Any herbal mixtures or teas he could have eaten?"

Nancy shook her head.

"We just arrived," said Louise, "and found him sicker'n a. . . a alligator, I guess, seeing as how this is Florida."

"We called the ambulance," added Nancy.

"We're going to keep him another night." Dr. Meadows eyed Nancy.

"Of course," said Nancy.

The doctor nodded at them and walked over to the nurses' station as she studied the clipboard in her hand.

Nancy turned to Louise. "I'm going to go in and tell Peter he can probably go home tomorrow."

Louise nodded and turned towards the waiting area.

But Peter had other ideas. "You can use my car, but I should have listened to you and gotten out of there," he whispered. He took several breaths but still lay limp in the bed. His arms stretched out under the cover, but he made no attempt to move his body.

"The next time may be fatal," he added. "If they find out about you, they'll come after you, too, so watch out. At least you know what you're doing. Not like me. Find out what's going on there, but tell everyone I'm out of town."

Nancy smiled down at him in relief. No fight, then, to get Peter away from that apartment.

Peter took another deep breath and added in a stronger voice, "Maybe they'll buy the idea that you needed to get away while your place is renovated, and I invited you to take care of the dogs while I'm away. You didn't use your real name, did you?"

Nancy shook her head. "It's Nancy Davis."

"Good. And let people think we know each other only casually." He reached for Nancy's hand. "And play dumb."

Nancy nodded. "Where will you go?"

"I'll get a place not too close but not too far away either. That way, you can let me know what's going on, and I can be nearby to help out." He closed his eyes. Had he gone to sleep? Nancy turned to the door but hesitated as she saw Peter peer at her through half-closed eyes and raise his hand.

"Pompano Beach. That's where I'll go. Just up I-95 about ten miles or so. Not likely to meet anyone I know up there."

"You should get some rest, take it easy for a while. You've been under a lot of stress." Nancy studied his face. The haggard look was gone, replaced by weariness. He needed to sleep, get his strength back, but he was beginning to seem more like the Peter she remembered.

"I plan to." His eyes were closed as he spoke. "Book me a suite with kitchen at the Pompano Vista Hotel. It's on the beach, but far enough away from the city pier and the center of town. Should be safe there." He opened his eyes. "And then pack a suitcase for me." He lifted his arm. "Put the folders on my desk into it, too."

"All right. Now we should leave." Nancy walked to the door.

"Wait," Peter said. He tried to sit up but sank back down on the bed. "Thank you for coming, Nancy."

"Of course I came." She looked at him. "Seems like we got here just in time."

Peter didn't respond, but he thrust out his jaw. Nancy waited. He seemed to be thinking hard. "We need to plan a strategy, but I need to rest. Pick me up as soon as I can get out of here, and I'll tell you what to do next. But play dumb. Play old and feeble. Doddering. Gaga."

"At least I look the part." Nancy patted his hand, but his bossy tone rankled. She didn't need him to tell her how to proceed. "I'll discuss strategy with you tomorrow. But you're not telling me what to do, Peter."

"Sure, sure. You're the pro. You're the reason I'm still around." He sank back to the pillow and closed his eyes.

***

Pompano Beach: A Jewel on Florida's Gold Coast
Named for a species of tropical game fish, Pompano offers some of the world's best sport fishing, beautiful and challenging golf courses, horse racing at the world-famous Pompano Harness Track, and miles of sun-drenched golden beaches. Living or vacationing in Pompano Beach is a dream come true.

Pompano Beach Tourism Brochure

Chapter 6

Nancy paused, pen in hand and notebook on her lap, to admire the effect of the purple chair against her teal slacks and white blouse. Peter always did have an eye for color and design. Just for a moment, she rued her own furniture, a random collection of odd pieces picked up at garage sales. She looked up to see Louise smiling at her.

"So what now?" asked Louise.

"We have two problems to solve in twenty days," Nancy said. "Gotta get cracking. I'll go along with Peter's idea that whoever is trying to kill him lives here, so the first thing we need is a directory of the residents."

"The management office should have one." Louise stood and grabbed her cane. "I'll go down and get it."

"All right." Nancy tapped the pen against her cheek.

In a few minutes, Louise was back with a photocopied booklet. "It's accurate up to three weeks ago. When did Peter's troubles start?"

"I'm not sure, but recently. That should do for our purpose." Nancy took the directory and leafed through it. "Unfortunately, we don't know any of these people yet." She walked to the back of the apartment, which extended the living room into a closed-in balcony with tiled floor. Two lawn chairs and a three-foot orange tree soaked up the sunshine there. Nancy stepped to the balcony window and stared down at the patio and pool, glimmering in a clear and tempting aquamarine. Louise leaned on her cane as she joined Nancy at the window.

"Looks inviting, doesn't it," said Nancy.

"People to talk to, too," Louise added, eyeing Nancy. "I know what you're thinking."

They spent the rest of the day at the condo pool. They had slathered on the fifty-plus sunscreen and then pulled their chairs into the shade. The Fort Lauderdale sun was hot enough to melt their sandals. Occasionally other residents plopped down in one of the plastic beach chairs near her, and Nancy greeted them, hoping to find out more about the people and activities going on at Riverside Acres. Maybe someone else had become mysteriously ill.

As Nancy watched the residents come and go, a short, heavy woman with a large mouth painted in wobbly red lipstick climbed out of the pool, wrapped a towel around herself, and pulled up a plastic chaise longue next to Nancy.

The woman wheezed softly and patted her chest as she looked over at Nancy. "Heart problems," she said. "Gotta be careful." She took several deep breaths. "I'm Abby Summers. You the gal staying at Peter's place? He okay? Saw the ambulance."

"He'll be fine. Stomach upset." Nancy gave her name as Nancy Davis, adding "I know Peter casually. I heard he needed a dog sitter while he went on vacation, so I volunteered. Louise and I are from West Virginia."

"Escaping the winter, eh?" She poked Nancy in the arm with her finger. Nancy flinched. "Pleased to meet you. Of course a lot of the gals here are gonna be jealous," Abby said. "They'd like to be his special friend." She laughed. "If you get what I mean." She winked at Nancy and glanced at Louise, who stared blankly ahead.

Abby lay back in the chaise longue and gazed up at the sky.

"Would you believe I'm 85 years old? Can't believe it myself." She patted herself on the chest.

"Looking good," Nancy said, glancing at her, but she didn't add that she was ninety. If she weren't observing the residents, she'd be swimming laps. Lots of exercise kept her in shape.

Louise pushed herself out of the chair with a groan. "Can't take this sun. Too hot for me. Gonna go inside." She picked up her towel and cane and tottered toward the elevator.

"Lotta stuff going on here, you know." Abby reached over and put a cold, pudgy hand on Nancy's arm. Nancy willed herself not to shake the hand off. "Since you're staying in Peter's place, you and your galfriend are welcome at whatever's going on in the clubhouse. We had a potluck luncheon there yesterday."

Nancy's ears perked up. "Potluck luncheon? Everyone invited?"

"Oh yes, my dear." Abby's bright eyes looked Nancy over. "We had a lot of people, including Peter, of course." Abby smacked her lips. "He always brings some Turkish dish. Delightful man."

"Sometimes I worry about potluck dishes," Nancy said, casting a line. "You don't know how people make them. . ."

Abby sniffed. "I've been going to potlucks for seventy-odd years, and I haven't been sick yet! And no one's gotten sick on one of ours here either."

"So everyone is okay?"

"Far as I know." Abby leaned forward and whispered, "'Except for a coupla people, but they're always sick with something. And Peter, of course. Is he all right?"

"He's very sick." Nancy said. "Don't know when he'll be released from the hospital."

Abby frowned. "Must have been some kind of stomach flu."

"Shame too," added Nancy. "Just when he was going off on vacation. At least he doesn't have to worry about the dogs."

"Those dogs." Abby sniffed. "Misfortunes, both of them. How Peter can tolerate. . . ."

A slim woman in crisp and spotless white slacks and striped navy top came up to them. She seemed much younger than Abby—and a whole lot younger than Nancy.

"Now, Abby," the woman said, "it's time for your medicine, and then I'll take you out for dinner. Early bird special."

A fleeting expression of amused cynicism crossed Abby's face, but then Abby smiled and placed a hand on the woman's arm. "This is my friend, Susan Withers. She keeps an eye on me. Keeps me on track." Abby pushed herself out of the chair. "I'll let the others know about Peter. Shame to get so sick."

Susan turned her guileless blue eyes to Nancy. "How is Peter? We saw the ambulance."

Was she a 'special friend' wannabe? Peter was quite handsome still, for his age. "He's in the hospital," Nancy said. "We're not sure when he'll get out."

Susan frowned. "I'm so sorry."

She took Abby's arm, but Abby held her ground. She waggled her finger at Nancy. "Anything you want to know about what's going on here, just ask me. I've got my eye on everything." Then she turned and waddled away with Susan, leaving Nancy to wonder how safe such a statement could be at Riverside Acres.

Louise left the shade near the elevator, where she had been talking on her cell phone, to walk back to Nancy, stabbing her cane on the sidewalk at every step. When she reached Nancy's side, she leaned over and whispered. "You detectives have a hard life. Talking to that old gossip. Hope you pulled out everything she's got and didn't tell her nothing."

Nancy laughed. "I was circumspect."

Louise nodded. "Good. I've got news."

She glanced from side to side as if searching for eavesdroppers, then she gave Nancy a thumbs up sign.

Nancy patted the abandoned chair next to her. "What's going on?"

"The 90s Club is invading Riverside Acres!" Louise took the chair. Her eyes sparkled. "I just talked to George."

Nancy raised an eyebrow. "George?"

Louise blushed. "Yep. It's only been two days, but he says he misses us, so. . . ," she paused.

"So?" said Nancy, beginning to smile. Louise's joy was contagious.

"So he called the Riverside Acres management office and rented a vacant unit for the three weeks we'll be here." Louise coughed to hide her embarrassment. "Not quite the tourist season yet, so lots of places are available. He'll be arriving in a couple of days."

"Wonderful." Good ol' George. He was a founding member, along with Nancy and Louise, of Whisperwood's 90s Club. "I didn't realize how much I'd miss him," Nancy added.

"Me too," said Louise. "And don't look at me like that."

Nancy turned away to hide her smile. George and Louise were becoming an item, but Nancy couldn't help a fleeting sense of envy.

***

Later that evening, as Louise and Nancy finished their dinner, Nancy heard a loud thump from next door followed by an outburst of profanity.

"What on earth. . .?" Nancy looked at Louise.

Louise leaned on her cane as she hobbled to the wall and put her ear against it. "I don't hear anything."

Nancy walked over and listened too. "Neither do I."

"What was that about? Sounded like someone got hit or hit something." Louise glanced at Nancy. "I'm going over there to find out what happened. I don't mind playing nosy neighbor."

"Someone may be hurt and need help," said Nancy.

"I've worked in a domestic violence shelter. I know what to look for." Louise's chin jutted out. "Always good to let people know others are paying attention."

"I'll stay by the phone in case there's trouble."

Louise stalked out. From the doorway, Nancy watched her knock on their neighbor's door. No response.

"I know someone's there," Louise called out. "If no one comes to the door, I'm calling the police." She looked over at Nancy.

The door opened a crack.

"Are you all right?" Louise asked.

Nancy couldn't hear what was said, but Louise nodded and said, "We're next door if you need help." The door closed, and Louise returned to Peter's apartment.

"Couldn't see her too well through the crack in the door." Louise tapped her cane. "But she said she was all right. Just dropped something. Couldn't see who else was in the place." Louise tottered past Nancy to the living room. "Too bad I'm not a cop. I shoulda called them."

"She said she was all right."

"Yeah, but a cop would have made her come out of that apartment and down the hall. He'd talk to her alone in case someone inside had a gun to her head." Louise clenched her teeth. "Or knife or something. And that reminds me. . ."

Louise disappeared through a doorway into a small room off the hall. Nancy followed.

"You only peeked in this room when we were looking around, but I took a better look. What do you make of that?" Louise pointed to a bulletin board covered with flyers describing criminals wanted by the FBI.

"I used to see these in the post office," Nancy's eyes darted across the twenty flyers lined up in two rows of ten and tacked to the bulletin board. Sixteen men and four women stared sullenly at the camera. Their photos were dark with contrast. Nancy read the descriptions on two of the flyers. "Here's a brother and sister act wanted for mail fraud, drug trafficking, and murder."

Louise brought her eyes close to the flyer and peered at it. "I don't think I'd ever recognize one of these people on the street no matter how much I studied these flyers. All he'd have to do is lose weight or gain it, shave his head or let the hair grow, dye it, anything like that would throw me off."

"Hard to see beyond the superficial. And on these printouts, you can't even tell if the people were blond or brunette." Nancy read the print under the photos. "The brother was older. Kid sister. Maybe he dragged her into a life of crime."

"Maybe," said Louise. "Or she dragged him. Or maybe their parents set them up. Or maybe they got into drugs. . . ."

"Okay, okay. I get the idea." Nancy walked over to Peter's desk. She flipped open a manila folder that lay on top. Inside were portrait-sized, full-color glossy photos of each person whose picture was pinned to the bulletin board. Pasted on the back of each photo was a full page of background information. Nancy handed one photo to Louise. "Peter wants me to pack these. Do you suppose he got them from the FBI?"

Louise looked at her. "I don't know, but what's Peter doing with them?"

***

Leave the Old You Behind

You're in South Florida now! Throw out that drab winter wardrobe. Color your hair a sassy blonde! Revamp your make-up and your style. Stop by LaMode Salon, just a few blocks away on Las Olas Boulevard, for a free facial. When you step out of LaMode, not even your best friend will recognize the beautiful new you! Discounts for Riverside Acres residents. 954-555-6332.

Notice approved by Riverside Acres Management

Nancy walked into the kitchen the next morning and put water on for tea. Louise already sat at the breakfast table, eating cereal and studying the local bus schedule.

Nancy tapped a finger on the schedule. "What are you doing?"

Louise didn't look up. "I'm going out to visit the local domestic violence shelter. Want to find out how the system works here. Good to know," she nodded toward the next apartment, "in case our neighbor needs help." She glanced at Nancy. "You'll be busy with Peter. Won't need my help, and you know I'm always getting into some kind of trouble."

"Usually for a good cause." Nancy smiled as she peered into a canister of tea bags. "You're an activist, Louise. The world is a better place because of you. I'm proud to have you as a friend."

She pulled out a bag labeled English Breakfast. "I could drive you around later. After I see Peter. But I only have nineteen days to solve the mysteries. Have to put a plan together."

"Let me know what I can do, but you don't have to get involved in my project." Louise picked up her cane. "Anyway, I'd like to try their public transportation." She stuffed the bus schedules into a vest pocket, a determined expression on her face. "A lot of people our age don't drive and have to use it, you know. It's how I measure whether a town is civilized." Then she hobbled out the door, clutching her cane.

Nancy had worn a navy sweater and khaki slacks when she walked the dogs before breakfast, but the day was quickly warming up. She took off the sweater. Short sleeves and the bright pink-flowered shirt suited South Florida weather better. The alert brown eyes of the dogs followed her every move. She reached down to pet them. Their receding jaws revealed teeth dripping the ever-present slobber. Nancy gave them an extra pet. They were both sweet little guys, despite their looks.

She dawdled over breakfast as she made notes in the residents' directory. She took it and her tea cup into the den to Peter's copier. She had known Peter was a fastidious sort, but the den was as neat and tidy as his hospital room. Nothing like Nancy's own den back at Whisperwood with its clutter and dusty piles of papers and magazines. He was certainly busy, whatever he did. The den was supplied with copier, fax, computer, file drawers. She made two copies of the directory and checked her watch. She didn't want to get to the hospital before ten—give the nurses and doctors a chance to take care of Peter first.

She spread the Fort Lauderdale map out on Peter's desk and traced the route to the hospital, but her eyes kept straying to the flyers on the bulletin board. She walked over to them and ran her eyes over each one, seeking some unusual and unchangeable characteristic. Nose, jaw line, ears, and lips would be difficult to change, but there was nothing unusual about any of those characteristics on any of the flyers. Hard to identify anyone on the street from such flyers. Even the color glossies were problematical. She gave up for the time being and packed a suitcase for Peter.

The gate attendant pointed out Peter's car, and Nancy eyed the vintage Mustang doubtfully. Stick shift just like her car back at Whisperwood. The familiar shifting gear gave her confidence, and she found that, unlike her own car, Peter's started without balking.

She drove it out to the street and used her map and the familiar blue "H" signs to find the hospital.

She tapped on the door of Peter's room and entered. She almost laughed to see Peter, no longer an invalid, glaring at his breakfast tray. He looked up. "Nancy! Thank God you're here. Spring me outta this joint!"

Nancy smiled at him. "Did Dr. Meadows say you're okay to leave?"

"Sure, sure. I'm just a little wobbly. I vomited out the poison before it could get to me. Let me get dressed, and you can take me out for a real breakfast."

"We should wait for the doctor first."

"I'm okay, Nancy." He sat up and put his legs over the side of the bed. "All I gotta do is get dressed and sign the papers, and they'll let me go."

Nancy turned to the door. "I'll wait for you down the hall while you dress."

She stepped over to the nurse's station and asked the woman on duty, "Is Peter Stamboul okay to go home?"

"Let me check." She paged the doctor as her eyes traveled from Nancy's feet to her head, put down the phone, and pointed to a small lounge area. "Please wait over there," the nurse said. "Dr. Meadows would like to talk to you. She'll be up shortly."

Nancy took a seat in the empty nook. The doctor wanted to talk to her. That didn't sound good. She hoped nothing was seriously wrong. In a couple of minutes, she saw the doctor flying down the hall towards her, the ubiquitous clipboard in her hand. She smiled at Nancy perfunctorily, then sat in the chair opposite her and pursed her lips. "I contacted the police because Mr. Stamboul insists he was poisoned."

"He has reported other threats to his life," Nancy said.

Dr. Meadows ignored her comment. "It could have been a suicide attempt, since digitalis was not prescribed for him, and you tell me you found no other possible sources for it. Has he been depressed lately?"

Nancy shook her head. "I haven't seen him in a long time, but I have talked to him on the phone. He didn't seem depressed." Terrified, maybe, but not depressed.

"I see." She peered at Nancy over her glasses. "Well, I think he needs friends right now." She hesitated as if she wanted to say more but instead she rose and shook Nancy's hand. "He's ready to go home. Are you picking him up?"

Nancy nodded. The doctor led the way to Peter's room and rapped on the door.

Nancy heard a robust "Come in." She followed the doctor in to find Peter dressed and sitting in a chair, putting on his shoes.

"The lab results came in," the doctor said. She glanced at Nancy.

"Nancy's a close friend," Peter said. "She can hear whatever you've got to say."

"You ingested digitalis, a medication prescribed for heart patients. Where did it come from?"

Peter stared at her then lifted his chin. "Someone gave it to me, that's where." said Peter, tying one of his shoe strings. "I didn't take that stuff on purpose."

"You didn't borrow someone else's medications?"

"Of course not."

The doctor stared at him a moment, then wrote a long note in the file on her clipboard. She glanced at Nancy before looking back at him.

"Fortunately," the doctor went on, "digitalis is one of those medications that if taken by the wrong person or in the wrong amount, causes so much vomiting, the victim usually gets rid of it before serious harm is done. How have you been feeling lately? Any depression?"

"If I were depressed," Peter tied the second shoelace and sat up, "I'd find something better to take than digitalis, I can tell you that."

Nancy watched Peter. Could he be depressed? He had been badly frightened, but Nancy had never known him to mention suicide. "Maybe you took it by mistake," she said.

"Not a chance. Heart patients might use it, but my heart is in great shape." He turned to the doctor. "I'm okay now."

"All right." The doctor scribbled a note on the clipboard. "Just don't go taking anyone else's prescriptions ever again."

"Sure, Doc. Never again. Learned my lesson." Peter picked up a bag of belongings and pushed Nancy ahead of him out the door. They headed down the hall, leaving the doctor behind, still writing notes on her clipboard.

"She doesn't believe someone poisoned me, but she can think what she wants," he whispered to Nancy. As they walked toward the hospital exit, he looked back. "Nobody following us." He picked up his pace. "Good. Narrow squeak back there. She was getting ready to recommend psychiatric care for me, I could see it in her eyes. I'm not spending any more time here than I have to."

"But where did you get the digitalis?"

"Somebody fed it to me. I don't have any heart problems, therefore no digitalis, prescription or no prescription. So," Peter leaned forward, "I don't know where I got it, but I'm going into hiding now. They won't get to me again."

***

A quick drive up I-95 to Pompano Beach and an hour later, Nancy and Peter were seated in a beachside hotel restaurant. The peach and green decor seemed dated, but the cool and quiet room soothed her spirits. Nancy asked for tea and relaxed while Peter ordered coffee and then added bacon and eggs. "The works," he told the server. He leaned toward Nancy.

"Still feel a bit wobbly." He held up a hand and watched it tremble. "See?"

Nancy nodded. "What's this all about, Peter?"

"I told you. Somebody's after me." He watched the server pour coffee into a cup. When she left, he added sugar and cream and took a long sip. "That tasted good." He fiddled with a fork as he scanned the dining room. "You tell everyone at Riverside Acres I've gone to St. Thomas." He looked back at Nancy and pounded his fist on the table. "But I'm going to stay right here. You were right."

Nancy glanced through the dining room doors toward the hotel reservation desk. "St. Thomas. Virgin Islands." She sat back. Despite the terrible siege of vomiting that had sent him to the hospital, he seemed downright cheerful. Easy to see why. He was getting away from Riverside Acres and the threat it posed.

Peter raised an eyebrow. "You've known me how long, Nancy? Sixty years? Seventy?"

Nancy nodded. "A long time."

"I was an electrical engineer till I retired." He stared off at the ocean. "But do you know what I really wanted to be?"

"I can't imagine," said Nancy.

"A private detective." He pointed his fork at her. "Like you."

"I always thought so." Nancy almost laughed. "But it's mostly a boring job. Not glamorous or exciting at all." She shook her head, remembering the stake-outs. They were the most boring—hours in a car trying to stay awake. Perusing courthouse records wasn't too bad. Feeling that you'd helped some deserving person—that was the best part when it happened.

Nancy's thoughts had wandered, but Peter's words snapped her out of her daydreams.

"What made you think I wanted to be a private dick?"

She shrugged. "You were always asking me about the cases, how I worked them. . . ."

"Yeah, well, that's what I wanted to be." He sat back as the server brought his breakfast and refilled his coffee. He began to eat, glancing up once to wink at her.

Nancy smiled, knowing the wink was a symbol of all they had shared through the years, but they needed to do some serious talking. "Why do you think someone wants to kill you, Peter?"

He pushed his plate away and picked up the cup. "I've thought and thought about that. They can't want to scare me out of my condo. Not like there's hidden treasure in it." He sipped the coffee. "I don't have a million bucks to give anybody. No heirs anyway. What I think is that I've told too many people about my hobby."

"Hunting down wanted criminals?"

"You saw the flyers." He rapped the table with his knuckles. "Those flyers are just the latest crop. I keep a file of murderers, spies, and war criminals who've escaped capture. I research them, and I've taken trips to track down some of them." He saw Nancy's raised eyebrow.

"I did tip off the FBI about one criminal and I was right. Bought the white couch with the reward money. Couldn't help bragging a little around Riverside." He sat back with a grin. "Now I think I've come too close to somebody and that somebody is at Riverside Acres." He looked away, sipping his coffee. "Did you know there's a $100,000 reward for some of those people?"

"Tempting," said Nancy. "Not enough if you get killed, but that hobby of yours could be motive enough if someone at Riverside is one of the 'most wanted.'"

Peter put down his cup and folded his arms. "You're saying I could be right? You're not poo-pooing the suggestion? Now I am scared."

"You didn't take digitalis or get shot at by accident."

"That damn potluck luncheon. Someone dosed my plate when I wasn't looking."

"So that someone needs digitalis or knows someone who does. Have other residents seen your bulletin board? Heard you talk about this hobby of yours? What other motives might there be?"

"Sure. I've shown those posters to other people there. Interesting stuff. Like to talk about it. Other motives? My poisonous personality, I guess."

Nancy laughed. Peter was one of the most generous, kind people she knew.

He shrugged. "I haven't rejected any possible lovers there— because there aren't any. No money to leave anyone."

"Any idea who at Riverside would feel threatened?"

"No, I don't. But I made a mistake."

Nancy watched him blush. "What kind of mistake?" she asked.

He cleared his throat. "I wasn't getting anywhere, so," he hesitated, "so I started dropping hints." He flicked at a crumb on the table. "Like, you know, that I knew something about one of the people at Riverside, something shady."

"That was dangerous." Most people had something to hide. Nancy knew she did, but of course nothing shady, just stupid or embarrassing. She thought of the romances on her Kindle. She'd hate Louise to see the kind of books she read.

"That's why I asked you to come visit. You know what to look for. You've got experience, Nancy."

She pursed her lips. "Not recent, though. And I'm not up on the latest technology." A tremor of fear swept through her body. She really shouldn't be passing herself off as a detective anymore.

Peter needed someone up to date, not her. She was about to say so, when Peter broke in on her thoughts.

"Maybe not, but you believe me and you understand. I don't care how skilled and up to date they are if I have to fight their disbelief and snide remarks about my age."

Sounded like he'd read her mind, but Nancy nodded. He was right.

Peter shook his head. "Anyway, we may be swimming in the middle of the shark pool, which the FBI is not." He folded his arms and spoke with determination. "I'll be working on it here, where the bad guys can't get to me. They won't know you're also on the job."

Peter snapped his fingers. "One more thing, Nancy. You gotta bring my laptop. Can't do anything without a computer. You can use the desktop in the den."

"Okay." Nancy's mind raced ahead, thinking how she might proceed. Excitement stirred within her. A strategy was taking shape in her mind. Maybe she could do this job. She stared off at a distant corner of the dining room and tapped her chin. "You can do the computer work, since you're stuck here in this motel. First, check on cost, feasibility, and effectiveness of face recognition software."

Peter grinned. "Now you're talking. Good idea. Never thought of that. How much would it cost?"

"No idea." She shrugged. "Have you contacted the FBI about your suspicions?"

Peter reared back. "Until I get something more definite, they'd only laugh at me. Even though I gave them one good tip, their memories are short. I'd just be one more old guy wasting their time." He leaned toward her and whispered, "Anyway, if I can give them enough info to actually catch the killer, I could get another reward—maybe as much as that $100,000 I told you about."

Nancy arched an eyebrow.

Peter saw the look. "Oh, I don't need the money, just the satisfaction." He winked at her. "I go after the drug pushers and smugglers. The destroyers. You remember Aflie?"

Alfie. So many years ago. Red-haired, freckle-faced kid. One of their gang in college. "I remember him," said Nancy.

"I loved him," Peter said. "But he got into drugs. Been dead a long time now." Peter frowned and stared down at his hands.

Nancy looked at him. Now she understood. Peter had been a rabble-rouser, agitating for social change—integration, equal housing and opportunity—and other causes way before the sixties. There were occasions in his past when he would have shied clear of any involvement with the police or FBI or anyone in authority. Life had been painful and difficult for him. Knowing him, she understood. "Be careful, Peter."

Peter summoned up a laugh. "Sure, I'll have me a nice, safe beach vacation," Peter leaned back in his chair, "and you get to stay in warm and sunny Florida for a few weeks. Not a bad deal." He took her hand. "This is your kind of thing, Nancy."

Underneath the jocular attitude he'd adopted now that he felt safe, Nancy sensed a serious resolve. She shivered. "All right, Peter. But I think we should have a system." She pulled the residents' directory out of her purse. "I want you to go through every name in this directory and weed out the impossibles—the people you know who couldn't be responsible for the attacks on you. Subscribe to one of those criminal database checks and run the possibilities through it. Consider possible motives and opportunities too. Then number the possibilities from one to three. One means most likely; three means least likely. Email me that list."

Peter sat back, open-mouthed. "Good, Nancy. I'll get right on it." He rubbed a hand across his chin. "But what if I weed out someone I shouldn't? What if I make a mistake?"

"We'll deal with it, but we're up against a formidable task, and we only have nineteen days for me to help you, so we'll stumble along as best we can. Once you've got the pared-down list, seek out more information about them through the computer. Develop a folder on each resident. I will email you digital photos of everyone I can to add to the folders and maybe," Nancy crossed her fingers, "I can even get fingerprints." She sat back as she realized that the job was taking shape. She could do this!

Peter stared off into the distance, nodding. "Good. I like that. We'll be a team. Just be careful. Don't let them see what you're doing. When you have questions or want me to check anything out on the computer, send me an e-mail." He waved his cup at her. "Or come up here and ask me. I like that better." He sat back. "Okay?"

"Okay, but. . . ." She might as well make this clear at the beginning. "I will do things my way. I won't be following anyone's orders. Our first priority is keeping you safe. The second is to develop a short list to turn over to the FBI. They can follow through and pin down the criminal and make the arrest. When that's done, you can return to Riverside."

"Sure. Sure." Peter waved her comment away. "I'll be like that guy in the detective stories, Nero Wolfe, solving the mystery up here from the stuff you and Louise dig up."

Nancy frowned at him. "But I won't be your Archie Goodwin, and we're not making any dramatic arrests," she said.

***

Computer Classes Begin Soon!
Register now for two computer classes beginning March 1 in the club room. Margaret Dunn, our resident computer expert, will teach Beginning Word, a word processing program, at 10 a.m. and Beginning Excel, a spreadsheet pro-

gram, at 11. Cost is only $49 per class. For more infor-
mation, drop by the Management Office.

Riverside Acres Resident Coordinator

Chapter 8

Nancy returned to the condo and walked the dogs, reflecting on their unfortunate fate. No one she met fawned over Oscar and Rupert. Most people shied away from their slobbery little faces. That puzzled the poor little guys. Nancy hoped their feelings weren't hurt.

Louise was still out, so Nancy ate a quick lunch alone. She was too unsettled about Peter's problem to stay home. She'd gotten him started laying the groundwork on his problem, and now perhaps she could see about Amelia Cantwell's granddaughter. By this time, Jessica might have called her family and reassured them. Nancy called Amelia.

A quavering voice answered the phone. "Hello?"

Nancy slipped past the status updates to ask about Jessica.

"I still haven't heard from her." Amelia hesitated. "It's been over eleven days now, and I am worried more than ever. Something is not right."

Nancy reassured Amelia as much as she could, but Amelia would not be comforted. Nancy hung up the phone and perused the local telephone book, skimming through pages of marina listings. She called several without success. Restless and wanting to explore Fort Lauderdale, she made a note of several marinas that had bought large ads in the book. Perhaps she might find the boat and

Jessica by driving along the river and visiting some of the marinas.

She waved good-bye to the dogs and stepped out the door, almost colliding with a frumpy little woman wearing a simple beige dress with thin black stripes. The woman mumbled as she hurried by, but she limped and Nancy could see bruises on her arms. Were those the result of a beating? Appalled at the thought, Nancy caught up with the woman.

"Excuse me," Nancy said and introduced herself. "I'm watching Peter's dogs." She gestured toward Peter's apartment. "Couldn't help but notice your bruises. Are you all right? Anything I can do to help?"

The woman blushed. "Perfectly fine, thank you. No problems." She hurried past, and Nancy watched her enter the unit next to Peter's. Ms. Sandstrom. Nancy felt sorry for the woman. The direct approach scared her off. Nancy would have to get to know her to find out what was going on next door.

Peter's vintage Mustang didn't have such a modern innovation as a GPS, so she studied the map of Fort Lauderdale with her magnifying glass, noting how the town was laid out, and then spread out the map on the passenger seat. She found her way back to Pompano Beach to deliver the laptop to Peter, then returned to Fort Lauderdale.

Since the city was laid out in a grid pattern and she had the map, Nancy felt confident that she could navigate the city, but she soon found that a grid was deceptive when railroad tracks and canals and the river intervened. Within ten minutes, she became lost in a maze of roads that ended or turned unexpectedly. In half an hour, she still hadn't reached the first marina on her list. She laid her head on the steering wheel and groaned at the end of another dead-end street. After an hour, she straggled back into the Riverside Acres parking area, burning with frustration. Instead of returning to the apartment, she walked over to the pool and sat in a plastic beach chair shaded by a large umbrella to calm down.

A group of women were playing cards around a nearby table also shaded by an umbrella. With their brightly colored shirts and shorts, they resembled a carousel. Each had a tall glass of iced tea, and a pitcher of tea rested on a small side table. All of them glanced up as she arrived.

"How's Peter?" asked one. "I saw the ambulance. Hope he's okay."

Nancy smiled and nodded. "He's fine. Just a stomach upset. He's off to St Thomas now."

Another one laughed. "He's always traveling. Nothing keeps him down."

One of the women peered at Nancy over her glasses, and Nancy recognized Susan, Abby's friend. Today she seemed more relaxed, an attractive fiftyish with flattering make-up and well-groomed blonde hair. Susan smiled at her. "Do you play bridge?"

"I love bridge. Is there a group I might join?" She remembered Peter's admonition. This wasn't Whisperwood. "That is," she amended, "I don't really play very well, you know, but I do like a good game." And the gossip. Gossip was always so useful in investigations.

"Absolutely. And we're often short someone so we'd enjoy having you join us." Susan picked up her glass and walked over to sit next to Nancy. "I'm dummy so I'm out this hand. I'm glad Peter's well enough to go on his vacation. I'm Susan Withers. We met yesterday."

"I'm Nancy. My friend Louise is touring the town right now."

Susan raised an eyebrow. "Peter always says he's going to St. Thomas. Wonder where he goes for real."

"I guess he just likes St. Thomas." Nancy made the comment

casual. Why would Susan question whether Peter really went to St. Thomas. A suspicious mind? Susan's open friendliness made that hard to believe, but Nancy had noticed Abby's subtle reservation. How well did Susan know Peter? Nancy glanced at the other women. Could any of them be a poisoner? Or one of the FBI's Most Wanted?

"Are you familiar with Fort Lauderdale?" Susan circled her hand in a gesture that included the whole city.

"I'm finding it more difficult than I thought," said Nancy. "Canals, one-way streets, railroad tracks. . ."

"Hard to get to know this town." Susan laughed. "If you need any help getting around, just let me know. I have a lot of time on my hands."

Nancy hesitated. She didn't like drawing a complete stranger into this doubtful situation, but searching for Jessica had nothing to do with Peter's problem at Riverside. "You'd be a godsend," Nancy said. "I found out this morning that I need someone like you. I was stopped at every turn by dead ends." She added a dithering "I just can't seem to read maps at all."

Susan laughed. "Been there." She sat back. "What were you looking for? Grocery store?"

"That, too, but I'm also trying to do a favor for someone I know at home."

"What kind of favor?" Susan asked. "Don't mean to pry, but maybe I could help."

"A friend asked me to check on her granddaughter." Nancy laughed to keep it light. "You know how it is. Daughter just out of the nest. Family worried. She came down here on a boat with some man the family never met."

Susan laughed too. "Young people do that kind of thing all the time. A lot of parents would love getting any kind of phone call."

"Do you think so?" Nancy put a note of gratitude in her voice as she noticed the oversized wedding ring on Susan's finger. Married but probably no children. A mother would understand the fear.

"If she came down here on a boat, do you think she might be at one of the marinas in town?"

"It's a good possibility."

Susan grimaced as she heard her bridge partner call her name. She stood. "They're all on the waterways that twist and turn through the county. No wonder you got lost." As she walked back to the bridge players, she added, "I'd love to help. Sounds like fun. Besides, I can show you the town as we drive around. Let's try again this afternoon. We usually finish our bridge session around three-thirty. I'll meet you out front at four."

"Wonderful! See you at four then." Susan could provide knowledgeable help, but Susan was sharp. *I'll have to be careful what I say around her.*

Nancy walked away from the pool area, sensing that hanging around while the bridge game continued would be distracting to the players, and she needed to walk the dogs.

As she approached the elevator, a short, thin woman in a flowered house dress and tight, white curls raised a hand from the walker she was leaning on, waved at Nancy, and greeted her with a nod. "You're that gal who's staying at Peter's now, aren't you?"

Nancy smiled. "That's right. Nancy Davis."

The other woman inched forward on the walker. "Iris Higgins. He's all right, isn't he? Saw the ambulance."

"Oh yes. He's off to St. Thomas. On vacation."

"Yeah. That's what we heard." She winked at Nancy. "But Abby and I bet he's up to something, isn't he?"

Nancy kept her face deadpan and shrugged. She'd have to ask Peter about Iris and Abby.

"You met my friend Abby?" Iris asked.

"I met her yesterday at the pool."

"That's what she said. You're new here, so if you want to know where anything is or what's going on around here, you ask Abby. She knows everything and everybody. Better'n me. I can't see so good, but she's sharp as a tack."

"I'll certainly keep her in mind," Nancy said. She waited until Iris crept into the elevator before she joined her and pressed the button for the third floor. "Third floor okay?"

"Second's my floor, but I don't mind a detour." Iris leaned on her walker as they passed the second and the elevator door opened on the third floor.

"Nice meeting you," said Nancy as she exited.

"See you around," responded Iris. "Come visit me." The door closed.

I certainly will. And Abby too. How could she caution them to be careful what they said? Knowing what was really going on around Riverside Acres might be dangerous to their health. Didn't they ever read mysteries?

As Nancy walked to the apartment, she bumped into a distinguished-looking man with silver hair dressed like a business executive. He was carrying a martini glass and teetering on his feet.

He raised his glass in a salute. "Beg your pardon, Miss."

He nodded at her as she passed, but when she unlocked the door to Peter's apartment, she looked back and saw that he had stopped and was staring at her.

***

Stay Active! Stay Alert!

Take part in the many activities available at Riverside Acres. Swimming, tennis, ping pong, bridge, shuffleboard, and golf are just a few of the games and sports you can enjoy here or at our partner, the Westover Country Club. Join a team or find partners at the sign-up sheets in the lounge. Questions? Contact Connie Stevens, Riverside Acres Activities Coordinator at 954-555-6534.

Riverside Acres Recreation Committee

Chapter 9

Nancy walked the dogs, shooed them into the apartment, and checked her watch. Plenty of time to visit Abby before meeting Susan. She walked down the stairs to the second floor. Ninety years old and still using the stairs. Nancy congratulated herself and remembered all the hours spent in swimming, tennis, and walking.

Nancy found Abby's apartment, pushed the doorbell, and waited. She could hear someone inside making her way slowly and heavily to the door. Abby leaned on the wall, catching her breath as she opened the door. She ushered Nancy into the living room, waving with a dish towel toward the couch. The smell of lavender suffocated Nancy, and the knickknacks, dolls, souvenirs, decorative throw pillows, and magazines that covered every table and shelf—even the couch—crowded around her. She pushed aside a couple of throw pillows as she sat. But, unlike the stuff in her own apartment back at Whisperwood, everything in this apartment was dust-free, clean, and well cared for.

"Tea? Coffee?" Abby asked, using chair backs for crutches as she walked into the kitchen and then brought out a plate of cookies, setting it on the table in front of the couch. "I'm so glad you came by."

"Tea would be nice," Nancy said, trying not to cough from the lavender.

Abby joined her in a cup of tea. "So Peter's in St. Thomas now, is he?" She huffed as she spoke, but her eyes twinkled. How much did Abby know? Surely Peter hadn't confided in her.

"He hasn't been himself lately," Abby said. "It's that hobby of his, you know." She leaned forward. "I told him, be careful. You don't know these people. What if one of them is your most wanted killer?"

Nancy almost dropped her tea cup. "He told you about that?" Nancy laughed, deciding that treating Peter's hobby as a long-standing joke among friends might defuse the threat it posed to someone here. "He's been doing that for years. Harmless, really." She sipped her tea, peering at Abby over the cup.

Abby straightened the antimacassar on her armchair. "I don't think so, my dear. He's usually so full of fun, but ever since that evening when he brought out the flyers on the latest crop of killers and showed us what to look for to identify faces, he hasn't been the same. Worried. Tense. I think he was too close." She ran a napkin across her lips.

"Were you there that evening?"

"I was, but I don't think it mattered if you were there or not. I heard people talking about it at the pool, you know." She sipped her tea. "Making fun of him and his ideas, but maybe someone here found his ideas too dangerous."

"Can you think of who that might be?" Nancy added a bit of flattery. "I know you keep an eye on what's going on here. You might have seen something. . ."

Abby was sharp. She'd be a good ally, if she could be trusted, but Nancy didn't know that yet. She'd have to ask Peter. Nancy retreated to dithering mode. "All the people I've met here seem so nice. I can't imagine any of them being dangerous, can you?"

Abby raised an eyebrow and smiled. "Not all the people here are what they seem," she said.

"Really?" So one of them might be Peter's dangerous criminal. "Who do you mean?"

"I'm not sure yet. I'm keeping my eyes open. We'll see." She took another sip of tea. "We'll see."

"I love mystery stories," Nancy said, trying to maintain the dithering mode but genuinely concerned for Abby's safety. "You've got to tell me. Who is it? Protection, you know. In a mystery, anytime someone says they know what's going on, they get murdered. I would sure hate to see that happen to you."

Abby raised an eyebrow. "That sounds like a threat."

Nancy shook her head and tittered. "Of course not, I'm just worried about your safety." She reached for Abby's hand and held it, looking directly into her eyes, abandoning the act. "If you do know anything, you should tell me now, and I'll contact Peter. If someone dangerous is living here at Riverside, we should alert the authorities."

Abby wouldn't meet Nancy's eyes. "I'll be careful," she mumbled, "but I told you, I'm not sure yet. Just seen glances, heard stuff, and I'd hate to malign someone who is innocent." She pulled back. "I'll keep my mouth shut and wait till Peter comes back. If he does come back." She lifted her chin. "For all I know, you've done away with him." She wasn't smiling.

Nancy almost laughed. Of course it might seem that way. They arrive and Peter disappears. "He's fine, but I'm worried about you. Please, no more hinting that you know everything that's going on around here." Nancy's tone was stern.

Abby cast her eyes down at her lap as if chastened, but Nancy could see a glint of humor in them.

Nancy set down her cup and looked at her watch. "I have to meet Susan who's going to show me around town." She smiled at Abby. "Thank you for an enjoyable chat. I hope you'll come visit us." *Maybe then I can find out what she knows. If anything. Maybe she's just playing this game for the attention.*

***

"Would you like to hear the bad news now?" Susan asked as she smoothed the folds of her pristine blue summer dress.

They were driving out of the condo parking area, shaded by the heavy foliage of spreading ficus trees, into brilliant, clear sunshine. Nancy halted the car to put on her sunglasses. She glanced at Susan. "Bad news?"

"Fort Lauderdale, the Venice of America, boating capital, gateway to the Bahamas, deep sea fishing paradise." Susan sat back and raised an eyebrow at Nancy. "What does that tell you?"

Nancy groaned. "Boats. Lots of boats."

"And marinas, boatyards, anchorages, houses with docks on the New River and on all the canals. Lots of places for a boat to hide."

"This isn't going to be easy, is it?" Nancy stopped at Las Olas Boulevard. "Where to first?" She looked over at Susan who was wrestling with the seat belt. Nancy glanced in the rear view mirror. No one behind them, so they could wait.

Susan got the belt buckled and sat back. "If they're staying here in Fort Lauderdale for some reason, it could be that they're having repairs done. I suggest we head for the south fork of the New River and see what boats are in the yards there." Susan pointed to the left. "That way."

Fifteen minutes later after Susan had directed Nancy in a number of turns that left her bewildered, they arrived at a gravel yard crammed with boats propped upright on land in wooden frames of two-by-fours. The sound of electric sanders, saws, and other tools pierced the air. Men and women in paint-stained, ragged cut-offs and T-shirts sweated in the hot sun working on the boats or scurrying across the yard. Susan and Nancy stepped around the equipment and debris scattered on the sandy ground.

"You say the boat was named the *Bonny Scot*?" Susan asked. "We could just call the marinas."

"I could, but I'll leave that till later." Nancy shielded her eyes. "I really want to see Fort Lauderdale first. Get my bearings." She glanced at Susan. "So to speak."

"Of course. You've just arrived."

"Let's find the office." Nancy searched the yard for a likely structure. She hoped Susan wasn't going to start being "sensible." Nancy loved to poke around and explore, but she'd met too many people who considered that a waste of time.

The first person they asked pointed to a small, shabby trailer sitting against a rusted chain link fence that bounded three sides of the boat yard. The fourth side was the river. An air conditioner in the window next to the door rattled. Nancy and Susan entered.

A slim, middle-aged man with a graying crew cut sat behind a scarred wooden desk littered with papers. He was eating a banana and stared at them as they entered. He swallowed. "Can I help you?"

Nancy smiled at him. "I hope so." She explained their mission. "They might need boat repairs. Have you met anyone like that here?"

He shrugged. "What is this? A missing persons thing?"

"The family is just wondering, that's all," Nancy replied.

"I see." He frowned and pulled open a desk file drawer. He rummaged through the drawer, pulled out a sheaf of papers, and leafed through them.

"Nope. Nobody named Slocum, but that sounds like a fake name to me. A boat captain named Slocum? Come on. And I don't remember a young woman named Jessica," he leered at them, "who wasn't spoken for, that is." He sat back. "Sorry."

Nancy gave him a card with Peter's phone number. "If you happen to see them, would you call me?"

"No promises. They probably went on down to the Keys or maybe the Bahamas. Better hope not, though." He steepled his fingers and grinned at them.

"What do you mean?" Nancy asked.

"Bad storm came through here a week ago. Tough if you were out in the Gulf Stream. A lot of boats were busted up out there, but I haven't heard of any fatalities." He winked at them. "Yet." He tapped a pencil on his desk. "And there's the drug trade. Wrong place, wrong time, you know." He ran a finger across his throat.

Nancy's first inclination was a cold "thank you," but then she remembered that Susan was an audience too. "Do you really think so?" she asked in her dithery voice, but the man was already shuffling through the papers on his desk. She nodded at Susan, and they returned to the car.

"You see?" said Susan.

"We might as well try the next boatyard." Nancy slid behind the wheel and turned on the car and its air conditioner.

"And then we can talk to the city dock master." Susan smiled at Nancy. "This is going to be fun! I have been so bored down here. Thank goodness you came along."

Nancy pushed down a feeling of relief. She wouldn't have to negotiate these visits with Susan. "You moved here from somewhere else?"

Susan examined her fingernails. "Didn't everyone?"

Nancy could see the effort Susan made to keep the tone light. "My husband and I sold our stationery business in Ohio. We'd been planning our retirement for years," she laughed, "so we drove to Fort Lauderdale, bought a house on the golf course, and a week later," she paused and turned to stare out the window, "he died."

Susan sounded as if she'd repeated that story many times. "I'm so sorry. . ." Nancy began.

Susan shrugged. "Hell of a note. He worked hard so he could retire and play golf. Then he had a heart attack on the course. It's been difficult, not knowing many people here. I sold the house and bought the unit at Riverside."

Nancy glanced at Susan. Hers was probably a common story in south Florida. Too common, maybe, considering how many retired people settled here. Nancy remembered the months and years she spent grieving as a two-time widow, but then long-time friends had surrounded her. Even so, they couldn't fill every lonely hour. Nights were the worst. She glanced at Susan. "Sounds like you'll stay down here."

"They don't have weather like this in Ohio." She smiled at Nancy. "Now you need to make a left turn into the yard there." She pointed to an overgrown, graveled lot similar to the last boatyard.

Dust, heat, and noise followed them past landed boat hulks as they walked to the office. Inside, a young woman sat at a desk behind a counter, drinking a soda.

She put the bottle down and walked to the counter. "Can I help you?"

Nancy told her of the search, but the woman shook her head as she leafed through a ledger. "Don't remember anyone like that, and I don't see anyone named 'Ray Slocum.'" She raised an eyebrow at Nancy, closed the book, and yawned. "We keep careful records."

Nancy pulled out another card and gave it to her. "Please call me if anyone like that comes here. It's very important."

As they walked back to the car, the sun beat down on them in the shadeless dust of the boatyard. Nancy was beginning to feel tired and dispirited and all of her ninety years. She regretted telling Amelia that she would take on this impossible task. The couple had probably left Fort Lauderdale by now.

As if sensing Nancy's mood, Susan made another suggestion. "Let's park downtown near the city marina along the New River and try the Riverwalk. It's shaded and pretty, and we can ask the boaters there as we sightsee."

Nancy found parking, and Susan led the way to the Riverwalk. "See?" She smiled at Nancy. "How can you feel depressed with all these flowers and greenery around?" She waved her hand at the hibiscus blooming along the walk.

Nancy agreed. The muted greens of the West Virginia summer faded in contrast to the sun-splashed clarity of color around her. And it was January! Sailboats and powerboats, small to luxurious, lined the riverbanks. Some were still decorated with holiday wreaths and colored lights. She held a hand over her eyes against the sun, but much of the walk was shaded by trees, and in the shade the breezes felt cool and balmy. She could smell the fresh-mown grass and the tropical flowers around them as they walked. Waves splashed against the concrete sides of the river and lines rattled against the sailboat masts. A drowsy sense of euphoria crept over her. She shook it off. She had work to do.

"When we see anyone onboard, let's ask them if they've seen Ray or Jessica," suggested Susan. "This is a good time, late afternoon, cocktail hour."

They approached a yellow catamaran. A young man sat reading in the cockpit. Nancy walked to the boat and rapped on the side. "Excuse me."

He looked up. "Yo?"

"Have you seen a trawler called the *Bonny Scot* with two people on board named Jessica and Ray?"

He stood and peered up and down the river as if he could spot the boat they were searching for, but he shook his head. "We got in a couple of days ago, and no, don't remember seeing the *Bonny Scot* and haven't met anyone named Ray or Jessica."

Nancy and Susan strolled on. "A beautiful walk," Nancy said, "but we might as well find the dock master's office and ask him."

Susan snapped her fingers. "Of course. They must have records." She looked sideways at Nancy. "Including next of kin."

Nancy could see that Susan was waiting for the obvious question, but she stopped to admire an odd tree with several waxy white blossoms past their prime still clinging to the stems. She pulled one over and sniffed its delicate fragrance.

Susan smiled. "That's frangipani. In Hawaii, they make leis of those flowers. Lovely, aren't they?"

"It's going to be hard to go back to West Virginia," Nancy said. "So why do they collect next of kin information?"

Susan shrugged. "Common story. People dream of retiring and bringing their boat down here, so they wait too long, the trip is too much for them, and they die when they get here."

"I see." Nancy remembered Susan's own situation, but that wasn't the case with Jessica and Ray, both young people..

A short while later, they entered the dock master's office and rang the bell on the counter, which brought a gray-haired man with a paunch out from the back room. Nancy told him what they were looking for and stood at the counter while he sat at a desk behind the counter and peered at a computer screen. "I ain't the real dock master," he muttered, "but I'll see what I can do."

He paused to look at them, his hand on the mouse, and frowned. "Lots of boats come through here, you know, I'm checking the other city docks too." He went back to the computer screen. "Just go sit over there," he waved at the two captain's chairs against the wall. "Don't crowd me here or I'll miss somebody."

Nancy and Susan sat in the two chairs for visitors. The varnished oak chairs, countertop and wainscoting shone as if taken from a luxury yacht. The carpet was a deep blue, and a steering wheel, rope knot display, and other nautical decor decorated the walls.

"Corny, isn't it?" Susan whispered.

"Aha!" The dock master looked up. "I've found a Ray Slocum here on a thirty-six-foot trawler, *Bonny Scot*. One crew member, Jessica Cantwell. They were here at the New River dock two weeks ago and left after one day."

Nancy's face fell. "They left after one day?"

"Sure. Young couple? Trawler?" He peered out the window to the river. "Living on a shoestring, no doubt. Couldn't afford more than one day."

Susan stepped forward. "So where would they go then?"

He stood and leaned on the counter. "Hundreds of marinas in south Florida. Probably found a cheap place behind a house up the river or on a canal someplace. Unless they went to the Bahamas or the Keys or," he shrugged, "wherever."

Nancy walked behind Susan back to the car feeling tired and depressed at the immensity of trying to locate one boat among the thousands in Fort Lauderdale. Finding Jessica seemed even more hopeless. She could be anywhere.

∗∗∗

Boat Slips Available

Riverside Acres offers boat slips at special rates to residents. Boats cannot exceed twenty-six feet in length and must have a draught of less than four feet. Contact Skip Foster at the Riverside Acres marina to reserve a slip for your boat.

Riverside Acres Management Office

Chapter 10

That evening, Nancy sat on the couch with the dogs on each side. All three moved their heads back and forth as they watched Louise pace the living room, describing her day at Fort Lauderdale's shelters.

"Makes me mad to think we need such places." Louise fumed. "I like to help out, but they didn't have anything for me to do, so I went to the homeless shelter a few blocks away. Volunteered to straighten up the place for the day. It helps the mentally ill, drug addicts, alcoholics, ex-offenders, disabled. People with no skills, no jobs, and no place to stay." She tossed her long, gray braid. "Shit. The lost ones in our society."

Nancy squelched her long-held desire to lop off Louise's braid. "At least they're going to a shelter," Nancy said, "where there are services for them."

"Yeah." Louise stopped pacing.

Nancy got up and walked into the kitchen. She poured two glasses of Chardonnay and brought them out.

"I'm worried about our neighbor." Louise nodded toward the apartment next door. "Is her husband beating her? Those thumps and bumps we hear through the walls are suspicious, I'd say."

"I saw her in the hall," said Nancy. "She had bruises."

"You saw her with bruises. Okay. She does need help." Louise flopped into a chair. "So what did you find out?"

Nancy handed her a glass of wine. "I had an interesting tour of the town." Nancy described the excursion to the marinas. "We only visited three and there are hundreds. It's a hopeless task. I wish Amelia had heard from her."

"But you learned a lot in just one day."

Nancy sat back on the couch and sipped the wine. "Susan was helpful. I would never have found the boatyards and the Riverwalk without her."

"How long has she been here? Does she know Peter?" Louise paused as if an idea just struck her. "Maybe she's the culprit."

"The thought had occurred to me. I'm being careful what I say to Susan about Peter since so many people here know each other. The potluck lunches and other activities would help with that. Susan can help search for Jessica, since Jessica doesn't have any connection to this place or to Peter."

"Most of the people are around all day, being retired," said Louise.

"A few work, though. I've seen them suited up and heading off when I walk the dogs. The person I worry about is Abby."

"Abby? The woman who knows everything about this place?"

Nancy nodded. "I talked to her about it. I hope she'll backpedal and keep her mouth shut."

"She's asking for trouble." Louise sat on the couch next to Nancy and reached out to Oscar who came over to her, tail wagging. She scratched his ears. "All kinds of activities go on here. I even saw a sign downstairs for a driving service."

"Driving service?" Nancy stroked Rupert's back to give him equal time.

"If you don't want to drive your car north, you take it to them, and they find a driver for it. Then you fly home and wait for it to show up." Louise sipped her wine. "I guess they figure they've got a pool of possible customers here. Drivers, too. If anyone here signs on as a driver, they'll probably drive slow and safe."

Nancy smiled. "Driving slow and safe is a good bet if they've lived long enough to afford this place."

Louise leaned back against the sofa cushion as Oscar settled at her feet. "So what's next?"

"After I call the hospitals about Jessica, I'll start calling boatyards." Nancy grimaced. "Tedious, but I told Amelia I'd help. Had no idea there'd be so many boatyards and marinas here."

"They've probably left the area."

"Or moved to a cheaper place. The city docks are probably expensive."

Louise sipped the wine. "What about Peter? How's he doing?"

Nancy studied her wine glass. "Peter's all right now, and I gave him an assignment." She sighed. "I just hope he stays put."

"Keep him busy there. Call him often," said Louise. "Whoever the culprit is has got to wonder how much he told us." Louise glanced at the den with its display of "Most Wanted."

"We're just dithering friends who came to dog sit." Nancy pursed her lips. "That's all. We should contact the FBI, but he's afraid they'll blow him off. He wants to give them something more substantial, and I'm helping him do that. He's just been stumbling around—a rank amateur. Too bad whoever the bad guy is here apparently doesn't know that."

"So what are we going to do?" Louise reached over and pushed Nancy's arm playfully. "You're the expert."

Nancy laughed to cover up another tremor of fear. She didn't feel like an expert and said so. "Not any more." That was the problem, wasn't it? How much had she lost since she retired?

She sat back and gazed at the ceiling. "We can take digital photos of everyone here and get their fingerprints. Work up files on them. I asked Peter to look into face identification software, but at least we can work with all the characteristics used for facial identification. None of us is sophisticated in that technology, though, and there are too many ways a person could change his or her appearance. Even a simple hair cut can make a difference to the average person."

Louise chewed on her lip. "I suppose you're right." She stared at the floor. "Did the police question Peter about the poisoning?"

Nancy shook her head. "He didn't have anything to tell them. He doesn't know how he got it or where, and he was worried they'd want to keep him in the hospital." She pushed Rupert's head away from her wine.

"I suppose they're inclined to think it was an accidental overdose of a medicine he had around."

"Or an attempt at suicide," added Nancy, remembering how Peter had rushed to get out of the hospital. "He was afraid they'd lock him in the psychiatric ward."

Louise wiped the slobber off Oscar's chin and stroked his fur. "Plenty of people use digitalis for their heart problems."

Nancy nodded. "It would be easy to add a dose to Peter's plate at a potluck."

"Peter's so old, they thought he'd succumb and no one would ask questions."

"They just didn't know how tough a bird he is."

"Have there been any other poisoning cases? The Health Department must have records of them."

"I'll call tomorrow morning," Nancy said. "The hospital should know, too, though the doctor would have mentioned that. If there aren't any other such cases," Nancy added, "then we have to agree with Peter that someone picked him out to deliberately poison."

"That's the way I figure." Louise smiled at Oscar whose alert brown eyes had shifted back and forth with their conversation.

Rupert now lay dozing against Nancy.

"And we have to consider a motive," Nancy said, "Right now, Peter's cold case hobby seems to be the most likely motivation."

"He didn't raise anyone's dander here?" Louise arched an eyebrow. "Maybe a widow felt rejected."

Nancy remembered how embarrassed Peter would get when a woman pursued him. She had been attracted to him herself, but she soon picked up on the clues he gave about himself. Nancy had learned his secret but never revealed it. Even as recently as ten years ago, he'd kept it hidden out of fear of losing his job or his friends. Now he was out and open about his sexuality. She felt tears brim. The memories kept flooding in. Peter. His partner Michael. Bill. The sadness could overwhelm her if she let it. She couldn't let Louise see her weakness. She looked away until she could gain control of herself.

"Do you think a widow was after him? Felt rejected?" Louise repeated.

Nancy shook her head, swallowed, and willed herself to speak. "Didn't mention it, and no one's indicated any such thing." She reached over to pet Oscar, lying on the couch next to her. "Except Abby, but she was just joking."

Louise snorted and flicked her braid. "Plenty of women here would find Peter attractive, and he would have been neighborly. Could have been misconstrued."

"Of course, but there wouldn't have been any reciprocation. Hard to keep a one-sided passion alive." Nancy stared at her glass and remembered her own crush on Peter so many years before.

"Some women do, though."

"I'll ask Peter, but time is a'wastin'. We lost time with Peter in the hospital, but today was well-spent. We can't afford to dawdle at the pool, but we can use pool time and other social times here to listen to the gossip, take photos—casually, of course—of the residents, and email them to Peter to include in the folders on each suspect."

Nancy walked into the kitchen, setting her glass down on the table. "Let him play with them. Maybe he'll find a match with one of the most wanted. He's holed up in that hotel room trying to help." She eyed the glass, picked it up, and studied it.

"Sure." Louise snickered. "But I'll bet he's lying on the beach."

"I don't think so. He's serious about this." Nancy set the glass down again. "The glasses here are plain and smooth. Perfect for usable fingerprints."

"Great idea!" Louise stood, accidentally kicking Oscar who hopped off the couch with an injured air. She tottered into the kitchen and picked up the glass. "You're right. Fingerprints will show up just fine."

Nancy casually reached for the newspaper lying folded on the table. She glanced at the front page, then flipped through to the local news. "Oh no," she said.

"What?" asked Louise.

Nancy held up the newspaper. "They found Ray."

***

An Important Notice

None of us likes to think about death and dying, but for the consideration of your family, we suggest that you file with our office your wishes for your memorial service, disposal of your remains, and information about the location of your will, bank, and investments. You may pick up a form at the office that will make this necessary task easier. Your family will be grateful.

__Management, Riverside Acres__

Chapter 11

Nancy read aloud from the newspaper. "Slocum's body was discovered in the Everglades. He'd been shot in the head."

Feeling sick, Nancy looked at Louise. "Killed about two weeks ago, they think. A fisherman found the body caught in some mangroves." Would the police find Jessica's body too in a few days? The prospect of telling Amelia the news sank to the pit of her stomach. This was the kind of thing she hated and feared about her job.

Louise peered over Nancy's shoulder. "What was Ray doing in the Everglades?"

"Let me see." Nancy scanned down the page. "The owner came down to claim the boat and found no one on board. The guy who owned the dock, Stan Jaworsky, said that both people on board had disappeared three days after tying up at his dock. Didn't know what happened to them, but figured they'd gone off somewhere. They'd paid up so he didn't worry about it."

"How'd the police identify the body?"

"The boat owner came down a couple of days ago and couldn't find Ray. Seems Ray was a long-time friend and should have been there."

"So the boat owner reported Ray missing and then identified the body?"

Nancy nodded.

"Don't envy him that job." Louise took the paper and perused the article. "They've got a local street address for the boat here. The owner was from Baltimore." She frowned at Nancy. "It says Ray moved his boat from the city marina to a private dock behind a house. That's why the street address."

Nancy pulled out a kitchen chair and stared glumly at Rupert who cocked his head at her. "The question is, where is Jessica?"

"She isn't mentioned at all." Louise peered over the paper at Nancy.

"She could have left the boat before Ray was killed, I suppose," said Nancy, "but why hasn't she called her family?"

Louise nodded. "Or maybe the murderer is keeping her prisoner, or she's the killer, or she escaped and is hiding somewhere."

Nancy frowned. "But if she's hiding out, we've got to find her before the murderer does."

Louise dropped the paper on the table. "Shit, shit, shit. I'm just sick about this."

"Me too," said Nancy. "Tomorrow we need to go see the boat."

"Yep." Louise picked up her cane and stalked towards her bedroom. She clenched a fist. "They better not have hurt that girl."

Nancy sat a moment, then reached for the phone and tapped in Amelia's number.

A timorous voice quavered, "Hello?"

"Amelia? Nancy. I'm calling from Fort Lauderdale."

"Nancy! I'm so glad to talk to you. We've just heard from Jessica!"

Nancy sat back with relief. "So she's all right?"

The voice took on a doubtful tone. "She *said* she's okay. She said she's staying down there for a couple of months since it's winter and all. She likes the beach."

Did Amelia know about Ray? Nancy didn't want to upset her. "Is Jessica still staying on the boat with Ray?"

"She said she'd left the boat and didn't know what happened to him."

Nancy hoped that was true. "Where is she staying?"

Nancy heard a long sigh. "She had to go. Told me not to worry and to tell the family she's okay, then she hung up."

Not good. No address. And she didn't stay on the phone. To Nancy, that sounded as if Jessica were trying to hide something. Nancy had to find her, but where could Jessica be staying?

"Doesn't she have a cell phone?" Nancy asked.

"Of course, but I've called and called, and she doesn't answer it."

"It probably has a GPS. You could have the company track it."

There was a long pause before Amelia spoke again, even more tremulous than before. "I don't know anything about that."

"Her parents might know. Check with them."

"I will, but right now I'm so relieved she called."

"Amelia, if she calls again, try to get an address or phone number or something. Give her my cell phone number. Tell her to call me. That it's important." Nancy spoke slowly and loudly to give Amelia the number. "Or use caller ID when she calls."

"Caller ID?" Nancy cursed Amelia's frail timidity. Of course she wouldn't know about caller ID. Nancy explained the service.

"I'm still worried about her," said Amelia. "The police have called here, too, asking about her. They wouldn't tell me anything, and I can't imagine why they called. There isn't anything wrong, is there?"

"I'm trying to find out everything I can," said Nancy. Should she go to the police herself? They already knew about Jessica and were searching for her. Did she have any information that would be helpful to the police? Probably not. *I really need to talk to Jessica first.* Why hadn't she left a phone number or address with Amelia?

***

Louise wandered into the kitchen the next morning while Nancy was eating breakfast. The dogs sniffed the floor hopefully, leaving trails of slobber. Louise frowned at them. hands on her hips. "We're going to slip in that slobber and break a hip if we're not careful."

Nancy nudged Rupert away with her foot. "The Health Department should be open in an hour. I'll call them about any digitalis cases. Then we can go find out what we can learn about Jessica and the *Bonny Scot*."

Louise stretched, yawned, and nodded. "Hate to mention this, but if we're going to get home in time for my party, we've only got eighteen days to go."

"Wish you hadn't mentioned it," Nancy said.

She spent an aggravating hour on the phone, being transferred from one office to the next before she had her answer. Other than Peter, a confirmed case of digitalis poisoning, the Health Department had not received notice of any other such incidents in the past two weeks. Nancy couldn't pry any other information out of them.

She reported this to Louise and added, "I'll call Susan to come with us. She knows this town and can get us to the dock easily." She waved the map. "I looked up the address, but the river runs through the area, breaking up the streets into dead ends." Nancy picked up the phone.

In half an hour, Susan was at their door, and the threesome headed down to the parking area. Walking between Nancy and Louise, Susan held their arms as if they couldn't stand upright on their own.

Louise shook her off. "I ain't crippled yet," she grumbled.

Nancy saw the glint in Louise's eye that meant she was preparing to trip Susan with her cane in response to the patronizing help. Nancy frowned at Louise and shook her head. Louise stuck out her tongue at Nancy but drew in her cane.

The breeze ruffled their hair as they strode down the covered, outside walkway. Two men sauntered toward them. Susan stumbled and moved behind Nancy to let them pass. Nancy recognized the well-dressed man from the day before, but he'd left his martini at home this time. The other man, balding, paunchy, and wearing a blue guayabera, swaggered past them, according Nancy a brief nod. Nancy turned and watched them walk past Peter's door. She heard the dogs bark, then the men turned the corner.

"Where do you suppose those guys are going?" Louise whispered. "Do they live here?"

"The older one does. Bob Connolly, the condo drunk." Susan spoke with distaste. "Dresses well and quite handsome, but not to my taste, frankly."

Nancy reached for her phone. Too late. She made a mental note to take photos the next time she saw those men. They seemed too dapper, like confidence men. Scam artists. Both of them.

"This is the first time I've seen him without a drink in his hand," Susan added. "The other one is Harv Johnston. He's quite wealthy. Real estate, I think. A nice guy. Doesn't live here, though." She glanced at Nancy. "He runs the driver service. You might have seen the notice downstairs. "

"I told you about it, remember?" said Louise. "I bet their slogan is, 'Old Fogies Drive Safe.'" She laughed at her own joke.

Susan joined her in laughing, but added, "I really don't think they feel that way, Louise."

Louise frowned at Susan. "Why not? Probably true enough."

Susan shrugged as they got on the elevator to go down.

The elevator stopped at the second floor, and Abby Summers crept in, moving her hands from hall rail to elevator rail. "Going out gallivanting?" she asked. She nodded at Susan.

Nancy smiled. "We're going to look around town."

Abby turned to Nancy. "Glad we could chat the other day. I'll remember what you said."

Nancy hoped Abby wouldn't elaborate. "I enjoyed it too."

At the parking lot, Susan insisted on driving. "Lot easier for me to drive than to give directions," she said.

Louise glared at her. Nancy shrugged and handed her the keys. She knew why Susan wanted to drive. Tiresome, but Nancy was used to younger people's presumption that they were somehow more skilled and competent. Nancy could stand the patronizing as long as Susan could get them to the dock quickly.

She caught a glimpse of herself in the car window and grimaced. She did look all of her ninety years, and now her white wispy hair had gone all frizzy because of the humidity. No wonder Susan seemed to think she and Louise were feeble. The thought would have depressed Nancy if the day hadn't been so bright with sunshine and flowers and the smell of the grass so fresh and wet from the sprinklers.

Susan navigated the back streets like a city cab driver. In fifteen minutes, they reached the address given for the boat dock. Nancy surveyed this block of seedy, neglected houses overrun by weeds with misgiving. A tall hedge on both sides of a curving gravel driveway hid the house they sought from the road. Nancy checked the address again. Hard to believe this house could have a dock on the river. They walked down the drive to a wide area where the drive ended and two cars were parked. A worn, unpaved path led to a green, stuccoed concrete block house and past it down to a dock and the river. Birds rattled the branches overhead and lazy waves gently slapped the riverbank.

"I don't think we should go any farther," said Susan, hanging back and looking distastefully at the wet, patchy grass.

"Nonsense." Leaning on her cane, Louise hobbled ahead. Nancy followed, and then with a look of disapproval, Susan joined them.

They passed the house on their right and crossed the lawn down to the dock where three boats floated placidly. One of them was the *Bonny Scot*, appearing closed up and deserted.

Susan turned to Nancy. "North fork of the New River. People who own places like this sometimes rent out dock space to transient boaters."

Nancy stepped onto the dock.

Susan hesitated. "Why don't we just wait here and see if anyone's around."

"Hell, no," growled Louise, already stepping toward the *Bonny Scot*.

"Wait. You don't want to trip on those boards. Break a hip." Susan took Louise's arm, but Louise shook it off.

Nancy followed. "We'll be just fine," she assured Susan. "Bless your heart. I do so want to talk to the other boaters." Nancy was finding it difficult to maintain the dithery old lady image in front of Susan.

The *Bonny Scot* appeared to be roomy, sturdy, and well-maintained. The white trim, varnished brightwork, and blue hull all looked freshly painted. Perhaps Ray and Jessica had worked on the boat during their stay here, sprucing it up for the owner's arrival.

A houseboat was tied behind it and in front floated a sleek, open boat with two huge outboard motors hanging on the transom. Nancy rapped on the side of the houseboat. "Anyone home?"

"Just a minute." A man's voice called out. The houseboat rocked as the person moved within. A couple of minutes later, a tanned young man with stringy blond hair emerged, dressed only in a ragged pair of cutoffs. "Can I help you?"

Nancy stepped forward. "We're looking for the young woman who was on the *Bonny Scot*."

He squinted at her. "You heard what happened, didn't you? The cops were all over this place."

"What happened, do you know?"

"Hell, no. Never talked to the guy but if you ask me, I'd say he got drunk, fell overboard, and drowned. Happens a lot around the water. The cops say he was shot, and he was found miles from here in the Everglades. Probably got caught in a bar fight." He shrugged. "Whatever. I'm looking to get out," he glanced down the river, "I don't like the comings and goings around here, but a place like this is so cool and hard to find."

Nancy took in the river and the mangroves along the banks, the sparse yard, the massive ficus tree by the house. Just a back yard with a dock. No security here and not what she'd call a good neighborhood. She glanced at the young man. "What about the young woman who was with him?"

The man jumped onto the dock and leaned against a piling. "She was cool. Pretty too. Nice. Sure hope she's not in the river." He frowned down at the water.

Louise stepped forward and peered up at the man. "Any idea what it could have been about? If he was shot here, I mean."

He squinted at her in the bright sunlight. "Nope and I don't like it one bit." His eyes darted from the house to the *Bonny Scot* and then beyond it to the power boat. "I've got my suspicions," his eyes drifted along the shoreline toward the inlet that separated this yard from the next, "and I want out of here. Been convenient, though. And cheap."

He glanced furtively at the house across the inlet.

"What's going on over there?" Nancy asked.

He shook his head. "Nothin' as far as I know, and that's all I'm saying." He jumped back onto his boat. "Got things to do. See ya."

Susan stepped off the dock and turned back. "Come on, let's go. This place gives me the creeps."

Nancy shook her head. "Just a minute." She pulled a pen and notepad out of her purse. "Can you tell me who owns that boat in front of the *Bonny Scot*," she called out, "or the house?"

"I'll wait for you in the car," said Susan.

"That's fine," Louise muttered and turned her back.

"Don't know about the fast boat." The young man spit into the water. "And the old guy who owns this place is pathetic. He's okay, though." He lowered his voice. "It's those guys in that house over there." He nodded toward the inlet and the pink house on the other side as he turned his back on them. "Don't look at it," he added urgently.

Nancy kept her face toward the houseboat but studied the other side of the inlet out of the corner of her eye. She could barely see the house through the mangroves and hedge. No boats were tied up at the dock.

"You don't want to mess with those guys. Too tough for me." He kept his back to the house as if afraid someone watched them. "I hear some fat cat owns the house. Never see him, though." He walked over to a coiled hose and glanced back at them. "And I don't look. Anyway, they took all the boats out of there like maybe a week or two ago." He picked up the hose and turned on the spigot. "Damn birds. Always got to shit on my boat." He began washing large white splotches off the deck.

Stopping for a moment, he stared out at the water. "That place over there," he gave a slight nod toward the house across the inlet, "is more like a depot than a marina."

"What do you mean?" Nancy studied the house in question.

"Just saying." He went back to scrubbing the white blotches.

Nancy stepped back. She reached into her purse and pulled out a card. "If you see Jessica, the young woman on the *Bonny Scot,* would you give her this card?" She handed it to the man, pleased that she'd made so many business cards on her computer, even if she wasn't in business. They came in handy.

"Sure. Doubt she'd ever come back here." He slipped it into a pocket as he sprayed another large white splotch. He glanced at the *Bonny Scot.* "Not with her friend getting murdered and all."

Susan honked at them from the car. Annoyed, Nancy shook her head at Louise and together they walked over to the house. Louise rapped on the front door with her cane. No response. They heard another honk as they walked back down the drive to join Susan.

"Where could Jessica be?" Louise punctuated the words by thumping her cane on the gravel drive.

The sweet young face in the photos surfaced in Nancy's memory. "I hope she's still alive, but if she is, I think she's in great danger." A young woman who should have a long life ahead of her.

"She's gotten involved in something fishy, that's for sure. Nothing about that Ray person or this house or that boat over there," Louise pointed to the powerboat, "smells right to me."

***

Drivers Wanted

Drive cars north, all expenses paid, for their owners while they fly back. If you have a safe driving record and would like a cheap way to travel, contact us at Drivers Unlimited. Car owner pays for gas and motel bills with a daily stipend for meals. Please call 954-555-8890 between 1 p.m. and 8 p.m. As long as you have a safe driving record, you're good to go!

Notice approved, Riverside Acres Management

Chapter 12

Nancy, Louise, and Susan sat in Peter's living room, sipping iced tea and idly watching the two dogs roll on the floor. The three women had hashed and rehashed the visit to the *Bonny Scot* but had reached no conclusions.

Susan sighed, flicking an invisible speck off her spotless white slacks. "I can't come up with any new ideas about that boat, and I have to get back home. By the way, are you two going to be around this evening?" She shrugged self-consciously. "Meant to ask you this before."

Nancy relaxed and sat back. "Far as we know."

"Why?" asked Louise, suspicion in her voice.

"There's a cocktail hour in the club room at five tonight. You both would be very welcome. Snacks are free but a cash bar." Susan smiled at them as if this were a sought-after invitation.

"Thank you," Nancy said quickly before Louise could turn Susan down. "We'd enjoy that, wouldn't we, Louise?" She stared at Louise, hoping her expression sent a message to agree.

Louise bent down to wipe Rupert's chin. "Sure. Like to meet the people here."

"Do most of the residents come?" Nancy's eyes turned toward the den. The cocktail hour would be a good way to see if she could spot any resemblance to the flyers. Susan's eyes followed her glance.

"That den's a nice feature in this unit." Before Nancy could stop her, Susan walked into the den.

"What in the world?" Susan perused the flyers as Nancy stood behind her. "What was Peter doing with these?" Susan pointed to the "Wanted" flyers.

Her question sounded a shade off, as if she had known about the flyers before. As if she wanted to know what Peter—and Nancy—were doing with them. Nancy stepped back to the living room. Susan followed.

"Just a hobby," Nancy said. "Don't know anything about it."

"I find this fascinating. Peter is such an interesting man. Has he tracked down anyone?"

"Not that I've heard," Nancy said.

Susan smiled as she turned away. Was her interest in Peter or in his hobby? Nancy supposed Susan hadn't been here at Riverside very long. She may not have heard Peter talk about Michael, his lover and partner for many years. And Peter could be very charming.

"He is such a card," said Nancy. Perhaps Susan's interest in Peter explained her willingness to befriend Louise and Nancy.

"He certainly is," said Susan, patting her perfect blonde hair into place.

Nancy's thoughts shifted to the cocktail party. Would she be able to take more photos of the residents? She might learn what she wanted to know just in the conversation. She'd have to plan a strategy with Louise. She repeated her question to Susan. "Do most of the residents come?"

"A lot of them do." Susan seemed to be thinking. "Your neighbor, Mrs. Sandstrom, doesn't. Too shy, I think. But most of them come if they're in town."

"Then I'd enjoy meeting them," said Nancy.

"Me, too," Louise chimed in.

"I've been wondering, Susan, if you have any ideas about where a young woman would go in this town if she were looking for a cheap place to live." asked Nancy. She twiddled with a straw in her glass of iced tea.

Susan sat back and pondered the question. "How much money do you suppose she had with her?"

"She could have taken whatever stash Ray had onboard," Louise suggested, leaning forward, her face alive with interest. "He probably had to pay cash for expenses." She flicked her braid.

"If she had money, then a motel? Apartment? Rooming house?" Susan shrugged. "Anyway, why wouldn't she just go home? Or at least let them know where she was staying."

"I gotta ask that too," said Louise. "Doesn't she know how worried her folks are?"

"Do you suppose she was injured?" asked Susan. "Lost her memory? Maybe she's in a hospital."

"But she called home and said she was all right," put in Louise. "If we believe her, we could drop our search."

Nancy shook her head. "She's hiding from the people who murdered Ray. Are they looking for her? Would she worry that they might go after her family? Ray's family? Or is there some other reason she's hard to find." Nancy walked over to the dining room table and picked up the newspaper. "We should talk to the owner of the property where the *Bonny Scot* was docked."

"I'm more interested in the house on the other side of the inlet," said Louise. "Did you see the way that guy on the houseboat tried not to look at it?"

Nancy nodded. "Like he was scared. Something odd there."

Susan sighed. "That ol' place is too creepy for me. Anyway, how could it possibly have anything to do with Ray Slocum. He probably wasn't even killed anywhere near the boat. Probably got all boozed up at some bar and taken for a ride like the guy on the houseboat said."

"You don't have to go back there," put in Louise. "We can find it by ourselves."

"I'd better go along," Susan shrugged, "just in case."

Louise glared at Susan. "In case of what?"

"Never mind. Anyway, I'm happy to play chauffeur." Susan's hands fluttered as if that took care of her concerns.

Louise clenched her jaw. "Nancy and I been doing this kind of stuff a lot longer than you been around."

Nancy laughed. She'd have to talk to Louise. "Driving, she means," Nancy said. "We've been driving a long time."

Susan stared meaningfully at Louise. "I know."

"Girls, girls," put in Nancy. "Let's go out and talk to this Stan Jaworsky, the dock owner, tomorrow. What kind of person do you suppose he is?"

"Have no idea," said Susan.

Louise arched an eyebrow. "Hard to judge a person just by their name."

Susan walked to the door. "See you at the party."

Nancy picked up Susan's glass and took it into the kitchen. Louise and the dogs followed her, pausing to check their food bowls.

"Good thing I brought my fingerprinting kit," Nancy said, as she blew black powder onto the glass sides. Then she pressed a piece of tape against the fingerprint imprints to lift them onto the tape before affixing the tape onto a white index card. The fingerprints stood out clearly. Nancy labeled the cardboard with Susan's name and put it into an envelope with Peter's name on it.

As she stepped back, she slipped in a puddle of dog slobber on the floor but caught herself on the counter before she fell.

"I told you," said Louise, wiping up the puddle with a paper towel. "You gotta watch out for that slobber."

That evening, Nancy and Louise set out for the condo clubhouse. Louise wore her usual khaki pants and polo shirt but arched an eyebrow at Nancy's outfit.

"You need to carry knitting if you're going to wear that dress," Louise said, her hands on her hips.

Nancy smoothed out the flowered, short-sleeved, cotton housedress. It had large pockets on each side and a zipper up the front. "It's a bit dowdy," she agreed with a smile. "Makes me appear harmless, don't you think?"

"All you need is a fluffy pussycat."

"I always pack an outfit like this, just in case. Worth a thousand words."

Susan met them at the clubhouse door, wine glass in hand. She glanced at Nancy's dress and her eyes widened. Behind her the buzz of conversation ceased. Nancy heard a few snickers. Apparently her outfit was a success.

Nancy hadn't been in the clubhouse before. With the red ceramic tiles on the floor, matching red draperies, paneled walls, and black furnishings, the designer must have gone for a Mexican look.

Someone had pushed the long tables against the wall, but comfortable chairs were clustered around small coffee tables across the room. The unimaginative hors d'oeuvres—potato chips, dip, crackers and cheese, carrots and celery—were set on the tables, while a bartender dispensed drinks at a portable bar in one corner.

Susan took Nancy by the hand, drew her in, and introduced her around. Bob Connolly lifted a glass to her and winked. "So how's our new neighbor?" His voice slurred the words.

Nancy smiled. "I'm enjoying myself," she said.

"What about your boyfriend?" Connolly asked. "Heard he wasn't well."

"He's doing fine." Nancy made her voice carefree. "Just a minor gastric upset. He's off on his vacation now."

Was it her imagination or did Connolly seem surprised. He covered whatever he felt by raising his glass and turning away.

Other residents crowded around her. Most of them looked as though they'd retired many years before.

A stout little woman with a heavy German accent also asked about Peter. "He didn't seem so good at supper." Others nodded their interest and waited for Nancy's response.

"Peter is fine," Nancy repeated. "I'm sure he's having a good time in St. Thomas. We're taking care of his dogs for him."

The German woman pushed in closer, took Nancy's hand, and peered up at her. "My name is Maria. Maria Schmidt. I live here now five years. I was so worried about him. He didn't look so good to me."

"And I'm Nancy Davis." She retrieved her hand. "I'll tell him you were worried—if he calls."

Susan stepped over to them and put her arm around Maria. "I see you've met my favorite person here." She smiled at Maria and winked at Nancy.

"No need to tell Peter." Maria rushed the words and backed away.

Nancy glanced at Louise, who had withdrawn to a dark corner and was talking on the cell phone. At least she appeared to be talking, but using a wine glass as cover, she was taking photos.

Their eyes met. Good. Their plan was working. Nancy's job was to meet and talk with the residents and distract them from Louise.

A gaunt man with a large nose tottered over to Nancy. "The

doctor tells me I got to gain weight." He chuckled. "Ain't that a stitch now. Been fighting fat all my life, but that ain't all. . ."

Nancy excused herself to meander over to the snacks table. A cluster of men were chatting there, and Nancy hovered. She gathered that one was a retired engineer and another had been a pharmacist. Nancy studied the pharmacist. A pharmacist would know about digitalis. A third man didn't say much but laughed on cue. She felt a tap on her shoulder.

"I hear you're a new addition here," the man said. "I'm Harv Johnston." His smile was ingratiating. "Welcome. I don't live here, but I have friends who do." He held out his hand.

Nancy shook it. "Thank you. This is a very pleasant place." The hackles rose on the back of her neck. Something about this man didn't feel right, and she could usually trust her instincts. She'd met used car and time-share salesmen—and con artists—who gave her the same trepidations. Did he look like any of the men in the flyers? Hard to say.

"I hope you enjoy your time here." He leaned toward her.

Nancy backed away.

"I hear Peter's okay," he said. "Off on a well-deserved vacation, I'm sure." Johnston seemed to be studying her. "Are you keeping busy?"

"We're having a wonderful vacation, thank you," Nancy replied. "Not a care in the world." She added a titter for good measure and shifted her position to give Louise a good shot at Johnston.

"Yessir," he rocked back on his heels. "This is a relaxing place. Warm weather. Pool. Palm trees. Just put your feet up and let the worries go." He paused to sip his wine. "We sure miss Peter around here. Good man at poker." He eyed her with pursed lips. "You be sure to let us know when you hear from him." His laugh was forced. "Don't want him to forget us."

Nancy fidgeted with her glass under that penetrating gaze. He seemed to want something more from her. "I'll certainly let everyone know if I hear," she said lightly.

He nodded and leaned toward her. "You need anyone to drive your car north, you talk to me." He raised his glass again. "I can take care of that for you."

"Thank you, but we flew." Nancy stared down at her glass, then glanced up at Johnston. "That's a good service you provide, though."

"Yes, it is." He stroked his chin, then dismissing her, he turned away. Nancy saw a calculating gleam in his eye as he surveyed the crowd. Was he looking for potential drivers or customers for his new business? Or something else?

Abby Summers came up and pulled at her sleeve. "Some of these people aren't what they seem," she whispered. "Watch out."

Nancy turned to her. "Like whom, for instance?"

Abby was about to say more when Susan appeared at Nancy's elbow. "Do you need anything? Or you, Abby?" She took Abby's empty glass, then nodded at Nancy's.

"Not me, thank you," said Abby, winking at Nancy. "Just telling Nancy she can come visit me anytime."

Susan raised an eyebrow. "I'll bet you know everybody here, don't you."

"I know what's happening, that's all I'm saying." Abby patted Nancy on the hand. "See you," she said. "Got to make the rounds."

Nancy watched Abby's progress, again wishing Abby would be more cautious. Nancy turned to Susan and smiled. "Enjoyable party. Interesting people."

"Very pleasant people," added Susan. "I can't imagine what Peter was worried about."

"I'm sure he wasn't worried about anyone here," Nancy said.

As she mingled, trying to memorize names and faces, hoping that Louise was capturing these people on camera, Nancy again felt overwhelmed at the task. They all seemed so ordinary. Even Harv Johnston was a type, although something about him seemed dishonest and vaguely familiar. She couldn't put her finger on it, though. In her experience, the feeling often sprang from some trivial individual quirk rather than an indication of something wrong.

She watched Johnston set down his glass. Nancy walked over, casually picked it up at the top and returned to Peter's apartment. She lifted Johnston's fingerprints, washed the glass, and took it back to the party. She found a seat near the wall and sat back to observe the assembly of residents, most of them elderly. Her eyes panned the room. Who had a shady past? Who was desperate to avoid recognition? Who was so afraid of what Peter might know that he or she poisoned him? Did anyone resemble a wanted criminal pictured in Peter's den?

As her eyes rested on each face for a second or two, she saw only an ordinary group of senior citizens, engaged in friendly banter and enjoying a simple social event. An ordinary group—the thought disturbed her and triggered her own fear.

Had she lost her edge?

***

Staying Well at Riverside Acres

We all enjoy our pot luck dinners and happy hours, but let's not forget to practice good hygiene habits. Scrub your hands well before eating and drinking. Help prevent the spread of colds and flu so prevalent in the winter, even here in sunny South Florida. Let's all keep healthy!

Riverside Acres Health Team

Chapter 13

Nancy sat at the computer early the next morning, e-mailing the photos they'd taken so far to Peter. "File these in the folders with the appropriate person," she typed. "Also, find an obituary of Susan Withers' husband. I'd like to read it." She pressed "Send," as she reached down to pet Oscar's head. "Just another minute, boys," she said. They looked at her puzzled. Why wasn't she getting their leashes for the morning walk? The question was written all over their slobbering faces.

Nancy felt good about her strategy. Peter was safe, and they were pulling together solid information to give the FBI. It was only at the beginning of cases that she felt overwhelmed and afraid. Once she began working, the step by step process broke the case into manageable bits. She looked up as Louise padded in, yawning.

"Already on the job?"

"Just want to keep Peter busy," said Nancy as she leashed the dogs. "We only have seventeen days left to solve this problem. Be back shortly."

When Nancy returned, Susan was sitting at breakfast with Louise. Her crisp white slacks and equally pristine light blue polo shirt made Nancy glance at her own navy slacks and flowered shirt. They were adequate. She didn't need anyone to salute.

Nancy took a place and reached for the teapot. She smiled at Susan. "Are we ready to return to the *Bonny Scot?* I'd like to talk to the owner of that place."

"Again?" Susan protested. "We've seen all there is to see there."

Nancy sipped her tea. "Not quite."

They arrived by nine o'clock that morning. Louise wore her usual khaki pants and running shoes. Nancy wore running shoes, too, in case she wanted to snoop around. She hoped the early hour would ensure the owner was home and not out on errands.

She knocked on the door of the pastel green house. The paint was patchy, and dirt and cobwebs obscured the corners of the doorway.

She knocked again and heard, "I'm coming, I'm coming, keep yer pants on." She hadn't heard that phrase in a long time. Louise snickered behind her. Susan hung back about ten feet from the door, frowning at the damp grass clippings clinging to her white sandals.

The voice came from the other side of the door. "Who are you and what do you want?"

"We're friends of the young woman who was on the *Bonny Scot*. Her family is very worried about her." Nancy noticed movement behind the peephole in the door. He was observing them. Probably terrified after what happened.

"I don't know nothin'."

"Please open the door and talk to us," Nancy said.

There was a long pause. Then they heard someone unhitch a chain and draw a bolt back, and the door opened. An elderly man stood in the doorway, gaping at the three women. "Thought you was the police again," he coughed, "or them murderers. You ain't sellin' nothin', are you? I ain't buyin'."

Nancy laughed. "We just wanted to ask you a few questions." She stepped forward. "About the couple on the trawler. We're looking for the young woman."

The old man stepped aside. "Come in, come in."

Nancy and Louise walked in. Susan followed but continued to hang back as if the whole business were distasteful. He led them into the kitchen and gestured at the chairs around a square table covered in a stained white vinyl tablecloth. "You family of that young lady?"

"Friends of the family," Louise said. They introduced themselves.

"Pleased to meet alla ya. Stan Jaworsky, semi-retired, kinda." He turned to the coffee pot on the counter, looking back at them. "Coffee?" He reached into a cupboard and brought out three mugs, all with Disney motifs.

Surprised at the cleanliness of the kitchen and its neatness, Nancy said yes. Louise echoed her. Susan mumbled, "No thanks." They all sat at the table as Stan filled their mugs and topped off his own.

"So what can I tell you ladies?" he asked. "I don't know much."

Nancy smiled. "Do you have any idea where the young woman on the *Bonny Scot* might be?" She gestured toward the dock.

Stan shook his head. "If I did, I woulda tol' the police, wouldn't I? But I don't." He sipped his coffee. "A young lady like that. Had no call to be on a boat with that Ray guy. The police are lookin' for her too. She coulda done it, you know."

The thought had crossed Nancy's mind. Could Ray have attacked Jessica? And she retaliated? But then how would she get him to the Everglades?

"Course I don't really think she done it," Stan added.

"You didn't hear them talk about going out?" Louise asked.

Nancy glanced at Louise. "Maybe to a bar? Any bar around here?"

"No, ma'am. All residential. Some people bring their boats here, then go back where they came from. Long as they pay their fees, I got no problems with that. But that Ray feller was waiting for the boat owner, then him and the girl both disappeared, far as I knew."

He set down his coffee and peered at them. "I'm wondering too. Nice-looking little thing. What happened to her? Where is she?" He scrunched his nose and peered at them. "So why are you looking for her?"

Nancy watched Stan for any deviousness as she explained Amelia's request. "We just want to make sure Amelia's granddaughter is all right."

Stan scratched his chin. "That girl doesn't have to be in Fort Lauderdale anymore, does she? She could be anywheres."

Nancy nodded. "That's true, and a couple of weeks have passed since you saw them last, but I'm not sure she had much money." She sipped her coffee and kept an eye on him. So far he seemed as puzzled and open as she would expect from a retired old codger, but then, people often assumed she was harmless, too.

"Probably holed up somewheres. Lotta people here don't have much money. Shower on the beach. Live in their bathing suits. Lotta fruit growin' in people's yards and a lotta them snowbirds ain't around even if it is January." Stan stuck out his chin and looked at them with wise old eyes. "Did that myself when I first come down here," he examined his fingernails before adding, "that was a long time ago."

"But that's awful." Susan shuddered. "And dangerous. A lot of crazy people live in the bushes around here." She frowned.

Louise folded her arms and stared at her. "Where else they gonna go? Not enough shelters or programs to help them." She sent a scathing look Susan's way. "Or jails."

Nancy broke into what was shaping up as a fight. "Those possibilities hadn't occurred to me," she said to Stan. "If Jessica is resourceful, she's probably finding a way to survive."

"Yeah, but you need to find her fast." Stan set his mug down hard as if to emphasize the point. "If she didn't kill that Ray feller, maybe she was with him when he got killed and somehow escaped. Whoever killed Ray might be looking for her too." He scratched his chin. "Seems to me."

"We know," said Louise.

"Do you have any idea what happened to Ray? Why he was shot?" asked Nancy.

Stan considered the question. "I don't, no ma'am." Stan shook his head. "Must have been a bar fight. Couldn't have happened here. This place is pretty quiet, and I'm choosy about who I give a slip to. Shocking, that's what it is." He sipped his coffee. "I ain't like those people across the way. Comings and goings all hours, day or night. That's the more likely place for murder, if you ask me." He squinted an eye at Nancy over his mug. "And I guess you asked."

Louise sat back and folded her arms. "Know anything about those people?"

"They want to buy this place, but I ain't selling. They look like they play rough, but I don't bother them," Stan clenched his jaw, "and they don't bother me. So far." He stood. "I got work to do, if you don't mind."

Nancy took his cue, followed by Louise and Susan. Nancy reached out to shake his hand. "Thank you for your help."

"Don't mention it." Stan walked with them to the door.

Susan was the first back to the car. "Glad to get out of there," she said.

"He was okay." Louise looked back at the house. "On the rough side, that's all." She climbed into the car. "Sounded like a Florida cracker, but he had a slight accent. Polish, maybe, considering his name. Long time ago, though."

Nancy slid into the passenger seat. "Let's go over to that house across the inlet."

"What?" Susan sat back. She pushed her hands away in disbelief. "Why do you think they had anything to do with it?"

"Why not? Their dock is a straight shot," Louise paused, "so to speak, from the *Bonny Scot*." Louise glanced at Nancy. "Anyway, they may have seen something."

Susan's eyes flashed. "He wasn't shot here. He was shot in the Everglades."

"He was found in the Everglades." Louise stuck her jaw out.

Nancy gave Louise a warning look. They didn't need to alienate Susan with all her knowledge of Fort Lauderdale and the people at the condo. "I'm sure the police have talked to the people who live over there. . ."

"Sure they have," said Susan. "Those neighbors wouldn't know anything." She sounded adamant.

"Still, we need to find out more about them." Nancy continued. "They may tell us what they told the police or maybe remembered something important after the police left."

"They may not want to contact the police even if they did remember something important," added Louise.

Susan clamped her jaw shut and backed the car out of the drive. She drove along the curving road to the other house. A tall, thick hedge of something with thorns concealed the house, and the gravel drive into the property was barred by an iron gate. A call box was attached to the left gate post. Susan looked at Nancy.

"Press it," Nancy said.

Susan pressed the call button. They waited. No response. Susan pressed again. Still no response.

"No one home," Susan said, relief in her voice. "Let's leave."

Louise opened her door and stepped out. "Coming, Nancy?"

Nancy turned to Susan. "Park along the side of the road over toward Stan's place. If anyone drives to the gate, honk. We'll hear you."

Susan shook her head. "I have bad feelings about this," she grumbled. "But if you're going in, I am too." She pulled the car to the side of the road and stepped out. "I really don't think this is necessary."

Hands on hips, Nancy stood looking at the wrought-iron gate.

Behind her, Louise whistled. "Hell of a lot of work went into that with all those fancy curves and points."

Nancy nodded. "It's only held up by a post on each side and not attached to a fence."

"The hedge comes right up to the posts, though." Louise eyed the narrow gap between hedge and post.

"Those thorns look nasty." Nancy began squeezing through the gap. "Good thing we're skinny."

Susan backed away from the gap dubiously. "This is trespassing."

"No, it ain't," Louise looked back at Susan scornfully. "Even if it is, we're just going up to the door like normal people and knock."

Once through the barrier at the gate, Nancy and Louise stepped down the drive toward the house. At first they walked carefully to avoid making noise, but their shoes crunched on the gravel and rustled the long needles and cones that dropped from the Australian pines lining each side of the drive and casting a dark shadow over them. Susan followed behind, clutching her purse.

"They can hear us a mile away," she said.

"I know." Nancy abandoned the effort. "No way to surprise them."

Louise swished her cane in the air. "I love this warm weather," she said. "Hardly need my cane at all."

Nancy tried to peer through the dense hedge. "The inlet between this property and Stan's must be on the other side and behind the pines."

"Can't see it from here," Louise said.

The breeze ruffled the pine needles overhead, adding a gentle touch to the peace and quiet. Not even a bird chirped. The quiet seemed strange for a property so near downtown Fort Lauderdale. Nancy led the group as they rounded a bend and came to the house they could barely see from Stan's property. The pink, concrete-block house had larger windows than Stan's and a screened-in pool with patio, but the water in the pool was murky with leaves floating on top. The whole place seemed abandoned.

Louise scanned the setup with her arms folded and scorn on her face. "Yeah. That's what they need. Five miles from the ocean, and they got to have a pool."

The drive ended at a self-standing, two-car garage. Louise peered into it through a side window. She whistled. "Garage is empty," she said, "but it's got a couple of pits in the floor."

"For car maintenance, I guess." said Nancy.

"At a private home?" Louise stepped away from the garage. "This is a regular setup for an auto mechanic."

Nancy held a finger to her lips for Louise. They studied the house for a few minutes, listening and looking for any signs of life. Nancy stepped up to the front door and rang the bell. She waited, then rang it again. She turned to Louise. "Nobody home."

They tiptoed along the house to a window and peered in.

"You shouldn't be doing that," Susan warned.

"These windows are filthy." Louise snorted. "I got dirt on my nose." She swiped at the window.

Nancy pulled a tissue out of her pocket and cleaned a large spot on the window so both she and Louise could peek in. The living room seemed stark. Only a couch and two armchairs on a terrazzo floor. Dining room table and chairs were pushed against the wall at the far end. Nancy picked up a handful of dirt to smear over the spot she'd cleaned.

Moving around to the side, they peered into the two back rooms. One was barren. The other contained a double bed and a chest of drawers, more terrazzo flooring, and no rugs.

Nancy stepped back from the house. "Not very comfortable. No homey touches."

"Seems like a regular house to me," Louise said. "What kind of person lives here?"

"I didn't see any photos or knickknacks or anything personal at all, did you?"

Louise took another look through the window. "You're right. Maybe a bachelor who's out a lot. Could be a rental. It's still early in the season. Maybe whoever owns this place just hasn't shown up yet."

Nancy pursed her lips. "I suppose that could be it. Most people leave personal items in a house if they rent it. Bill and I used to do that when we rented our cabin. That way renters might feel more inclined to take care of the property."

Louise flicked her braid. "Sure. I'll bet that works. I'm going to check out the shed around back." Louise walked toward it. "No windows. Yard tools, I guess." She tried the door. "Shit. Locked."

Nancy eyed it speculatively. "I could come back with my lock-picking tools."

"Lock-picking tools?" Susan screeched.

"Just a hobby," Louise told her. "We forget our keys a lot." She glanced at Nancy.

Nancy nodded, still examining the door. "In fact, I should. Something odd about this place. Doesn't exactly display the buzz of activity Jaworsky talked about." She glanced out at the river. "And that young man on the houseboat said there were boats in and out over here, but you'd never know that to look around this place. Seems deserted as if no one has been here for months."

Louise shook her head. "But he also said it's been quiet here the last week or so."

Nancy's eyes swept across the garage and the house. "Since the murder."

"I suppose the police were over here after they ID'd the body," suggested Louise. "Checking with the neighbors."

Nancy nodded. "There's nothing here—at least not right now." She walked back down the drive toward the road. Louise and Susan followed.

They passed through the gate and got into the car. "I hope you're satisfied. How could this place have anything to do with the *Bonny Scot?*" asked Susan. "Owners are probably out of town." She started the car.

Nancy stared back at the locked gates as they drove away. She had a lot of questions about that property.

***

Designated Car Spaces Available

Riverside Acres offers designated car spaces to residents for a small monthly fee. This is your chance to ensure a space in the parking area most convenient for you. All spaces are numbered, and you can select any space not reserved by someone else. Hurry or the space you want may be taken!

Riverside Acres Management

Chapter 14

Back at the condo, Nancy brought a pitcher of lemonade and a stack of clear plastic glasses down to the pool. She set them on a table between Louise and Susan and poured lemonade for each of them before pulling up a third chair. She set her phone on the table too to keep it ready for photos. She looked at Louise. "I'll go online later and check out who owns the property next to Jaworsky's place."

"Go ahead." Susan swept a hand across her perfect hair. "But why? I'm sure an ordinary couple lives there with a home mortgage and their pet cat. Nothing suspicious at all. Just because they weren't home doesn't mean anything."

Nancy watched a white-haired African-American woman and small boy ambling toward the pool. The boy carried an inflatable ring and began running. Nancy surreptitiously took a photo of the woman.

"Walk! Stop running!" the woman called out to the boy and smiled at Nancy. "Regular Aqua Man, he is," she said.

Louise pointed to an empty chair under the umbrella. "Join us."

The woman hesitated, glanced at the others, but they smiled in welcome.

"Thank you," she said. "I'd like a bit of adult talk, if you don't mind."

Louise nodded. "I remember those days."

Nancy didn't say anything. Years ago, she would flinch at the easy conversations her friends had about their kids. Not that she missed having kids—her life was too full for that—but sometimes she did wonder what her life would have been like with children.

"Yep," the woman said, "this the second time 'round for me." She shaded her eyes with her hand. "I'm Eveline Kwame, and that's my grandson Dashaune."

"He's very cute," said Susan, watching the little boy twirling in his water ring.

Nancy leaned forward. "I'm Nancy Davis." She introduced Louise and added, "You probably already know Susan." She gestured toward the lemonade. "Help yourself."

"Thank you." Eveline poured a glass and smiled at Nancy. "Glad to meet you."

Louise never let awkward questions stop her. "Where's the boy's mother?"

Eveline stared at the pool. A bitter look crossed her face, and she hesitated before answering. Finally, she said, "Not around any more." She glanced at Susan.

"I'm sorry. . ." Nancy began as she handed Eveline a glass of lemonade.

Eveline turned to her. "Drugs done her in. If I ever lay my hands on a pusher…" She spoke softly with one eye on the boy. "Well, I'm used to it by now. Didn't expect to be a mom again, but I'm adoptin' him seein' as how she's gone. Don't trust those foster homes and nobody else is gonna take him."

"He'll have a good home," Susan said. "I've got to go. See you later." She picked up her towel and strode toward the elevator.

"Yeah, he'll have a good home." Eveline stared down at her hands. "Now," she muttered, so softly that Nancy wasn't sure she heard right. Eveline shrugged as she smiled at Nancy. "Not what I expected when I retired, and I'm sure not gonna travel or enjoy myself. I'll be lucky to get to stay here, now that my grandson's living here too."

"He seems like a nice little boy," proffered Nancy.

"Oh sure. He's a love, he is." Eveline sighed and looked over at Nancy. "Of course he is. It's just that. . ." She didn't finish the sentence but turned instead to Louise. "So how do you like Fort Lauderdale?"

They chatted for another hour in the shade of the umbrella, but Louise eventually tired of the idle talk and left for their apartment. Nancy stayed awhile longer, hoping to draw Eveline into talking about the residents. Susan had told her what she knew of Bob Connolly. Would Eveline know more?

"Connolly?" Eveline shrugged. "Drinks too much. And then he gets to talkin'. Most of us don't believe any word he says."

"We've seen him with Harv Johnston," Nancy said.

"Oh. Yeah." Eveline squinted at Nancy in the bright sunlight. "He's real estate, I heard. Developer. And now he's got that driving business." She laughed. "I'm thinking of hiring on to drive somebody's car north. Only way I'm gonna travel now." She turned to Nancy. "He tries to act real nice, but you gotta watch him." She laughed. "Tough man. And that is not good, nosirree."

Nancy saw the quick look of appraisal Eveline threw at her.

"I wouldn't trust neither of 'em." Eveline grimaced. "Sorry. Mouth runs away with me sometimes. Don't pay me no mind." She sighed and glanced over at Nancy. "You staying in Peter's apartment while he's away? Is he all right?"

Nancy nodded. "He's fine and off on vacation."

"Sure was odd the way he took sick. Nobody else been sick like that." Eveline shook her head.

Nancy didn't respond. Eveline had given her a strange look just then as if Peter were a questionable character. She hadn't seen him in some years, and she knew he'd gone through hard times. She surveyed the landscaped gardens and lawn, the sparkling pool, the pleasant poolside terrace. He'd done quite well for himself. What was that odd look about?

"Did ya hear 'bout Abby Summers?"

"I've met her," Nancy said, sitting back and admiring the huge puffy clouds building up in the sky. She'd never seen such beautiful clouds and brilliant blue skies anywhere else.

Eveline leaned back, too, with a sigh. "Yessir, she was one nice lady. We'll be missin' her, all right."

Nancy froze, the chill of foreboding crept up her body. "What happened to her? Did she leave?"

Eveline glanced at Nancy. "Nobody told you? They found her in the river. Early this morning. Drowned. She musta fallen in last night. Had an attack or something. Stroke, maybe."

Drowned. Dead. Her ears buzzed in shock. She stared up at the sky, unable to speak. Drowned. Dead. She knew this would happen. She had warned Abby to be careful. What else could she have done? How else protect a nosy, gossipy old woman who knew too much? And now she was drowned. Dead. "I was afraid. . ." she whispered.

"What?" Eveline glanced at Nancy.

Nancy came to herself and shook her head. "I'm so sorry. . ." Nancy began but couldn't complete the sentence. She remembered Abby's assurances that she knew what was going on here at Riverside Acres. Who else had heard her? Probably everybody the way she bragged about it. She didn't think Abby's death was an accident. Nancy still held the glass of lemonade in her hand but had lost all taste for it. She felt sick.

"How did it happen?" Nancy managed to ask.

"She always liked to sit on the bench next to the dock along the river's edge." Eveline pursed her lips. "No harm in it, but you know how wobbly she was sometimes."

"Is the bench so close to the river that she'd fall into it?"

Eveline shook her head. "Not at all. But if you went on the dock and tripped or wobbled at the wrong time, you could."

"I see."

"Once you're in, there's nothing to grab onto and the water's deep."

"Wouldn't someone hear her cry for help?"

Eveline stared up at the sky. "It was probably late, you know. Dark. Sometimes when Dashaune is asleep, I'll walk down there at night by myself. I feel pretty safe on this property. Usually."

Everything consistent with an accident as well as murder.

Eveline leaned toward Nancy and lowered her voice. "You ask me, you wanna keep an eye on somebody, just watch that ol' Bob Connolly." Her gaze swept the pool area. "Works with tourism people. Hotels. Restaurants. That's the kind of business where a whole lot of drinking going on. Before I retired, I worked for the county and heard the stories." She sat back and flashed a grin at Nancy. "Gotta keep up with the gossip. Connolly's a womanizer, a schmoozer. Now why would they pick a man like Connolly for tourism? Bad choice for someone with his problem."

"I see him a lot with Harv Johnston," said Nancy, feeling like she'd tapped a barrel of information.

"They pal around." She glanced over at Susan who now hovered by the elevator. "She's always hanging around them. Looking for husband number two, my guess." She grinned at Nancy. "Johnston doesn't live here, you know. Got a place on the river, but he's always hanging around, talking up his driving service."

***

Pool Rules are for Everyone

Please note the rules for the pool posted on the towel kiosk. These are for your safety and protection. An adult must accompany all children. No running and no glassware of any kind are allowed in the pool area.

Riverside Acres Management

Nancy picked up the tray holding Eveline's and Susan's glasses and the pitcher and returned to the apartment. Louise was taking a nap and Nancy was grateful for the quiet. Abby's death weighed her down. *I warned her but too late.* Who had felt so threatened that he—or she—killed her? Nancy lifted the fingerprints from the two glasses and then called Peter and told him the news.

"Those goddamn sons of bitches," Peter said. Nancy heard a loud thud as if his fist had hit the desk. "She was harmless."

"Not to somebody," Nancy said. "And it must have been somebody here."

"We gotta find those people," Peter said. "I'm tired of this place, and I don't think I'm getting anywhere."

"At least you're safe there. Have you been checking the names with a criminal database? And googling them?"

"I'm going through everyone in the directory in alphabetical order, one by one. Even the disabled who couldn't manage a doorknob by themselves. I don't want to assume anything."

"Right. Good." Nancy thought a moment. "I sent you the photos we've taken so far."

"Got those, and I'm examining each one by facial characteristics."

"Did you check into facial recognition software?"

"I had fun looking that stuff up." Peter's enthusiasm bounced across the phone line. "Do you know you can buy voice recognition software too? Didn't think that would work for our purpose, and the facial recognition stuff isn't advanced enough yet for us. Take too long to get it anyway, at least nothing we could purchase, download, and learn how to use. You'd probably have to be part of some spy agency to get the real stuff. Would be fun to get our hands on it though."

Nancy smiled at the energy in Peter's voice. She could imagine him pacing as he talked. "Okay. I thought they might have developed that more since I last heard about it."

"But we're moving forward, Nancy."

"We are, but I hope we get a break soon."

Only fifteen days before she returned to Whisperwood. They had to move faster. She turned on Peter's computer. Peter was going through the directory from A to Z. But what about the people she'd already met? Surely the culprit was in the circle of people surrounding Peter, the ones he knew—and Nancy was getting to know—on a first name basis. She began googling names. Her spirit lifted, but then Louise padded out of the bedroom.

"What's up?" she asked.

Nancy told her about Abby.

Louise sank to the couch as if she'd been punched in the stomach. She didn't speak for a long time, just stared ahead grimly. Nancy moved over to sit next to Louise and patted her hand.

"They got her," Louise whispered at last. "Shit, shit, shit."

"Yes," said Nancy.

"Excuse me." Louise reached for her cane. "I gotta go for a walk." She flashed a grim smile at Nancy. "And not next to the river either." She called to the dogs. "I'll take them with me. At least they're nice people."

Nancy spent the next three hours on the computer, googling the people she had met so far as well as Ray Slocum and Jessica. She found a short item about his murder, which included a paragraph saying the *Bonny Scot* was registered in Maryland to a Johnson MacDermid of Baltimore, and police were searching for anyone with information. The article also included a grainy photo of Jessica as a missing person. Googling MacDermid brought up his brokerage firm and a brief bio.

Googling Cantwell brought up a number of other Cantwells and one hit for a Jessica Cantwell who had written a paper on administrative systems that made its way to the Internet.

She found nothing on Amelia Cantwell as she expected. Amelia seemed to be one of those who froze at the sight of a computer and, for that matter, any kind of attention. Self-effacing, shy, and technologically ignorant.

Nancy googled the address of the house next to Stan's. The present owner, who had bought it three years before, was the Mandell Consortium at an address in Deerfield Beach. She'd seen Deerfield Beach on signs in Fort Lauderdale. Must be nearby. So exactly what or who was the Mandell Consortium? A name like that, hiding the people behind it, was a red flag to Nancy. An Internet search only turned up the same entry she'd read about the property sale and a brief legal item about its establishment. The names on the list of officers were unknown to Nancy.

She sat back. The Mandell Consortium needed more research. She printed out the page.

Then she googled Stan, Susan, Harv Johnston, Abby Summers, and Bob Connolly.

Connolly's name was included in several recent news releases about tourism but nothing else. How had he gotten the job? Stan's name had no references to anyone who could be the same Stan Jaworsky. Johnston's name didn't show up at all, which was odd considering he was supposedly in real estate and also had the driving service. Someone named Abigail Summers had many listings, but she was a young singer. Nancy found Susan's name in listings for women who were obviously not the Susan from Ohio who now lived in Fort Lauderdale.

Googling the names on the wanted flyers yielded additional information about their crimes and a few better photos, but nothing she turned up seemed at all related to anyone she had met. She finally checked her e-mail. Her friends at Whisperwood complained as usual about the ongoing construction work and the boredom now that she and Louise had gone off "like college kids to Florida." She logged off and drummed her fingers on the desk, gazing absently at a painting on the wall.

That night Nancy heard shouting next door. She looked up from the book she was reading to listen. The dogs ran into the bedroom. Louise sprang up and paced the floor. Nancy heard something thrown against the wall and crashing sounds, then silence. Louise put her ear against the common wall.

"I can't hear anything," Louise said, standing back from the wall. "I talked to Carla out in the hall yesterday. By the way, that's her son Quint who lives with her, not her husband. He was listening at the kitchen window, and I let him know I was watching. I think he beats her—when he's hopped up on drugs."

"On drugs?"

"Or alcohol. I'll bet his mother's worried sick about him. A real loser, I'd say." Louise snorted.

"So how are we going to help?" asked Nancy. Louise would have suggestions.

"Told her she could come over here anytime," said Louise. "I'll bet she's afraid to call the police or fill out a warrant against him."

"Let me know what I can do," said Nancy.

"Most people say you gotta hit rock bottom before you change your drinking habit." Louise glared at the wall. "But I say bullshit to that and to coddling the bastard. Throw him out is what she ought to do."

"But she's his mother—and she doesn't seem very strong," Nancy protested. "Maybe she needs his financial help."

"What she needs is a job. At least that would get her out of the house and away from him. And give her some self-respect." Louise sat on the couch and called Rupert. The dogs hovered at the bedroom door looking puzzled and worried. Rupert ran forward and jumped into her lap.

Putting Rupert aside, Louise stood and lifted an eyebrow at Nancy. "Keep your fingers crossed. Let's hope he doesn't kill her. Right now I'm going over to invite her here for tea and dessert."

***

Computer Services Available

Riverside Acres' own computer technician, Kevin Mueller, is Riverside's expert at fixing any problems you experience with your home computer. He's on staff, available Monday through Friday, and his rates are reasonable. Call him to set up an appointment, 954-555-3334.

Riverside Acres Management

Chapter 16

When Nancy stepped into the kitchen the next morning, she found Louise already on her second cup of coffee.

"Thought I'd drop by next door as soon as Carla's son is on the street," Louise said. Her eyes sparked. "Since she refused my invitation last night."

"She won't appreciate your interfering," Nancy cautioned, "and I think she's rather shy."

"I'm hoping she's had enough." Louise sipped her coffee. "Been pretty quiet this morning. Lucky if she's not dead." She stuck out her jaw. "Sorry. Can't get Abby out of my mind."

"Neither can I."

Louise glanced from the kitchen clock to her watch. "It's eight-thirty now. I'll give her another hour."

Nancy leashed the dogs and tucked a couple of plastic bags in her pocket for the morning walk. The dogs whined and tugged at the leash, pulling her out the door and down the outside corridor.

Behind her a door slammed, and heavy footsteps walked her way. Quint Sandstrom. Nancy moved to the side and pulled the dogs closer to let him pass. Quint looked like he might kick them. Hurting the weak and helpless seemed to be his style. He stalked down the hall as if he were angry. He had the muscular look of a nightclub bouncer along with carrot-colored hair and a matching scraggly beard. She stared at his back. A single blow from his fist could kill. He entered the elevator and the door closed. A dangerous man. Louise was right. They should get his mother away from him.

Exactly what kind of work did he do? She took her cell phone out of her pocket and leaned over the half-wall to focus the phone-camera down on his face as he exited the elevator on the first floor. In the parking lot, Harv Johnston walked towards Quint, greeted him, and stopped to chat. Nancy leaned forward to listen, but she couldn't make out what they were saying. She did see Johnston hand Quint something and then the baleful glance Johnston threw her way as she pretended to fuss with the leashes.

When Nancy returned to the condo, Louise was handing Carla Sandstrom a cup of coffee. Carla took it with well-kept hands and manicured and buffed fingernails. Nancy threw another look at the dumpy little woman wearing a floral housedress. Her hair didn't reflect the same care as the hands. It was mussed, short and curly, and an indeterminate color streaked with gray.

"We should get to know our neighbors," Louise said with a meaningful glance at Nancy. She turned to Carla. "You've met my friend Nancy Davis?"

Carla sat on the edge of the couch. She cleared her throat and spoke with a tense smile. "I passed you in the walkway. Are you enjoying your stay down here?"

"Yes indeed." Nancy released the dogs and smiled at Carla.

Carla reached down to pet them. "They're so sweet. I was here when Peter brought them home. That was before my son moved in with me." The dogs seemed to make Carla feel more comfortable.

Louise plunged in. "He been here long?"

"A year. Since he lost his last job." Carla sighed. "He's had such a run of bad luck. I feel so sorry for him."

Nancy poured herself a cup of tea. "What does he do?"

"He can do just about anything with his hands." Carla gulped.

"Right now he's working for Mr. Johnston who runs the driving service."

Louise leaned forward. "We've heard about that. Sounds like a great idea."

"Oh it is," Carla breathed. "Helps a lot of people travel when they can't afford to, really."

"Sounds win-win to me," said Louise, "doesn't it, Oscar?" She reached down to pet him. Rupert lay on the rug, boredom on his face along with the slobber.

"Did you know Abby Summers?" asked Nancy. She watched Carla over the teacup as she sipped.

Carla added a dollop of cream to her cup. "Not well. Terrible how she drowned."

"Surely accidents like that don't often happen here," said Louise.

Carla shook her head. "Not at all." A shy smile crept across her face. "We all try to be careful. Especially Abby. Especially after she broke her hip." She sipped her coffee.

Louise folded her arms on the table and leaned toward Carla. "Did she spend much time at the pool?"

Carla frowned. "Not that I noticed, but then I never went down there myself." She hesitated before adding, "Didn't want to get involved, you know."

"Involved?" asked Nancy.

"Some people hang around there all the time." Nancy watched Carla thrust out her lower lip. Her hands tensed around the cup.

"The bridge players, you mean?" Nancy asked.

Carla seemed troubled. "They're part of the crowd. Hate to push my way through in my bathing suit." She took a deep breath and drew herself up. "And then they all want me to join them so they can ask questions. Nosy bunch."

She set the cup down and brushed her hands.

"So I keep away. Not that fond of swimming anyway, but me and Abby—she didn't like it either—we would sit out on the bench by the elevator and talk."

"Abby didn't like swimming?" Nancy glanced at Louise. Abby was in the pool when Nancy first met her. Surely Abby would hang around the pool to be first in line for the gossip. Maybe Carla's shyness spurred Abby's interest. A fresh, untapped source of gossip. Nancy looked back at Carla. Did she have any understanding at all why Abby would take the time to talk to her?

Carla shook her head. "She liked to sit by the river, though. I guess she slipped and fell in and then couldn't get out. Deep channel there 'cause boats tie up on the sides."

"What did Abby like to talk about?" asked Nancy.

"She was a nice lady." Carla sighed. "I'll miss her. She was always asking about my boy and how his job was going. She was interested, you know." She frowned. "Nobody else here cared and only wanted to make trouble for him." She looked at Nancy. "He's trying his best, and he works hard for Mr. Johnston."

"I'm sure he does," Louise reached over and patted Carla's hand.

"He's got an important job." said Carla. "Makes sure the cars are okay so whoever's driving them doesn't get into trouble, and he does other odd jobs. Mr. Johnston pays him well." Carla rose and nodded to Louise. "Thank you so much for the coffee. I-I have to get back home now." She walked to the door.

Nancy followed her. "Let us know if you need anything."

"Thank you," Carla's hands trembled as she fumbled with the door knob. "It was nice getting to know you both."

Carla fled. Nancy closed the door behind her, picked up Carla's cup by the handle, and took it into the kitchen. "Do you get the impression she's hiding something?"

Louise grinned. "That's why I'm building trust."

"You're a good person, Louise." Nancy set about lifting Carla's fingerprints.

"Hah! A lot of people would tell you different." Louise limped over to her cane and brandished it at Nancy. "But they're the bad guys."

"Speaking of bad guys," Nancy put the fingerprint card aside and fed the dogs. "I would guess the police have their eye on that house across the inlet."

"If they know their business, they do." Louise leaned on her cane as she followed Nancy into the kitchen. She peered into the refrigerator. "By the way, George comes in tomorrow afternoon. I'll hang around to get him settled in."

"Terrific," Nancy said, smiling at the way Louise tried to hide her feelings. "The 90s Club meets again! I've missed George too."

Nancy felt a wistful sense of longing. At age ninety, love and romance were behind her. She had loved two good men and perhaps that was enough for one lifetime. At least she could enjoy reading romances, but she would not like anyone else, especially Louise, to know that those were the books on her Kindle not that she was ashamed to read them. They helped her get through the depression that plagued her every night so she could get to sleep.

***

Please Clean Up After Your Pets

Keep our waterways, our yards, and our sidewalks clean. Please pick up after your pets but take them out often enough so they don't use our halls and elevators for litter boxes. All of us appreciate thoughtful pet owners.

Riverside Acres Management

Chapter 17

That afternoon, Nancy drove twenty minutes up to Pompano Beach to visit Peter. She found him dozing in a plastic chair under an umbrella on the beach. "So this is how you're spending your days," she said as she bent down and kissed him on the cheek. She pulled up another chair to sit beside him in the shade.

He jerked awake, sitting up and looking around. "Good thing you kissed me. I was fixin' to slug you." He yawned and stretched. "Just taking a break. How's it going?"

"Interesting—and sad—developments." Nancy gazed at the boats far out to sea.

"Yeah. Abby was quite a fixture around the place." Peter said. "She was always buzzing around, nose in all the gossip. My source for scuttlebutt."

"Even I knew she'd found out something, but I couldn't pry it out of her." *I'm too rusty at this. Maybe I am too old.* For a moment, a sick feeling crept over her. How easy it would be to succumb to the world's opinion that she should give up, that she was no good anymore. The self-defeating thoughts clamored to be heard. She fought them as she had all her life.

When she was much younger, the world's opinion was that she was only good for cooking and cleaning and keeping house, or maybe teaching or secretarial work if she had to get a job. The interesting, high-paying jobs were for men only. She remembered those early struggles and took a deep breath. *Living the way I want to live is still a battle.* She reminded herself that at ninety she could still win at tennis. *And I'm still a good detective.* A quiver of fear ran down her back. Was she still a good detective or would she fail? She glanced at Peter. Would he die because his faith in her was misplaced? The thought threatened to bring on a panic attack. She took a deep breath and forced herself to calm down and listen to Peter.

"I should have talked to Abby before I left," he was saying, absently drawing circles in the sand with his cane. "Should have brought her up here, that's what I shoulda done."

"But what did she know?" Nancy reached over and patted his hand. "She saw something, I guess, that made her ask questions."

"And that did her in." Peter turned to Nancy. "I saw her talking to Carla a lot. My neighbor, you know. Feel Carla out," he paused, "but don't let Quint, that bastard son of hers know."

Nancy nodded. "We think he abuses her."

"Of course he does. I've heard the banging and the yelling, and I tried to help but he's her son and it's hopeless."

"I know."

"Maybe he'll move out soon." Peter squinted toward the ocean. "But he works for that driving service of Harv Johnston's. Too convenient for him now to stay at his Mom's. He's got to be close to thirty, you'd think he'd want his own place."

"What do you know about the driving service?" asked Nancy.

"It's a good deal and legitimate, I suppose." Peter picked up a bit of shell and threw it in the ocean. "I even used it once to visit a friend in New Jersey. Had people to see along the way so I didn't want to fly. Worked out well."

"Does seem like a good idea." Nancy watched the waves reach Peter's feet and obliterate the sand circles.

"They do okay with it." Peter picked up a few more shells. "So what else is new at Riverside?"

"What do you know about Harv Johnston?"

He frowned in distaste. "Too smooth. Like a con man. Raises my hackles. Doesn't live there but always hanging around. "

"Couldn't find much about him on the Net." She shivered. "Which is odd since he's in business, but he gives me the creeps."

"Yeah," added Peter. "Me too."

"What about Susan Withers? Or Eveline Kwame?" Nancy searched the hotel terrace behind her for someone who might bring her a soft drink.

Peter gestured to the bartender who nodded. Peter sat back. "You want to know about Susan and Eveline? Seem all right to me. Try to keep my distance from Susan, you know." He winked at Nancy.

Nancy laughed. "She is an attractive widow."

"Don't I know it," he grinned at Nancy, "but not on my team."

"Have to let her down easy," said Nancy. "Is there anything I should know about them or anyone else at Riverside?"

"That's what makes this so hard. Who would want to kill me?" Peter sat up and hit his chest with his fist. "Me, I'm a nice person. Delightful, in fact. No heirs waiting for me to kick off. No grudging enemies that I know of. The only thing it could be is that I'm onto a wanted felon at Riverside."

A shadow fell over Nancy. "Want anything from the bar?" Startled, Nancy turned around to see an apron-clad young man wearing sunglasses lurking behind their chairs with pen and pad in hand.

For a moment, Nancy felt threatened, then she pulled herself together. She was miles from Riverside. "Thanks. I'd like a Coke with lots of ice—and a glass of water."

"Me too," added Peter. "And put it on my bill."

"Yessir." The man departed.

"I've been sending you photos as I take them," said Nancy. "We also need to look at alibies, opportunities, and any other motives." She gazed out at the ocean, thinking aloud. "What about alibis for the night you were shot?"

Peter snapped his fingers. "Most everyone at Riverside goes to bed early, and it could have been a. . ." he hesitated, "a hired gun."

Nancy smiled at the phrase. Hired gun. Peter seemed to be getting into the swing of things. "I'll ask the guard if I can see his records for that night. Might be useful but you're right, looking for alibis is probably a useless exercise. Let's see what you come up with on the Net. It might trigger some little detail that will help." She remembered several cases, long past, where one significant detail, easily passed over, solved the case.

"Are you paring the list down?" Nancy asked. "We need to push forward. I only have fifteen days left."

"I've got the list down to one hundred but that's still too many."

"Make a spreadsheet—list residents down the side, then put motive, opportunity, alibi, and likely characteristics for a killer across the top. That will help."

"Get me more photos too."

Nancy nodded and looked up as the same waiter brought their drinks along with a bowl of peanuts. His sunglasses and expressionless face now seemed more bored and shallow than threatening. Seagulls screeched overhead, and waves gently washed ashore. Breezes dispelled the heat that radiated from the sun and sand.

"Pleasant here," said Nancy.

"Almost nicer than Riverside." Peter looked over at her. "But I'll be glad to be back there, once we catch the culprit."

"We're getting close." The killer had made a mistake with Abby; she was just a garrulous old gossip, but it showed how nervous and threatened he or she must be. That paved the road for bigger mistakes. She hoped they wouldn't be fatal for someone else.

***

Happy Hour Notes

Many hotels and restaurants on the beach from Pompano down to Dania offer late afternoon happy hour discounts and lavish hors d'oeuvres. See the Riverside Acres Management Office for a list. Discount coupons for nearby restaurants and bars, including the most sought-after places in South Florida, are also available.

Riverside Acres Management Office

Chapter 18

The next morning brought another warm sunny day to Fort Lauderdale. Louise's wrist, badly injured in the fracas at Whisperwood last summer, was bothering her, so Nancy left her in the sun by the pool with the camera, while she planned a walk into town. As she waited for the elevator, Susan stepped around a corner, pushing a grocery cart.

Nancy nodded at the cart. "That's handy. Does Riverside Acres supply them?"

"Not really." Susan tossed her head. "I brought it from the store. Use it to take stuff around as I need it. It is convenient. Grocery store won't miss it, you know. They've got way too many."

Nancy watched her as she pushed the cart down the hall and around the corner. Susan was wrong. Nancy remembered a case where a store hired her to ferret out such petty thefts because the money it lost had mounted to an amount too high to be ignored. Like shoplifting. Nancy tapped her chin. Actually, taking that cart was shoplifting. Did Susan really think it didn't matter?

Nancy stopped at the gatehouse. "Another lovely day," she said.

"Yes, ma'am." The guard waved his clipboard at her and stepped out.

"Do you keep records on all of us coming and going?" she asked as ingenuously as she could.

"That's my job."

"It makes me feel so much more secure knowing you're here," Nancy said, smiling to herself. *The very best butter.*

The guard grinned at her. "Thank you, ma'am."

"So you note down the car or the person and the times in and out?" Nancy asked.

"Sure do."

"How long do you keep those records?"

"Well, ma'am," he hesitated, "not long. If nothing's happening, we usually discard them at the end of the month."

The end of the month. Nancy looked up at the guard. "Thank you so much for taking care of us," she tittered, waving at him as she walked on in the heat and bright sunshine to Las Olas Boulevard. She ambled along the boulevard, pausing to window-shop and hadn't noticed how far she'd gone until she found herself feeling dizzy and weak. She must be dehydrated. She checked her watch. Eleven-thirty. Time for lunch.

She stood in front of a tea room swimming in plastic flamingoes, but then up ahead she saw Harv Johnston, wearing a broad-brimmed Western hat that was an odd match for his blue guayabera but perfect for the blistering sun. He carried a legal-sized manila folder. Nancy's curiosity propelled her towards him. She followed him into a cafe half a block down the street.

The lunch hour crowd was bearing down on the cafe, but Nancy found a small table and ordered a turkey sandwich with salad and iced tea. She glanced around the dining room as she saw Johnston sitting with Bob Connolly and two other men at an inconspicuous table in the back corner.

She'd never seen the other two men around Riverside Acres, or anywhere else, for that matter. The shorter one, wearing jeans and a black polo shirt, was swarthy with black hair. He sat with his elbow on the table, chin in hand, bored expression on his face. The other man, wearing jeans and a white T-shirt, resembled a male model or some handsome action figure, except for the angry expression and a scar down one side of the face. He had tipped his chair back and radiated insolence. Both drank Cokes. Nancy guessed they performed odd jobs or worked as handymen for Connolly or Johnston. Connolly's pink shirt and dotted bow-tie gave him a jaunty look next to Johnston's sober-looking guayabera.

Connolly and the two young men listened intently and nodded to whatever Johnston was saying as if he were the boss. Why would Connolly defer to Johnston? Odd. Questions ran rampant in her mind. Was some kind of real estate deal involved? Is that what the manila folder was about? Nancy took out her phone and pretending to text, took photos of all of the men at the table.

When her food came, she whispered to the server, "There's a draft here. May I move to that table?" She pointed to one near Johnston that was still vacant. Other tables were filling up fast, and the hubbub of conversation was growing.

The server nodded, picked up the placemat and packet of silverware, and headed for the designated table. Nancy hid behind her as they walked and then sat so she could watch the men without facing them. She kept her face averted and her eyes on her food. With any luck, Johnston and Connolly wouldn't notice her. Intent on their conversation, so far they hadn't, and Johnston continued to talk. She strained to hear the conversation.

"Got your men on those deliveries?"

"Yeah, boss," Scarface said. "We have to hold off awhile…cuz of the…you know."

There was a pause. Nancy munched her sandwich, staring blankly out the window hoping for more concrete information. Who were those other men? *A name. Give me a name.*

"What about the old guy?" This time Connolly was speaking.

"Under control," the swarthy man growled. Nancy risked a glance at their table. He was eyeing a young woman wearing a halter top and short skirt who sat down at a far table. What did Johnston mean by deliveries? Were they talking about his driver service business? And what old guy? One of their clients? Could they possibly mean Peter? What was under control and why?

Nancy glanced back and saw Scarface nod at the swarthy one. "Sergio here's got that problem nailed down."

"Nailed down tight," the man called Sergio added.

The way he said those words sent a chill through Nancy's heart. What had she missed? What was nailed down tight?

Their lunches arrived and the conversation descended to sports talk that continued through lunch. Connolly picked up the check and laid a credit card on it. A business luncheon on Connolly's behalf?

She was just finishing her iced tea when all of the men scraped their chairs back and headed for the door.

Nancy stood at the same time and teetered into Bob Connolly. He grabbed her arm, and she stared into his face. She gasped as if this was the ultimate of surprises. "Oh, Mr. Connolly. Thank you for saving me from a fall. How nice to see you." She simpered at his startled face and wobbled. Old lady to the core. She smiled at Harv Johnston. "And Mr. Johnston. I'm so pleased to meet people I know here. Remember me? I met you at Riverside Acres."

Bob Connolly shook her hand like the politician he was. "Don't mention it. So nice to see you again, Ms. Davis."

She fluttered her hands as if she were a bit flaky. "And who are these nice young men?" she asked ingenuously, bending over to appear frail. "You're friends of Mr. Connolly too? I'm Nancy Davis. So nice to meet you."

They laughed nervously, waiting for Connolly to respond.

Connolly waved a hand in their direction. "Mike Glazer and Sergio Carrera. We were just discussing some, uh, work they're doing for the county." He turned to her with a politician's smile. "Now if you'll excuse us…"

"Oh yes, yes, of course," Nancy tittered. "So nice to meet all of you."

They turned and walked out the door, and Nancy regained her seat. She wrote down the names. Mike Glazer and Sergio Carrera. Real names? Maybe.

Later, sitting under the umbrella at the pool with Louise and Susan, Nancy showed them the printout on the Mandell Consortium. "I've never heard of it, have you?" Nancy pointed to the name. "But then, I'm not local."

"I read the papers," Susan shook her head, "but I don't remember reading anything about it. Hundreds of those consortiums around, I'm sure."

"It's some kind of dummy corporation." Louise read down the list of officers. "Do these people even exist?"

"I googled them. Bank officers." Nancy's gaze shifted from Susan to Louise. "We need to find out more. Their headquarters is in Deerfield Beach."

"That's a short drive north." Susan sat up and frowned. "Wait a minute. They may be dangerous. You have no idea who they really are. Maybe they're Mafia."

Louise rolled her eyes. "You can stay out of it. Nancy and I are over ninety. We can act like doddering fools. . ." She paused, then stared directly at Susan. "Which we are not."

Nancy frowned. She should have talked with Louise. Doddering old fools is exactly the impression she'd like to present. Now Louise had blown it, but they'd been around Susan so much that she had probably formed her own impressions, for better or worse. Were they wise to let Susan know so much? She did help with local information, and she knew most of the residents here. She couldn't have abducted Jessica, but could she be Peter's would-be killer? Nancy glanced at Susan. If so, they'd have a better chance of catching her in a mistake if they kept her close. Nancy decided to wait and see and cut her loose if they had to.

"Of course not," Susan said. "But the murder victim—Ray, was it?—was found in the Everglades. He could have been shot anywhere. That house and even the boat probably have nothing to do with it."

Susan was right, but something in that whole setup didn't smell right. The young man on the houseboat said boats came and went all the time at the house across the inlet. Why weren't boats there now?

"Maybe not," Nancy said at last, "but if someone was in that house, he may have seen something that could help." She shaded her eyes in the glaring afternoon sun to look at Susan. "We have to find Jessica soon. Every minute she's missing may be dangerous for her."

Nancy turned to Louise. "We need to go back to that house, maybe this evening when someone might be home."

"Sure seemed deserted to me," said Louise.

Susan glanced from one to the other. She shook her head. "I'll stay here—not going back to that place--but I'll be by the phone in case you get into trouble. Anyway, I think you're trespassing and that's against the law."

"Fine. You don't have to go." Louise moved her chair so she could see the condo entrance. She sighed. "I can't imagine what's keeping George. He should be here by now."

"George?" said Susan.

Nancy winked at Louise. Even the thought of George made

Louise smile. "George is an old friend of ours from Whisperwood."

"That's where we live," Louise added. "The three of us formed the 90s Club since we're all ninety and over."

"We have a 90 Years' Club here too," said Susan. "Don't think they do much, though."

"How do you know? Do you talk to them?"

Susan shuddered. "Actually, I don't know, but they're all over ninety. What can they do?" She saw Louise's angry face. "Oh, but I didn't mean you. . ."

"Didn't you?" Louise said coldly, then turned her back and stalked toward the entrance. "I'm gonna wait for George by the elevators."

Susan turned to Nancy. "I'm sorry. . ."

"Don't mention it." Nancy picked up her papers. "I'm going to join Louise. We'll see you later."

As Nancy walked toward the elevators, a cab pulled up and George, still shrouded in a heavy winter coat, tumbled out. Nancy watched as he raised his hat to Louise, then turned to pay off the cab driver and retrieve his cane and suitcases. Louise hobbled up to him, and Nancy held back to let them greet each other. Once again, a wave of loneliness swept through her. But as if sensing an audience, Louise and George kept their greetings sedate. Nancy could see the beaming grins on their faces. Their relationship warmed her heart but left her feeling like a dandelion in a rose bed.

George spied Nancy and lifted his cane in greeting. "Did I get here in time to save the day?" he asked.

"I hope so," Nancy said. "We can sure use your help." She pulled a small wagon—not a grocery cart—from where it was kept next to the management office, and the three of them piled George's baggage onto it.

"Things been too calm back at Whisperwood," George said.

"Nobody falling down stairs or getting killed. Still dying off, but that's natural."

"Glad to hear it," Louise deadpanned.

Louise and Nancy stayed with the luggage while George hobbled into the management office, signed the papers, and picked up the keys to his rental. He returned, leaning on his cane as he waved a legal-sized sheet of paper at them. "Got more rules and regulations than city hall," he grumbled.

They spent the rest of the afternoon catching up on the news from Whisperwood. Then Louise and Nancy filled George in on events so far at Riverside Acres. As the sun set, Nancy suggested they go out to dinner. George looked at them in surprise.

"You mean they don't have a dining room here?" He lifted his eyebrows.

"Not that kind of place," said Louise.

"They've got a pool and a gym," added Nancy, "and a clubhouse for potluck suppers. . ."

"No, thank you." George shuddered. "Not for me from what I've been hearing."

"People tell me that someone plans trips now and then, and I'm sure there are clubs here." Nancy said. "Notices on the bulletin board."

"Whisperwood's looking better and better." George tapped his cane.

"Before we go," Nancy said, "I need to get a different purse." She retreated to the bedroom and returned, holding a large straw bag covered with red and yellow straw flowers. "I bought this in town." She dumped the contents of her more modest black leather purse into it.

Louise laughed. "Perfect."

As they walked out to the car, Nancy said, "We've an errand to run before dinner, George."

"And without Susan this time," Louise added with a stern look at Nancy.

"Good," said George. "Maybe we can have dinner at a decent hour then. I'm tired of the early bird dinners at Whisperwood."

"Better than cooking yourself," said Nancy with a smile.

Louise laughed.

In fifteen minutes they arrived at the house on the inlet. The gate was still closed. Nancy parked the car on the side of the road, and the three of them walked to the gate. Nancy pressed the buzzer, waited, then pressed again.

She heard static and then a man's voice. "McCall's residence."

Nancy jumped in surprise. She had expected the place to be vacant, but this was better. She gave their names. "May we come in and talk to you about the boat next door?"

"We don't know anything about any boats next door. And we don't rent out slips, if that's what you're asking." The voice sounded familiar even through the intercom.

"You've probably heard about what happened," said Nancy. The captain on a boat docked there was murdered, and now our friend, who was staying on the boat, is missing. I have her photo and would like to show it to you. Maybe you've seen her."

"Just a minute." Nancy heard the intercom click off.

They waited. A couple of minutes later, they heard the gate unlatch. Nancy turned to George. "You'd better wait here."

"I oughta go with you," he sputtered. "I've got a weapon." He brandished his cane.

"So have I." Louise held up her cane like a sword and poked George with it.

"Hey, watch that," George said, then his eyes widened. "Is that the cane that comes apart into a real sword?"

Louise nodded. "We're not helpless."

Nancy laid a hand on George's arm. "We need you as back-up," she said. "Here's my phone. Stay in the car. If you spot any trouble or something doesn't seem right to you, call the police."

Nancy and Louise stepped through the gate and walked down the driveway to the house. As they approached, Nancy glanced at the pool, still murky with leaves floating on top.

A woman waited for them at the door. She appeared to be in her thirties with blonde hair and heavily made-up face. She wore a short, skin-tight black dress and high-heeled cork sandals.

"Okay," the woman said. "Let's see the picture."

"May we come in?" Nancy asked, fanning her face and trying to look exhausted. "We need to sit down, and I'd like to ask you a few questions, if I may."

"What kind of questions?" She refused to move from the door.

Nancy heard chuckling, then a man appeared behind the woman. "Hello, Mrs. Davis, isn't it?" He peered behind her. "And I see your friend Mrs. Owens. Come in." He glanced at the woman. "Let these nice people in, Tiff. They're friends."

"It's nice to see you again, Mr. Johnston." Harv Johnston. Was he behind the Mandell Consortium or did he rent this place? "So this is where you live?" Nancy asked.

"I'm renting here while I get my business going," Johnston said. "Come on in." He gestured toward the living room. "Sorry about the furnishings. Haven't settled in yet."

The woman hung back. "They were just going to show us a photo."

Johnston's smile was reptilian. It sent shivers racing down Nancy's back.

"This is my friend Tiffany, ladies. Tiffany, these good people are from Riverside Acres." Johnston turned to Nancy. "Now have a seat and tell me about those photos."

Nancy and Louise sat on the couch. Nancy smelled mildew. Tiffany took a chair, folded her arms, and frowned at them.

Nancy sat up, not wanting to lean back against the mildewed fabric. "We're searching for a woman who is missing. She came on a boat that docked next door, and I thought you might have seen her." Nancy put the straw bag on her lap and opened it.

The woman looked at her watch and glanced at Johnston.

"Now honey," said Johnston, "these people are trying to find someone. I have to help them out." He turned to Nancy. "We were just going out to dinner. Would you like some coffee?"

Nancy seized the chance and simpered, "Oh yes, that would be so nice."

Tiffany glanced at Johnston irritably. "I guess I can make it. You got everything in the kitchen?" Her tone was not friendly.

Johnston nodded. "That would be real sweet."

"Nice place," Nancy said. "So the McCalls are the owners?"

"That's who I'm renting from," said Johnston. "I like it." He sat back in an armchair. "I don't know anything about this missing friend of yours."

Nancy made a show of digging in her purse, giving Louise time to elicit more information.

Louise smiled at them and asked in an admiring tone, "Beautiful spot you have here. Are you snowbirds? Down for the winter? I'm from West Virginia myself. Where are you from?"

"We're both from up north." Johnston folded his arms as he spoke.

"Up north," echoed Tiffany, coming out from the kitchen. "Coffee will be ready in a moment." She watched Nancy rummage through the huge straw bag beside her on the couch. She pointedly looked at her watch. "We have a reservation. . ."

"Yes, just a minute, I'll find that photo," Nancy said, still rummaging. "I know I've got it here."

Tiffany glanced at Johnston. "I'll go see about the coffee." She withdrew into the kitchen.

"Hate to impose on you like this," said Louise.

Nancy's eyes darted around the living room. Several framed photos and a couple of common Florida souvenirs were now displayed on a bookshelf, but they seemed like more window dressing to Nancy. She glanced at Louise and then at her own aged hand. There was nothing at all menacing about the two of them, but then the media made everyone suspicious. She finally dredged up a photo of Jessica. "Here it is."

At that moment, Tiffany appeared, carrying a tray with three cups and a sugar bowl. She handed the cups to Nancy, Louise, and Johnston, then set the tray on the coffee table.

Nancy picked up a cup and dumped a spoon of sugar in it. Plain white cups and saucers. The kind supplied with rentals or bought for second homes.

"No cream," Tiffany announced. She glanced at the photo Nancy had placed on the table.

"Nope," she said. "Never seen her before."

Johnston peered closely at it. "Me neither. Can't help you at all."

"I didn't really think you'd recognize her," said Nancy, adding a titter, "just thought I'd ask. Don't know where she's gone to. These kids and spring break. . ." she laughed.

Johnston laughed with her. "I know how it is."

"This is such a pleasant place you have," said Nancy. "On the water. Must be really nice—especially if you have a boat."

"No boat, I'm afraid," said Johnston. "I just like looking out at the river." He looked at his watch. "I'm afraid I've got to be going. I'll walk you to the gate."

"Goodness, the time just flew." Nancy rose. "Please don't trouble yourself. But first," she tittered, "may I use the rest room?"

Tiffany threw a quick glance at Johnston.

"Curse of getting old," added Nancy.

"I guess so," said Johnston. He pointed down a darkened hall. Nancy walked in that direction and opened a door at random. Johnston hurried after her. "Not that one." He threw open another door, farther down the hall. "This one."

"Thank you." Nancy closed the door behind her, peeked into the medicine cabinet, and found it empty. She then used the facilities before rejoining the others.

Johnston waited alongside Louise. "I'll go with you to the gate. Gotta check it anyway."

He wants to make sure we leave. As they ambled out to the gate, Nancy exclaimed about the hedge in a loud voice as if she were deaf. Thank goodness George got the hint and ducked down out of sight. In the rearview mirror, Nancy saw Johnston still at the gate, watching them drive away.

"So what did we get out of that visit?" asked Louise.

"We know where Johnston lives, and we know he lied. Boats are kept at that dock. In fact, the young man on the houseboat at Jaworsky's dock said they are a nuisance. Why did Johnston lie?" She glanced at Louise. "That was a stage set, you know."

Louise stared at her in astonishment. "Why? Seemed like an ordinary house to me."

"Those photos in the bookshelf were stock photos, and that door I opened accidentally? The room was empty. We know there's a bed in another room, but the furnishings are minimal. What is that place used for?"

"Maybe he just needs an address," said George, "and a place to stay. He has to live somewhere."

"Whatever the case," added Nancy, "I saw no signs of Jessica."

"Do you suppose that Tiffany and Johnston are the brother-sister pair in the "Most Wanted" flyers?" Louise asked.

"I wondered about that, too," said Nancy. "Didn't see a resemblance, and she seemed more like a girlfriend. She didn't live there." She shrugged. "Maybe she was a date for the evening."

***

Glad to Be in Fort Lauderdale

Here's a personal comment from Tom and Betts, Apt. 215:

We're so happy we moved down here. Don't know why it took us so long. The temperature back home in Michigan is 22 degrees. We thought our fellow residents would like to know what temperatures are like up north in other places.

New York City: 18 degrees F.

Cleveland: 30 degrees F.

Toronto: -5 degrees F.

Buffalo: -2 degrees F.

Fairbanks: -40 degrees F.

Happy you're here?

Notice approved by Riverside Acres Management

Chapter 19

After dinner, George went on to his apartment. "Long day today," he said, but Nancy and Louise were still keyed up speculating about their visit to the pink house. Louise paced the floor, stopping now and then to listen at the wall. "I don't hear anything," she said when she saw Nancy look up from reading.

Oscar and Rupert lay beside Nancy on the couch, heads cocked as if they also wondered what Louise was up to.

"I don't think Quint is home yet," Nancy said. "Too quiet over there. Maybe he's out of town."

"We'd all be happy if he stayed out of town," growled Louise.

She opened the front door and looked down the hall. "Nothing going on out there." She turned back to Nancy. "Do you think Eveline's daughter is really dead?"

Nancy paused as she turned a page. "That's what Eveline said."

"I know that's what she said." Louise flicked her braid. "But the way she said it makes me wonder."

"Why would she make up something like that?"

"Maybe her daughter's on drugs or alcohol or in rehab or prison or a runaway." Louise flopped into the arm chair. "That's usually why grandparents end up raising their grandkids."

"So tragic. But if her daughter isn't dead and shows up here, Eveline would have to explain that to all of us." Nancy reached over and hugged Oscar. Even though she had never had children, she still knew how difficult the job could be, even with two loving and capable parents. The more she thought of parenting over the years and seen the effects of inept and unloving parents, the more strongly she believed that parents should pass a test or at least get parent training before they had kids.

Nancy heard a door slam, then muted yelling and several thuds. She raised an eyebrow at Louise.

Louise jumped up and put her ear to the wall. "There's someone else in there. I hear Quint's voice and another man's. I know what I'll do."

She ran out the door. Nancy heard her knocking at the Sandstrom's door, then Louise's voice.

"Hello," Louise said, speaking loudly in a voice so syrupy it could catch flies. "I came to invite Carla over for tea. Carla, come on over."

Nancy sat back in surprise as Louise walked in with Carla behind her. This was a different Carla. She had exchanged her boring house dress for a loose T-shirt, cropped pants, and athletic shoes.

"Nice to see you again, Carla," Nancy said in as welcoming and warm a voice as she could muster while adjusting her impression of Carla.

"I'll put on some tea." Louise looked back at Carla as she headed for the kitchen. "English Breakfast all right?"

Carla nodded and sat down in one of the armchairs. She reached over to rub Oscar behind the ears. "Nice dogs," she murmured. Rupert rose from his place on the couch, yawned, stretched, and walked over to Carla for his share of attention.

"How is everything going?" asked Nancy.

"F-fine," Carla stammered. "Well, to tell you the truth, not so fine. Some of the gentlemen here," she paused, "aren't so gentlemanly, if you know what I mean."

Louise hovered at the kitchen door. "Ain't that the truth. Even if they're close relatives." She glanced at Nancy with a slight smile.

Nancy nodded. Perhaps Carla would tell them what was happening next door. Was her son beating her? That happened in the best of families. If Carla would only admit it, then Louise knew how to help her.

"I didn't mean Quint. He's a dear, sweet boy." Carla sighed. "I meant that Mr. Connolly." She leaned toward Nancy and whispered, "He drinks too much, you know, and when he drinks, he gets ugly."

"That's Bob Connolly yelling next door?" Louise raised an eyebrow in disbelief.

"It's not Quint," sniffed Carla. "Just because Mr. Connolly and his buddy, Harv Johnston, hire my son to run errands and fix their cars doesn't give them any call to yell at him."

"Certainly not," said Nancy.

"Quint is doing the best he can," Carla said, a secret smile on her lips.

What did that smile mean? It was gone in an instant.

"Seen my share of bad bosses," said Louise. She heard the kettle whistle and withdrew into the kitchen. A minute later, she appeared with three steaming mugs, tea bag labels hanging over the sides, and a sugar bowl on a tray. "Just gotta let it steep for a few minutes." Louise looked up at Carla. "Glad you could join us."

"I don't like staying around when they're," she nodded her head toward her apartment, "talking business."

"We heard all the yelling," said Louise. "They probably realized that and quieted down."

"Quint isn't going to be working for them much longer," said Carla. "And I'll be glad for that."

Nancy glanced at Louise who arched an eyebrow. "Getting another job?" Nancy asked.

Carla smiled. "Yeah. Out of town. He'll be moving in a couple of weeks." She leaned back and stroked Oscar, who lay in her lap.

Nancy handed her a towel. "Good for him if he gets yelled at by the people he's working for."

"I wouldn't stand for much of that," Louise said.

"He's finally had enough of it too," said Carla. "Just had to finish what he started. Wrap things up." She wiped slobber off the dog's chins with the towel.

Louise shot a quick look at Nancy. "I suppose you'll miss Quint when he goes."

"Have to expect that." Carla shrugged.

Nancy looked at Carla over her mug. "What does Quint do?"

"He's the mechanic." Carla folded the towel. "Checks the cars before they're given out to drivers. Makes sure there's no trouble on the road. Almost takes 'em apart sometimes."

"So Bob Connolly and Harv Johnston run the driving service business." asked Nancy. "Seems like such a good idea."

"Oh it is," agreed Carla.

"Where's the business office?" asked Nancy.

Carla laughed. "They don't really have an office. Do everything by phone and email, and people pick up the cars here."

"He can't keep the cars here." Most of the residents had designated parking spaces. Nancy hadn't seen many spaces for guests.

"No. They contract with some, ah, what is it now?" Carla tapped her cheek as if she sought to remember. "Consortium. That's it. The Mandell Consortium rents out warehouse space to Mr. Johnston. He has some place on the river to do the final outfitting before they bring the cars here for the drivers to pick up."

"I see," said Nancy. She had no doubt about where that place on the river might be.

***

No Commercial Vehicles Allowed

Riverside Acres is a private residential community and cannot permit commercial vehicles to park overnight in the residents' parking areas. Any commercial vehicles parked there for more than four hours will be towed by A&S Towing Company and can be retrieved from the A&S facility, 954-555-3156.

Management, Riverside Acres

Chapter 20

George popped in on Nancy and Louise for breakfast early the next morning. They sat around the table with a quart of orange juice and bagels Nancy had brought back from walking the dogs. The two bottom-feeders, slobber dripping on the floor, rummaged underfoot for crumbs.

"So Quint works for Johnston," said Louise, "and Johnston rents space from the Mandell Consortium."

"What's this?" George said, eyeing the bagels. "Quint is the guy next door? The bruiser?"

Nancy nodded and told him about Carla's visit the night before. "I think Harv and Bob Connolly are the Mandell Consortium."

Louise stopped chomping on a bagel. "That would make sense."

"And Eveline mentioned that Susan is buddies with Harv Johnston," Nancy added.

"I'm getting a glimmer," said George.

"So am I," said Louise, glancing at George. "But I'll bet Susan is buddies with all the bachelors here."

"As helpful as she's been, we don't know her that well." Nancy folded her arms on the table. "But I like to give people a lot of rope. See what they do with it."

"Oh boy, just like in a detective story." George rubbed his hands together.

"She could be buddying up with us to find out what we know," said Louise, pushing Oscar away with her foot.

"Or she could just be nosy or a busybody." Nancy spread cream cheese on a bagel. "In any case, we can feed her whatever might have useful consequences. Keep Peter out of it. Focus on the search for Jessica."

"There is a tenuous connection though."

"Yes," Nancy said slowly. "Harv Johnston and the pink house. I'm getting a vague suspicion about what he might be up to there."

"Me too," said Louise, "which reminds me," Louise tapped George on the wrist, "whatever happened to that novel you were writing?"

George wriggled uncomfortably. "It's in the works. Just need more material, that's all." He brightened. "That's why I came down here."

They heard a knock on the door. Louise opened it and walked back to the kitchen with a jocular "Look what the cat dragged in." Susan followed her.

"Last night we met the people renting the house next door to Stan Jaworsky," Nancy said.

"Really?" Susan seemed amused. "So who were they? A Mafia boss and his moll?"

Louise passed in front of Nancy, her back to Susan. Nancy could see the spark in Louise's eyes as she silently mouthed, "Don't tell her anything."

Nancy nodded and smiled at Susan. "We were surprised to find that's where Harv Johnston lives."

Susan stared at them, open-mouthed. "Harv lives there?"

"And he has a girlfriend named Tiffany," added Louise.

"Oh." Susan shrugged. "See? No mystery to that place at all."

Nancy watched Susan. She didn't seem shocked or dismayed at this information. Or was she covering up?

"Who owns that big muscled powerboat at Jaworsky's? The one with two huge outboards," Louise muttered. "That's what I'd like to know."

Susan leaned against the wall with her arms folded. "Why?"

"If I were bringing in drugs or had some other illegal stuff going on, I'd want a fast boat." She sat back and challenged Susan. "Wouldn't you?"

George sipped his cup of tea. "A plane. I'd want a plane."

"Nah. You'd have to land someplace." Louise tapped her cane.

Susan rolled her eyes. "I hear they drop the stuff into a field, and somebody there picks it up."

"Oh sure. I've heard that too. As if nobody'd see that." Louise's sarcasm cut the air. "Hundreds of hidden places to take a boat. Easy to hide. Easy to pick up anything by land or water."

Nancy watched this exchange as she stirred her tea. Even if they weren't sure about Susan, she knew Fort Lauderdale and she knew the people at the condo. She could still be useful.

"I've been reading about those fast boats on the Internet," Louise added. "Some people call them cigarette boats. Hard to detect by radar. Stealthy, fast, seaworthy, and difficult to intercept with conventional boats." She rapped the table. "Preferred boat of drug smugglers. Of course DEA knows that and so does the Coast Guard. So the smugglers keep coming up with innovations, like submarines and such."

"Good to know, but I don't see a submarine going up that river," Nancy said. She glanced at her watch.

"Have you talked to Jessica's grandmother recently?" asked Susan.

"Yeah. Maybe she's heard something by now," chimed in Louise.

"If she had, she would have called me." Nancy pulled a small address book out of her purse and walked over to the phone. She tapped in the numbers, and they waited. Nancy quickly came to the point. She stared at the wall as she listened.

"I see. Well, thank you." She shook her head at Louise. "No, we don't know where she is either. I'll let you know if we find out anything." She hung up and turned to the three expectant faces.

Louise summed it up. "Hasn't heard anything," she said.

"No word." Nancy walked back to her chair. "Amelia knew about Ray. The police have been in contact with Jessica's parents. Amelia said they all think Ray's murder has nothing to do with Jessica, that he tangled with some thugs in a bar or someplace, and they killed him and dumped him in the Everglades. The police just haven't identified the bar yet."

"Everyone in that bar would clam up," said George.

Louise frowned. "Jessica could have been taken prisoner."

"But she called Amelia and said she was all right." Nancy frowned in thought. "I'm going to talk to the police. They must be searching for her. We ought to tell them what we know, not that that's very much." She paused. "We should have done this before." She looked at Susan. "We passed the police station on one of our drives. I'm sure I can find it."

"You want to go there now?" Susan glanced at her watch.

Louise rose stiffly out of her chair. "I'll go too, but be careful what you say to the police about Jessica. They might think she killed Ray."

Susan stopped. "Maybe she did. You don't know anything about her, or even, from what you've told me, about her grandmother."

Nancy opened the door. "That's true, but until we learn different, I'm going to think of her as a bystander in all this."

They walked single file along the outside corridor toward the elevator, pressing against the wall to let Dashaune pedal past them on his tricycle as he made zooming noises.

Nancy turned to watch him speed down the corridor and stop at a door near the end. "Such a shame," she said to Susan. "He's a sweet little boy but even so, Eveline had hoped for a pleasant retirement without the responsibilities of raising a child."

"Guess that's not going to happen," Susan said.

Tottering along behind them, Louise added, "A lot of cases like that. The kid gets hooked on drugs or alcohol and then gets pregnant and grandma gets the baby. Terrible situation. Illegal drugs, the pushers and the users, destroy our communities and finance the terrorists. Just wish we could keep the addicts from having kids. Adds more tragedy."

"Poor little boy." George reached over and pushed the "down" button for the elevator.

"Poor grandma," said Nancy.

"Poor all of us. We're all paying for them, you know." Louise flicked her braid. "One way or another. Drunks, drug addicts, sadists, thugs, and any other irresponsible jackass can become a parent. The horror some kids endure is beyond belief." She clamped her lips shut and stuck out her jaw. "My opinion."

Susan looked at her, amused. "And we all know it now."

George chuckled. "That's our Louise, all right. Ya gotta love her."

Susan raised an eyebrow at this and held up her watch. "I'm afraid I can't go with you this morning, after all."

"What's the matter," George said. "Cops lookin' for you?"

Nancy watched Susan blush. "Don't mind George," Nancy said. "He's always joking."

Susan laughed, but Nancy didn't think Susan found George amusing. "I almost forgot that I promised to take Maria to the store today. She depends on me, you know."

"Don't worry about us," said Nancy, waving her map. "I'll find it." She hoped. After driving around with Susan, she felt she could avoid the worst dead ends and bottlenecks.

"All right, then." Susan waved as she walked back toward her apartment.

The elevator door opened, and Nancy and George entered, but Louise hesitated, still looking at Susan's retreating back. She turned to Nancy. "Did you see her reaction?"

"She turned red at George's comment," said Nancy.

"What? I didn't see anything." George frowned. "What'd I say?"

Louise laughed. "Never mind."

Getting to the police station was a straightforward drive taking ten minutes. They walked into the building, and Nancy headed directly to the information desk against the back wall in the lobby.

"We'd like to speak to the officer in charge of investigating the murder of Ray Slocum," Nancy said to the elderly man in suit and tie who sat behind the desk. "Smith" in large white letters on a green field stood out on his name badge.

He flipped through a loose leaf notebook as he peered up at them. "The man pulled out of the Glades? Shot?"

Nancy nodded.

"Okay. That's Detective Alleso." Mr. Smith picked up the phone. "Some people here to see you." He listened a moment, his eyes surveying the group from head to foot. "About the Slocum shooting." He nodded and hung up. "The detective will be right down. You can sit over there." He pointed to a long wooden bench against the institutional green wall. A woman, tears wet on her cheeks, and a teenaged boy with a sullen face already sat there.

"What are you going to say?" asked George, looking around with interest.

Nancy shrugged. "I'll tell them what we're doing. They should know we're looking for her too." She walked to the bulletin board on the wall near them and studied the "wanted" posters. She recognized several of them from Peter's own collection, but there were so many they were tacked to the board in a stack a half-inch thick.

"That's my Nancy," said Louise, sitting back, arms folded, watching a well-dressed young man pass by engrossed in conversation with a young woman in a bikini and flip flops. Uniformed police officers strode in and out, a few stopping to chat with other officers on their way.

Nancy and her fellow 90s Club members waited for twenty minutes before a gray-haired, stocky African-American man wearing creased gray slacks, white short-sleeved shirt and a blue striped tie walked up to them and stopped with his hands on his hips. "You the people inquiring about the Slocum murder?"

Nancy stood and smiled at him. "We have information for you."

Face blank, his eyes traveled from one to the other. "Let's get some privacy, shall we?" He ushered them down the hall and into a small conference room. Like the hall and the waiting area, it was painted in the same dreary institutional green. Gesturing to the seats around a long brown table marred by scratches and graffiti, Alleso took a seat himself. "Okay. Whatcha got?"

Nancy told him about their search for Jessica. "I know you're looking for her. She must be an innocent victim of whatever happened to Ray Slocum." She pulled a photo out of her purse and laid it on the table in front of him.

He glanced at it and nodded. "The family emailed us her picture." He wrote in a small notebook that had materialized from his back pocket. "Thank you." He stared at Nancy. "We have an APB out for her. We'll find her." He closed the notebook and slapped it against his hand. "What is your concern in this matter?"

"Her grandmother asked me to find her. She's been missing for three weeks. If we don't find her soon…." Nancy shook her head.

"Ray Slocum must have messed with some very bad people, and she may have got roped in on it, whether she knew what he was doing or not. We are looking for her as a person of interest. We hope she was not a victim, but we'll find her," he hesitated, started to say something more but stopped.

The fleeting expression on Alleso's face was odd. What had he been going to say? Nancy tried prompting him. "Did you find out what Ray could have been doing that resulted in his death?"

Detective Alleso pushed his chair back and crossed a leg over his knee. He shook his head. "We're on the case."

Nancy knew that body language. Alleso was barricading himself against them.

Louise leaned toward him. "We think you should investigate the house across the inlet. Something funny is going on there."

Alleso turned to her. "What makes you say that?"

"The guy on the houseboat behind the *Bonny Scot* was afraid of it," Nancy said. "He told us not to stare in that direction. He was planning to leave as soon as he could."

George spoke up. "Ray and Jessica could have seen something they shouldn't have seen."

"So then the murderers killed Ray and took him out to the Glades to throw you off," added Nancy.

Alleso wrote a few words in his notebook, then tapped his pencil on the table. After a moment, he frowned at Nancy. "So what happened to Ms. Cantwell?"

"We don't know, but she's in danger," Nancy said.

"If she's innocent as you seem to think, why didn't she come to us? Or go home?" Alleso stood and stepped to the door. "There's more to this than you think. We appreciate your help. If you hear from this Jessica, let us know immediately."

"If you'd fill us in," Louise sputtered, standing and stabbing her finger at him, "we could be of more help."

"We don't encourage civilians to get physically involved in solving crimes," Alleso said, frowning. "We appreciate your information, of course." He moved to the doorway.

"There's one more thing," Nancy said. She stood, too, and faced him eye to eye. "We're staying at Peter Stamboul's apartment in Riverside Acres. He filed a report with you about a drive-by shooting aimed at him. Shortly after that, he was poisoned with digitalis. Are you working on that case?"

Alleso pursed his lips. "We have nothing to go on for the drive-by. No witnesses. He left the scene and didn't recall exactly where it happened. The digitalis poisoning is questionable too."

"He thinks, and we agree with him, that someone at his home in Riverside Acres wants to kill him." Nancy explained about the "Most Wanted" flyers. "Peter has left town to escape these attempts, but I can contact him if necessary."

"Okay. I'll let you know." Alleso checked his watch. "Now I've got to go." He reached into his pocket and gave Nancy a card. "In case you come up with any concrete information," he said.

Nancy walked to the door. Louise followed. George remained where he was sitting, pushing his lips in and out, then he looked up with a start and followed Louise. Alleso waited for them to pass through the door, then ushered them back to the information desk.

"Thank you for dropping by." He gave them a perfunctory smile, his eyes elsewhere. "We appreciate citizen input."

Nancy watched him stride away. She turned to her companions. "That was a polite brush-off."

George shivered. "All business. Didn't tell us a thing."

"Not their job," said Nancy. "But the police haven't found her yet. I hope that's a good thing."

George frowned and shook his head. "Alleso's right, you know. If Jessica's innocent, why didn't she call the police or go home?"

Nancy bit her lip, thinking of Amelia and then of the bright young woman she'd met at Whisperwood. Jessica must know by now that Ray was dead. If she was all right, why hadn't she gone to the police?

Nancy drove them back to Riverside Acres. So far, they were scoring zero in finding Jessica and identifying who poisoned Peter. She wandered into the den to take another look at Peter's flyers of the "Most Wanted." They were all there, twenty flyers tacked to the board. Nancy took a second look. They were different flyers. The original twenty that Peter had posted were gone, replaced by a new set of felons she'd never seen before.

***

Don't Become Another Victim!

Riverside Acres is a gated community, which helps keep burglars, unwanted solicitors, and con men away from our doors. You can still become a victim of frauds and scams, especially over the phone or Internet. Don't give out personal or credit card information to anyone you don't know and especially not over the phone.

Riverside Acres Resident Coordinator

Nancy called Peter. "An interesting development," she told him. She kept her tone neutral, but her hands shook. Someone had invaded their apartment. *We aren't safe here.* Thank goodness the fingerprint cards she'd collected so far were hidden in an envelope that hadn't been touched.

"You found out something?" Peter said.

"Maybe." Nancy took the phone with her into the den. "Someone got into your apartment and took all ten flyers you posted on the bulletin board and replaced them with others."

"What?" Peter shouted. His voice rose. "That means I am on the right track."

"And that he or she does live here at Riverside." Nancy returned to the living room and sat on the couch. Oscar leaped up beside her. "Does anyone else have a key to your apartment?:"

"Just the management office." Peter sounded thoughtful. "No one else."

"Just a minute." Nancy went over to the front door, opened it, and inspected the lock. She nodded as she saw faint scratches on the outside and returned to the phone. "I think they picked your lock."

"Those locks aren't state of the art, you know," said Peter. "It's a gated community, security guard, cameras. And the residents are always wandering around. They'd notice anything odd going on."

"I could open your lock with my picks," said Nancy, "but I

think I could also do it with a credit card."

"Oh my," said Peter. "A credit card? I had no idea it could be so easy."

"You've led a sheltered life." Nancy knew kids who opened locks with credit cards. "You've got a list of the ten people in the missing flyers?"

"I've got the names here and when I realized I was targeted," Peter hesitated and cleared his throat. "I made copies, ordered glossies of the photos, and printed out the age progressions, although we're only talking a few years. They're all here in the folder you packed for me."

"I'll drive up there in a few minutes. I'd like to study them again now that I've met some of the residents. Fresh eyes." She glanced over at Louise, sitting on the couch, reading. Louise had uploaded a batch of photos of residents the night before.

"Louise has been on the job," Nancy added. "I'll e-mail you the latest crop of photos."

"I'll be waiting."

Nancy heard eagerness in his voice. Peter must be lonely and probably depressed up there by himself. She'd known him a long time—he'd cried in her arms as he dealt with the anxiety and frustrations of being gay, and she'd cried in his when she lost her husband Bill. She knew how fragile he was, despite the face he wore. *We have to find the killer and get Peter back here fast.*

She studied the den and living room. *The killer sees Peter as a threat, but we're just Peter's doddering old friends who came to dog sit.* Had the intruder found anything that might give them away? He or she had ruffled papers on the desk, but Nancy had hidden a sheet of notes in the telephone directory. She held her breath as she shook them out of the directory. Still there and in place. What a relief! The notes included Jessica's name, the boat's name, and a list with question marks next to three names: Harv Johnston, Bob Connolly, and Quint Sandstrom. All three were suspicious characters, but were they behind the attacks on Peter and Abby's murder and one of them the intruder? If so, what would they do if they had read this list?

She found Peter's bug detector in his desk drawer and used it. In the base of a lamp in the living room, she found a wire-tapping device. She disabled it and showed it to Louise. "I hope they put this in when they changed the flyers, but I'll be checking regularly from now on."

"Good idea. I wonder who put it there—and when." Louise stood in the doorway behind Nancy. "Seems like they're onto us."

"If they are," Nancy said, "we'd better keep an eye out for falling flowerpots and drive-by shootings."

"That's what I'm thinking."

***

Nancy arrived at Peter's twenty minutes later. He stood at the open door and ushered her in. "I've taped the flyers on the wall. We can both sit in front of them and brainstorm." He lined up two chairs facing the flyers and shoved a coffee table between them. A pile of manila folders lay on the table.

Nancy took one chair and Peter the other, tilting it back and tapping his foot. He drummed his fingers on the chair arm.

Nancy stole a look at him. The old Peter seemed to have revived, thanks to the rest and freedom from worry, but the foot tapping and finger drumming showed how restless he was.

She put her hand on his arm to calm him. "Relax," she said, speaking slowly. "We can study the posters and go through the folders you've set up so far."

"Good. I've been feeling stymied." Peter now drummed the fingers on both hands, but his foot had stopped tapping. "I've ruled out the people who have solid backgrounds and reputations—and the ones who obviously are no match for the flyers." He sprang up and flipped through the papers on the desk, bringing back a printed spreadsheet. "Take a look at this, Nancy." He handed it to her.

She stared at a list of names, each with notations across the page. She recognized the names now, having met many of the residents at the pool or the elevator or in the halls.

"This is my alpha list," said Peter. "I still need photos of some of them—I've noted that in the margin."

"We're working on that. And I'm collecting fingerprints too."

"Great!" Peter whistled. "When I compare the photos I've got against the flyers, Harv Johnston comes close to looking like the man in the brother-sister pair, but I can't get a make on the woman."

Nancy studied the spreadsheet. "The people I'm most interested in at Riverside are Harv Johnston, Susan Withers, Bob Connolly, Eveline Kwame, Quint Sandstrom, and Carla Sandstrom." All except Johnston had made the alpha list and the spreadsheet.

"Johnston doesn't live there, but he comes around so often, he should be listed. You sent me the photo of him." Peter riffled the folders. "Can't believe Eveline's in on this. She's got enough troubles, and the African-American woman in the flyers doesn't resemble her in the least."

Nancy nodded. "Could she be Eveline's daughter?"

Peter peered more closely at the flyer. "Possibly, but that would be a stretch. Eveline went to her daughter's funeral up north somewhere. She told all of us about it."

Nancy turned back to the flyers on the wall. Peter got up and paced back and forth behind her. "It's got to be one of these people, but so far, any resemblance is slight," he said.

Nancy studied each flyer. The hard faces didn't look like any of the friendly people she'd met at Riverside Acres. When she came to the brother and sister, wanted for murder, mail fraud, and drug dealing, she paused and scrutinized their pictures. The woman seemed younger than the man, but Nancy could imagine them being a congenial couple. They could pose as man and wife, she supposed, or they could separate. The sister had long, straight, brunette hair and was slightly overweight. She seemed vaguely familiar but not enough that Nancy could put a name to her. Ears were hard to change, but her hair covered the ears. Dark, heavy eyebrows but how easy to tweeze them down to a fine line. Eyes? Nose? Lips? Hard to change those and not without surgery.

She turned to Peter. "Know any brother-sister act at Riverside?"

"Never met any residents who claimed to be." Peter stroked his chin. "But if they're wanted as brother and sister, they'd be sure to split up."

"Of course."

Peter stopped pacing and sat beside Nancy to study the faces of the brother and sister. "I'd vote for these two over the others," he said. "The other criminals seem way too tough to live inconspicuously at Riverside."

Nancy nodded. "We are getting close. I leave in twelve days, so we can't waste time. I'll get photos of the other people on this alpha list, and I'm lifting fingerprints of the most likely people. That way, when we send our report to the FBI we can include our best guesses backed up by photos and fingerprints to confirm our suspicions."

"Great idea, Nancy." Peter snapped his fingers and grinned.

Nancy smiled at him. "Meanwhile, you can do a systematic study of facial features, using a list of features difficult to change, then comparing these features on the photos with those on the FBI flyers and photos."

"Right." Peter picked up another sheaf of papers. "I've tried doing it a different way--writing down their descriptions and then next to each person, writing the opposite description." He selected a sheet of paper and pointed to the first few lines on it. "Like this. Brunette hair? I put down blond. Short and curly hair? I put down long and straight."

"Good. Even eye color can be changed with contacts nowadays."

"Sure. Maybe you have to look at the bones. The jaw line maybe."

Nancy scanned through the papers. "Shape of the lips, eyes, nose, ears. Those are hard to change." She saw Peter's eyes stray to the laptop.

"I'll get on it right away," he said, sitting down at the desk. His fingers played over the keyboard. He was already absorbed in the Internet.

Nancy let herself out.

Late the same afternoon, Nancy systematically called every hospital and rehab center in the county. No doubt the police had already checked them, and since Jessica had assured Amelia that she was safe, this was probably a useless exercise. Either way, all the young women patients were properly identified and had relatives or friends standing by.

Louise dozed on the sofa, book in hand, with the dogs cuddled up on each side. George had gone back to his own apartment for a nap. "Don't do anything without me," he cautioned as he left.

Nancy hung up the phone after the last call. "It was a bust," Nancy said.

Louise sat up, startled. "Thought it would be." The dogs jumped off the sofa and stared expectantly at Nancy. She smiled at them. Their earnest little faces were somehow endearing

"She could be anywhere," added Louise. "I hope she's not dead."

Like Ray. Nancy didn't say the words out loud.

***

Riverside Acres Beauty Salon Opens

Janne Barnes welcomes you to her new unisex salon at Riverside with half-price specials on hair cuts, permanents, and coloring this week! Drop by for tea and cookies, meet the staff, and set up your appointment. The salon is conveniently located on the first floor, next to the management office. Your own friends won't recognize the beautiful new you that emerges like a butterfly from Janne's salon!

Notice approved by Riverside Acres Management

Chapter 22

The next morning, Nancy slept late but woke to the sound of sobbing in the living room. What in the world. . .? She threw on a robe and opened her bedroom door.

Louise glanced up from the living room sofa and made a show of looking at her watch. "Good morning, Nancy."

Nancy walked into the living room and nodded at the distraught woman on the couch. Carla Sandstrom. Today she was wearing gray slacks and white shirt, but her outfit looked like prison garb on her stout figure. Oscar and Rupert were lying on the rug, their heads on their paws, as if waiting for instructions.

Louise sat next to Carla and shook her head in warning at Nancy. "We heard some bad news, Nancy."

Carla burst out weeping into tissue.

"What happened?" asked Nancy.

"It's Quint," moaned Carla. "His truck ran off Pelican Road out near Alligator Alley early this morning. He went right into a canal." She wiped her eyes with the tissue. "Can't imagine what he was doing there."

"He was hurt but not badly," added Louise. "He was able to get out of the truck."

"Bob Connolly was riding with him," added Carla, "and he was killed." She blew her nose. "I just know they'll blame Quint."

"That's terrible," Nancy said. She took Carla's hand and patted it. Whatever they thought of Quint, he was Carla's son. She loved him. But Connolly was killed. Was it an accident or was there more to this than appeared? He drank too much and had a loose tongue. A liability, for sure. Did Quint deliberately stage an accident? Nancy could not see Quint as a man who would plan such a thing, but someone might have paid him to deliberately wreck his truck to kill Connolly.

"He's such a good boy," Carla quavered, "most of the time. And smart. He works hard." She twisted her hands together. "He's got a tough job, and he's been under so much stress. . ." She began weeping again. Nancy brought out a glass of water and gave it to her.

"I'm sorry." She hiccupped, taking the glass. "I shouldn't be talking to you like this. I shouldn't be talking to you at all." She took a deep breath. "Quint would be madder'n a messed-up yellow jacket if he knew I'd talked to you. It's such a complicated mess. I'm scared."

"Scared?" asked Nancy. "Why?"

Carla shuddered. "I don't know how much more I can take of this. They might come after me, too. At least I can protect myself."

Nancy glanced at Louise. Who did Carla think would come after her? Why?

Louise tossed her braid. "Protect yourself?" she asked, raising an eyebrow at Nancy.

"I'm working on my brown belt." Carla rubbed her hands together. "Karate, you know."

"Karate!" Nancy's surprise echoed Louise's.

Carla looked down at her hands. "I hope I haven't bothered you. Practicing can get noisy sometimes." She smiled blandly at Louise. "Must sound like a battle."

Nancy sat back, reassessing her opinion of Carla. She glanced at

Louise who stood rigid as if she'd been hit by a body punch herself.

Nancy pulled herself together. "That's wonderful! I've studied karate myself." Nancy remembered all the sore muscles those karate lessons had given her, but the skills had carried her through some ugly confrontations.

"Took lessons for years but lapsed, you know. Then Quint insisted I take it up again." Carla shrugged. "Sometimes we practice together, but he's careful with me."

So Quint insisted. "Was there any particular reason to learn karate? Was someone threatening you?"

Carla's face turned sheepish. "He just thought it was a good idea." She sat up, and her voice became pugnacious. "So do I."

Karate practice certainly explained Carla's bruises and the noises from her apartment, but who would have expected that? Perhaps Carla didn't need their help at all. "Where's Quint now?"

"He's lying down. The doctors told him to rest. I'm so thankful he wasn't hurt bad." She sighed again. "I feel terrible about Mr. Connolly, but at least I won't have him at my door anymore. Him and his drinking."

"You can stay here with us for a few days if that would help," said Nancy.

Carla sighed. "I've got to get back to Quint, and I'm expecting a call from the insurance company." She gave them a weak smile as she stepped out to the walkway, meeting Harv Johnston as he passed by. He followed Carla into her apartment.

Louise watched them and then closed the door. She turned to Nancy. "I'll bet Quint and Connolly were both drunk."

"I can't believe she knows karate," said Nancy. "And a brown belt too."

Louise shook her head. "Maybe the karate is just a cover-up. She knows we hear the banging around in her apartment."

"Far-fetched if it is," said Nancy. "Why does she really feel so scared she had to take up karate?"

"Shit. Do you suppose she's had near-miss accidents too?"

***

Please Drive Carefully

South Florida's canals, lakes, lagoons, and rivers are beautiful and make boating a popular sport here. For cars they can be a hazard. Please drive carefully and at reasonable speeds along the waterways, which are home to alligators and other predators. We've all read news stories about cars veering off into a canal, and neither the car nor its passengers and driver are found for months.

Management, Riverside Acres

Once Carla left, Nancy called George and the three of them hurried out to the car. "Maybe we can get to the truck before it's towed away," said Nancy.

She drove out to Pelican Road, without Susan's help this time but with Louise, finger on the map, as navigator. George sat in the back seat, fiddling with the GPS Susan had loaned him.

"Got it figured out yet, George?" asked Louise, glancing back at him.

He grunted. "Almost."

"We're almost there," said Louise. "Those newfangled gadgets can't beat a good map and brains."

Nancy laughed.

"Can't believe you gals wanted to turn down Susan's GPS. Soon's I get it figured out, we can bounce around Fort Lauderdale like pros."

"Sure," said Louise.

"The reason I turned it down," said Nancy, "is because I think Susan could track where we've been when we return the GPS to her."

"No kidding." George held it at arm's length and squinted at it. "You think she'd do that?"

"Don't know." Nancy pointed to the canal they were driving along. "Where I come from, you run off the road into a tree. Here, you run off into a canal and drown."

"Drinking and driving," rumbled George. "Bad combo."

Louise nodded. "You ever hear me talk about alcoholism?"

"Probably," Nancy said, smiling at Louise. "But shoot anyway."

"Surely you don't mean that," grumbled George. "Considering what's been going on."

Louise glanced back at him. "All right, George. Anyway, people laughed at Carrie Nation taking a hatchet to the saloons back in the early 1900s," Louise began, "but we just don't realize how bad it was."

"How bad was it?" asked Nancy, humoring Louise.

"She and a bunch of other people were tired of drunken men making laws, starting wars, and conducting business. Her first husband was a drunk. The song about the little girl who goes to the bar and sings, "Daddy, please come home," was just life for a lot of families. Carrie Nation and her friends weren't necessarily a bunch of killjoy prudes."

Nancy nodded, remembering the alcohol-driven parties of her youth. Not that she participated, of course. . . . She grinned. How long ago all that seemed now.

"When liquor was made legal again after Prohibition, moviemakers thought it was cute to show a hung-over comedienne with an icepack on her head." Louise tossed her braid. "How dumb can you get? "

Nancy laughed and glanced over at Louise. "I saw an old movie where a character says he had to drive around to clear his head because he was drunk."

"That's what I'm talking about." Louise peered at the map. "I like my glass of wine as much as anyone. Beer, too. But," she frowned, "in moderation." She looked up. "Turn here, Nancy."

Nancy turned onto a rough two-lane road and traveled along it for three miles before they came to the wreck of a truck on the roadside. A flat-bed tow truck, yellow lights flashing, was parked in front. Nancy pulled up behind the wreck, and the three of them got out of the car. George shaded his eyes with his hand and squinted at the canal running alongside the road for miles in each direction. "Tow truck winched it out of the canal, but the tires are busted so they're having to put it on a flat bed."

Louise whistled and pointed to the tire tracks cutting across the swale. Farther down, tracks from other vehicles had chewed up the ground.

"Ambulance," said George.

"Police," added Nancy.

They walked past the wreck. The tow truck driver glanced over at them.

"Bad accident," said George.

The driver nodded.

"What caused it?" Nancy asked.

The driver nodded down the road. "Drinking and driving, my guess. Racing on this road. Happens all the time."

"Thanks," said Nancy. She turned to the others, and they walked across the swale to the canal edge.

"Hood is too smashed up to open," George muttered. "Maybe a flat tire caused the accident."

"Stay outta that grass," cautioned Louise, walking in the car tracks. "Sawgrass cuts. Could be moccasins around here."

"Moccasins?" asked George, staring down at his feet.

Louise snorted. "Water moccasins. You know, snakes."

Nancy took the lead, studying the ground and the tracks. "Doesn't look as if he slowed down at all, just ran off the road and crashed into the canal."

"Going way too fast," added George. "What I'd expect from

someone Quint's age. No brains at all."

Louise peered back at the wrecked truck. "Maybe his brakes failed."

"On the way back, look for oil streaks on the pavement," Nancy said.

"Why?" asked Louise.

George nodded at Nancy. "Maybe someone fixed it so the brake fluid would leak." He bent down to pick off the sandspurs that clung to his pants.

"Bob Connolly was a known alcoholic," said Nancy. "Quint might have been into drugs or alcohol or both. Would make both of them unreliable."

The three walked back to the road. "This road hasn't been maintained at all." Louise kicked at the edge of a pothole.

George peered down the road, shading his eyes with his hand. "To run off the road the way he did, cross the swale still going pretty fast, and end up in the canal, you'd have to be going maybe seventy, eighty, a hundred."

"The truck is certainly totaled." Nancy walked around the wreck. "Even the wheels are bent."

Louise put her hands on her hips and surveyed the scene. "Are you thinking what I'm thinking?"

Nancy nodded. "Bob Connolly was probably becoming a liability. He drank too much and then he talked. When would he give away whatever game they're playing?"

"Quint isn't much better. He's a hothead too." Louise walked back to the car.

George puffed up behind. "Are you saying what I think you're saying?"

"Yep," said Louise. "Quint works for Harv Johnston who is buddies with Bob Connolly."

"An interesting mix," said Nancy.

George started down the road, "I'm checking for oil streaks."

"Should show up on the grey concrete they use for paving roads down here." Louise tapped her cane.

Nancy stopped. "Here, see this?" She pointed to a glistening trail on the pavement.

"See if it's wet," said Louise, brandishing her cane. "You're the only one who can get down low enough."

Nancy stooped to run her finger on the streak. She lifted it up and showed the reddish smudge to the other two. "It's still wet, and it could be oil or brake fluid, I guess."

They returned to the car and Nancy headed back to town. As they neared Riverside Acres, George leaned forward from the back seat. "What now?"

"Let's think about it." Nancy pulled up to the Riverside Acres gate as the attendant opened it and waved her through.

Louise looked at George and shook her head. "I thought about it, now tell me what you think about it," said Louise.

"Carla told us Quint planned to stop working for Johnston and Connolly."

Louise nodded. "Yeah, he'd bought his own truck."

"And Johnston and Connolly were behind the Mandell Consortium." Nancy smiled over at Louise.

"Where was I?" George leaned forward and folded his arms on top of the front seat. "I didn't hear about this."

Nancy parked the car. "And the Mandell Consortium owns that strange house next to Stan Jaworsky's."

Louise flicked her braid. "Bet the Mandell Consortium is involved in something crooked."

Nancy nodded. "Me too. Wheels are starting to turn."

George smacked his lips. "You know," he drawled, "if I were

out to kill somebody, and I knew you were after me, I'd want to stay real close to you."

Nancy glanced at Louise. "So who's been staying real close to us?"

Louise put her hands on her hips and spit out the name. "Susan."

Nancy thought about Susan. "She has been helpful, and she knows Fort Lauderdale. You could say we've been using her."

"Keep an eye on her," said Louise. "That's all I'm saying."

"If I need background on anyone at the condo, she's the person I'd ask." Nancy swung into a parking space. "And she lets us know about what's happening there." She looked at Louise. "So we remain friendly, right?"

Nancy didn't hear Louise's reply. She was surveying the parking lot as an idea struck her. The car door handles might be an excellent place to lift fingerprints. Plastic lemonade glasses at the pool were difficult to manage and to keep straight who had used which glass.

"Join us for lunch, George?" said Louise.

"Don't have to ask me twice. Then, after lunch, take me by the *Bonny Scot*." said George. "You gals had all the fun. How about letting me in on it?"

***

Car Detailing and Mechanic Services

The Management Office keeps a list of reliable car detailers and mechanics who will clean and do minor maintenance and repairs on your car right here. Keep your car shined, clean, and running right—without leaving Riverside. Contact the Management Office for more information.

Riverside Acres Management Office

<h1 style="text-align:center">Chapter 24</h1>

Nancy brought the car to a halt in Jaworsky's parking area. They walked down the drive, past Stan's house, and stopped at the lawn. The sun sparkled on the water but as she stood in the shade of the ficus tree, Nancy felt depressed at the faint whiffs of mildew and decay drifting from the *Bonny Scot*. The boat seemed lifeless and the cabin windows, curtains drawn, like dead eyes.

"The owner's come by and closed it up," said Nancy. "Guess he's keeping the boat here. Cheap dockage, I suppose."

"Let's see if Stan is around." Louise headed for the house.

"From what you've told me, he sounds like a character," said George.

Nancy stopped at the front door, hanging open on one hinge. "I don't like the looks of this." She knocked and called out Stan's name. They waited. Nancy heard no sounds of movement inside the house. She knocked again, louder this time. Again no response.

"Whoever did this might still be in there," whispered Louise.

"Stay outside until I see if he's here. Be ready to dial 9-1-1." Nancy motioned them back. She listened but heard nothing. Whoever had done this was gone, but where was Stan? Had they taken him too? She peered into the darkness of the living room, then stepped forward, around smashed furniture, broken glass, and papers strewn across the floor. "What a mess," she said aloud.

She heard a groan. "Stan?" It came from behind the overturned couch. She rushed around the couch to where Stan lay sprawled in a bloody heap on the floor.

"Louise! George!" She yelled the names.

"We're here," Louise said, casting her eyes around the wreckage. "Shit! Shit! Shit!" She propelled herself with her cane toward Nancy.

"What happened?" George followed, pausing at the doorway to whistle.

"Call an ambulance, Louise."

Stanley groaned and tried to sit up. "No ambulance," he croaked.

"You're hurt. You need to see a doctor." Nancy put an arm around him. "Don't move."

Louise hovered over the phone but took another look at Stan and called 9-1-1.

George pushed the couch away from Stan and turned it upright. "Is he going to be all right?"

Stan wiped hair out of his face and managed to sit up. "I said no ambulance. And no police. I been beat worse 'n this in the Navy."

"Who did this?" Nancy asked him and glanced at Louise.

She nodded. "The dispatcher asked questions." Louise inclined her head toward Stan. "I told them he'd been beaten. Medic unit— that's ambulance to the rest of us—is coming."

She frowned at Stan. "Now don't go into conniptions. A crime's been committed here, so they're sending police too."

Stan's face turned red. "I told ya no ambulance and no police."

Nancy patted him on the back. "What happened?"

"A coupla guys busted their way in. Seemed to be mad at some-body." Stan paused, spit out blood, and held his jaw. "Then they trashed the place and beat me up."

"Ever seen them before?" George asked.

"Maybe. Gotta think on it." He leaned back against Nancy's arm and surveyed the mess around him. "I know what they want, but they ain't getting it."

"But what…?" Nancy looked at Stan.

"Leave me alone. I'm all right, I tell ya."

Nancy heard sirens. "Don't worry. They'll patch you up, and you can come right back." Nancy glanced around at the debris. "If you want. Need to fix that door first. Do you have anywhere else you can stay?" She heard a knock. Louise and George stepped aside as two EMTs walked in.

Nancy waved them over. "He's here, behind the couch." She stepped aside.

One of the EMTs turned to Nancy. "What happened?"

"We came to visit and found this." She gestured around the room.

The other EMT knelt by Stan. "Where do you hurt?"

"I don't hurt no place," said Stan. "I told them I didn't need no ambulance."

"You got us now, pal, and looks like you could use some help." The EMT proceeded to take pulse and respiratory rate. Then he took out a stethoscope.

"I don't need that, I told you," Stan yelled. "Get away from me."

"Okay," said the other EMT. "Tell me your name."

Stan peered up at him. "Stan Jaworsky."

"All right. Where are you?"

"Where am I?" Stan groaned as he sat up, but his eyes sparked. "You ask me where am I? I'm home, that's where. And that's where I'm gonna stay."

The EMT scribbled a few more notes. "Now what day of the week is this? What time?"

"What kind of tomfool crap is this?" But Stan recited the date and day. "And for your information," he turned to Nancy, "let me see your watch."

Nancy showed him her watch.

Stan glared at the EMT triumphantly. "It's 2:10 p.m. Now leave me alone."

The EMT scratched his chin. "Seems to have no broken bones, and he's oriented x3 so he can refuse treatment," he said to Nancy.

Stan grinned at them. "Yeah. I refuse treatment."

"This is a crime scene," the EMT continued. "We're obligated to relay that to the dispatcher who'll alert the police. They should be here shortly."

At that point, a young police officer in uniform showed up at the door. He nodded at the EMTs. "They alerted me when they notified you. What happened here?"

Stan shrank back. "Nothing," he mumbled.

"His name is Stan Jaworsky," said Nancy. "His house was broken into, he was beaten, and his place vandalized."

The officer turned to Stan. "Anyone hold a grudge against you?"

"Leave me alone," Stan said, staring at the floor.

Nancy stepped forward. "He thinks the people next door are trying to buy him out. Maybe the beating was supposed to persuade him to sell." She stepped over the debris to a desk and pulled open the drawers. "They weren't thieves. Nothing inside the desk drawers seems to have been touched."

"Was anything taken?" asked the officer. Nancy peered forward to read his name badge. Dylan Smith.

"They didn't steal nothing," said Stan, not looking at the officer.

George craned his neck forward to see into the bedroom. "Bedroom doesn't look torn up."

Louise peeked into the kitchen. "They only trashed the living room. Nothing touched in here."

The police officer scribbled notes in a pad. "I'll get the crime lab to process this scene. I'd like all of you to wait outside." He nodded at Stan. "He going to be all right?"

"We hope so," said Nancy.

"He's oriented," said the EMT, "and he refuses treatment."

"We'll stay here awhile to make sure he's okay," said George. He turned to Stan. "Got anyone you can call to fix that door?"

* * *

Later, Stan was cleaned up, bandaged, and resting on the couch. Nancy had called Stan's handyman friend who had made a quick repair on the front door and gone off to buy supplies to make the house secure. The 90s Club returned to Peter's apartment.

"Why didn't Stan want the police to investigate?" asked Louise.

"Could be a holdover from wherever he came from," said George. "Police oppression and all that."

"He probably doesn't have a permit for live-aboard boaters," said Louise. "Afraid he'll lose his income."

"Or he's terrified of reprisal from whoever beat him," added Nancy. "The only people who seem to have a motive are the people who want to buy his place and that is. . ."

"The Mandell Corporation," said George and Louise simultaneously.

***

Live-aboard Slips Available

Boat slips available. Live-aboards accepted. Private home. No party boats. Boat length cannot exceed 42 feet; draft must be less than 4 feet. North fork, New River. Easy access to the Intracoastal. Call 954-555-6122.

Bulletin Board notice, River Cross Marina

Nancy checked her watch. "Still early enough to stop by the police station. See if they learned anything new."

"That we can ferret out of them," added Louise.

"Need the GPS?" asked George.

"We can ask about the vandalism at Stan's place," Nancy said. "There might be a tie-in."

Nancy checked in at the reception desk, and they were directed down the hall to the small conference room where they'd first talked to Detective Alleso. They sat down at the table and waited. After half an hour, Louise got up and gazed out into the hall. "Where is that man?"

Nancy glanced at her watch. Louise would be pushing to leave in another five minutes.

As if he'd timed his arrival to the brink of their patience, Detective Alleso came down the hall from the elevator. This time he wore Navy blue slacks with the white shirt and blue tie and carried a manila file folder.

Alleso walked into the room and sat down. "Weren't you here before, inquiring about the young woman missing from the *Bonny Scot?*"

Nancy introduced herself and the others again. "I've called all the hospitals and rehab centers. They don't have any record of receiving her or any unnamed young woman."

He pulled out a pen and opened the folder. "Doesn't look good for her, disappearing like that. If you hear anything from her, let us know at once."

"Of course, but I'm afraid she's in danger," Nancy replied. "She may have been kidnapped, or worse. I'm especially worried since she was on the boat at the Jaworsky place and someone broke into his house and assaulted him."

"So. How did you happen to be there?" Alleso glanced at the papers in the folder. "According to the report, Ms. Owens called for the medic unit."

"I'm Ms.Owens," said Louise, arms folded belligerently.

Nancy sat back. "We met Mr. Jaworsky a few days ago and stopped by to say hello."

Alleso pursed his lips. He riffled through the papers in the folder. "We don't see any connection to the Slocum murder."

"What?" Nancy couldn't restrain herself. "No connection?" Nancy was astounded. She had assumed a connection, but now that she thought about it, Alleso might be right. Slocum's body was found miles from the Jaworsky property. Jessica was still missing. And the neighborhood around Stan's place was not prime real estate. A shabby neighborhood, in fact. Still there was that mysterious house next door. . ."

"Have you checked into that house next door?" Louise asked. "Something's going on there, all right."

Alleso glanced at her. "Of course. We have our eye on that neighborhood. Don't you go getting involved in that."

Louise thrust out her jaw.

Nancy could see scribbled notes on a form in Alleso's folder, but she was too far away to read them upside down. A lot of notes. "Did Ray Slocum have a record?" she asked, hoping for Jessica's sake that if he did, it would be for something like shoplifting or check-kiting rather than murder and assault.

"No record. Applied for a security guard job. That's why his fingerprints are on file." Alleso laid down his pencil and sat back. "Probably a case of wrong time, wrong place. Was this missing young woman into drugs?"

"I have no reason to think so," said Nancy, looking at her hands. "I only met her a few times and saw no signs of it. She was a bright young woman, college graduate, well brought up." She could feel Alleso watching her, and she was glad Louise hadn't aggressively butted in as she usually did. That would probably get them thrown out in a hurry. "I liked Jessica. She simply took a job as crew on the boat for the adventure of it."

Alleso stroked his chin and stared at her for a moment, as if sorting, slicing, and dicing her comments into slots in his brain. He closed the file. "The boat owner hired Slocum to take the boat south. A lot of wealthy boat owners do that. Get someone more experienced than they are or with more time to ferry their boat." He gazed at them impassively. "Happens all the time."

Louise leaned forward, tossed her braid, and pointed a finger at Alleso. "He was in Washington, D.C. No way is that on the route south."

Alleso nodded, a faint smile on his lips. "You're right. It's not. We don't know what he was doing there, but he'd docked at a boatyard in Solomons Island, Maryland, for minor repairs. He probably got a ride into D.C. or maybe rented a car."

"Probably someone told Jessica he was looking for help taking a boat down to Florida," Nancy said, "and Jessica called him and got the job."

Louise looked over at Nancy. "Maybe he kidnapped her."

Nancy shook her head. "Her grandmother said she was excited about the adventure of sailing to Florida. She also sent a post card from Fort Lauderdale saying she was all right. When I was young, I might have done the same thing." She might look white-haired and frail, but in her heart Nancy was still an adventurous eighteen years old. She remembered the sailing races on the river when she was a teenager. What fun they'd had.

She brought herself back to the present. "What did he plan to do in Fort Lauderdale? Surely the trawler owner would expect the boat to be docked in a regular marina. Why would he take it to a shoestring outfit behind a house? It all seems odd."

Alleso closed the folder and sat up. "Now what was this information you had for me?"

Nancy glanced at Louise. "I wanted to make sure you knew that Jessica is still missing, Stan Jaworsky was assaulted, and we're very concerned. We need to know you're doing everything you can to find her."

"That it?" Alleso asked.

"What about the Peter Stamboul case?" asked Nancy. "He reported several attacks, including a gunshot, that could have killed him. And a poisoning, too. Has anything been done about that?"

"We've got someone on it." Alleso said stiffly.

"Haven't done anything," mumbled Louise. "That's what Peter was afraid of."

"People there know he studied "Most Wanted" posters," Nancy said. "We think someone at Riverside is a criminal, and Peter was getting too close."

Alleso narrowed his eyes. "We receive a hundred reports a day from people like Peter—think they've spotted a dangerous criminal or afraid they're being attacked. Most of them don't pan out," he said. "But don't you start thinking you're police detectives and getting yourselves killed."

He walked to the door. "Go to the beach," he said as he stalked out. "Enjoy yourselves. That's what you should be doing. Don't try to mess in our business. You could get hurt."

Alleso had dismissed them. Irritated and annoyed, Nancy followed Louise, who was already thumping her way to the door. George followed. It was going to be up to her, Louise, and George, the 90s Club, to find out what really happened to Jessica and Ray Slocum. Surely the assault on Stan Jaworsky was connected, despite what Alleso thought.

Outside on the street, George turned to Nancy. "At least the family filed a missing person report."

"Yes, they did." Nancy tapped her teeth. "I hope that was a good idea."

"Of course it's a good idea." George tapped his cane. "She's missing and might need help. People should be looking for her."

"But we don't know what's going on with Jessica. The police are posting her picture and looking for her. So are we." Nancy bit her lip. "Maybe so are the killers. And now everyone knows what she looks like."

***

Attention Seniors! Perk Up Your Power!

The Riverside Acres Health Team offers an exciting new empowerment seminar to help you get your needs met when confronting indifferent government and business representatives. This seminar will help you maintain your "cool" while assertively demanding your rights. Register now at the Management Office. Hurry! Space is limited. Cost is $35. Refreshments will be served.

Riverside Acres Management

Chapter 25

Louise yawned and pushed herself off the sofa. "What with Stan's beating and the visit to the police station, I've had a long day. I'm turning in."

Nancy looked up from the book she was reading. "Can you wait a little longer? I have a project I need help on."

Louise looked at her watch. "What project?"

"Change into something dark. I will too."

A slow smile appeared on Louise's face. "Now you're talking."

In a few minutes, Nancy and Louise hovered in the shadows at the edge of the parking area. "I've been trying to figure out how to get fingerprints to add to Peter's files on each resident," Nancy whispered. "So far, I have Carla's, Susan's, Eveline's, Harv's, and a few others. Difficult to manage getting the fingerprints and being sure I match them with the right person without anyone knowing what I'm doing."

"Okay. . ." Louise slowly scanned the parking lot. "So how will this help?"

Nancy handed her a towel. "We'll do this systematically, but," she nodded at the gatehouse guard, "don't let him see you. If he does, just tell him you needed to get something from the car."

Louise shook the towel. "What do I do with this?"

"Wipe down the door handles and the area around them to get rid of any fingerprints left in the last week or so. Then tomorrow night, I'll go around and lift the fingerprints on the handles. I've been identifying who owns what car as we've seen them driving in and out."

Louise nodded. "Might work."

"I can't ask them for their fingerprints," said Nancy, "and I can't get all of them to handle glasses in our apartment. This plan isn't perfect, but unless you can think of a better one. . ."

"Let's get to work," said Louise.

***

Nancy awoke the next morning to the feel of wet slobber on her cheek. She opened her eyes to see Oscar staring at her, his brown eyes an inch away from hers, his warm breath on her face, slobber dripping onto her pajamas. She pushed Oscar away and checked the time. Seven a.m. She groaned.

Louise was sitting up in bed, reading. She looked over at Nancy. "I told them to bother you this morning. Tired of them hitting on me."

Nancy walked the dogs and joined Louise for a quick breakfast. Then Susan knocked on the door. Nancy let her in and Susan joined them at the kitchen table, sitting carefully as if to avoid wrinkling her crisp navy blue slacks. "So what's on for today?" she asked.

Nancy waved the folder of computer printouts. "A visit to Mandell Headquarters in Deerfield Beach."

"I can't imagine what you'll find there," said Susan. "Just a big office building." She sipped her coffee. "Deerfield Beach never seemed like prime real estate to me."

Nancy shrugged. "Still, I might pick up more information there. I'm curious about the Mandell Corporation."

Louise pushed her chair away from the table. "I'll go get George."

As Susan and the 90s Club walked toward the car, Susan patted

Nancy's hand and said, "I can get us there faster if I just drive." Nancy acquiesced, but she could see the spark in Louise's eyes and just managed to derail Susan from tripping on Louise's artfully placed cane. Nancy glanced at George, who tottered along behind, apparently oblivious to the machinations in front of him.

Susan was a fast and competent driver, and she knew the area. "This is the street," she said, driving past warehouse-style, one-story buildings with storefronts and rear loading docks on a side street. The buildings were cheap and barren; all concrete surrounded by asphalt, no landscaping. Nancy read off the building numbers until they found the Mandell office. Susan parked the car two buildings away down the street.

"So now what?" she asked.

"I'm going in," Nancy said. "All of you wait out here. Back me up if anything happens."

"Wait a minute," Louise said in her raspy voice. "I'll go with you."

Nancy shook her head. "I don't want them to see all of us together. We may need to come back on another pretext. Then you can go in."

"Shit." Louise sat back. "Long as you have a good reason," she muttered.

"Call us if there's any fun," said George from the back seat where he'd been dozing.

Nancy walked to the Mandell office door. It was locked but had a window in it. Nancy peered through it as she rapped. A middle-aged woman looked up from her computer, removed her bifocals and let them drop to her chest, suspended by a cord around her neck. She hesitated, then she stood and walked to the door. Speaking through the glass, she said, "We're not open to the public."

Nancy fanned herself. "I'm so sorry. I've been trying to find where my son works in this complex, but the heat. . . ." She let herself sag. Now was the time to appeal to this woman's motherly instincts. Appearing old, weak, and fragile came in handy sometimes.

"Oh no. You poor dear. Come in and sit down." The woman opened the door and helped Nancy to a chair by her desk. "You just sit there a minute. I'll get you some water." The woman disappeared behind a door.

Nancy scanned the papers on the desk. Cryptic abbreviations and numbers. A list of names. She pulled a small camera with a special lens out of her purse and took a quick photo of the paper on top.

When the woman returned bearing a plastic cup of water, Nancy was sitting back fanning herself.

"Here now, dear. You just drink this and rest a minute."

The phone rang. The woman answered it with "3912." She listened a moment, then said "He's not in today. I'll take a message." Apparently there was no message. She hung up the phone. Nancy sat up and glanced at the numbers labeled on the phone next to the lines of buttons. A slew of different numbers.

"Where does your son work, dear?" the woman asked. She pulled a tattered book of yellow pages out of a shelf behind her.

Nancy kept her voice weak. She remembered the large set of offices they'd driven past on the next street. That would be a likely place for this fictitious son to work. "Bryan's Auto Parts Distributors."

"That's all right, then. They're on the next block."

"Thank goodness," Nancy said. "I'm almost there. If I could just rest a minute more."

"Of course, dear." The woman twirled her bifocals.

Nancy looked around her. "What do you do here?" she asked as if she were only being polite.

"It's a consortium, dear." The woman glanced at her computer. "We have different businesses. All very complicated." She stood. "I'm afraid I'm going to have to ask you to leave now."

"Of course." Nancy replied in a quavering voice. "I'm sorry I took up your time."

The woman shrugged. "Wouldn't do for the boss to find a stranger in here."

"I understand." Nancy walked to the door, emphasizing a stoop. "Thank you for your help."

"Don't mention it." The woman unlocked the door and let Nancy out.

Nancy could feel the woman watching her hobble down the street. She walked past Susan and Louise in the car and continued on around the corner. Then she signaled to Susan and waited while Susan drove around the block to pick Nancy up on the side street.

"So what happened?" Louise asked, leaning forward from the back seat.

"Yeah," George piped up. "What happened?"

Susan kept her foot on the brake for Nancy's report.

"Only one person there. Woman at a computer. I knocked and she let me in."

"Just like that?" Susan raised an eyebrow.

"She thought I was developing heatstroke." Nancy winked at Susan. "She went in back to get me some water."

"What'd you find out?" Louise asked.

"I only glimpsed the papers on her desk. Have no idea what they were about. A lot of numbers and abbreviations." Nancy pulled out her camera. "I got a photo of the top one. Then she came back and the phone rang."

Susan tapped the steering wheel. "And then what?"

"The woman answered it with four numbers." Nancy buckled her seat belt. "Not an extension. Last four digits of a phone number and only one of many numbers indicated on the phone console."

Susan and Louise both stared at her with puzzled expressions. "So what?" said Louise. "That doesn't tell you anything."

"Probably not." Nancy frowned. "Why didn't she answer it, 'Mandell Consortium'?"

Louise nodded. "Yeah. Why indeed. Unless they were hiding something." She flicked her braid.

"I don't get it," said Susan. "So what if they answered with a number? A lot of businesses might do that."

"But why?" Nancy folded her arms. "Most businesses use their name whenever possible. Helps get the word out. People remember it. And when they call, they want to know who they're talking to. Did they get the right number?"

Susan shrugged. "Pretty slim, if you ask me. Maybe the consortium involves several different businesses, but they all just use the one phone number but have another number as well."

"You're probably right," Nancy said. "We have to find out more about the Mandell Consortium."

Later that day after Susan had gone home, the 90s Club gathered around the kitchen table and studied the printout Nancy had made of the numbers and abbreviations on the paper in the consortium office.

"They're obviously keyed in to a master list or lists," said Nancy. "They could be renters and properties, or drivers and cars, or anything."

"Looks shifty to me," said George. "The whole operation."

"I agree with you." Nancy sat back.

"We could give this info to the police," said George.

"Let's wait and see what happens," Nancy said. "We're suspicious of the Mandell Consortium, but we don't actually know yet of a tie-in with Ray's murder or the attacks on Peter."

"Good day's work, though," said Louise.

Nancy glanced at her watch. "Now I've got another job to do. She retrieved her box of black powder, lifting tape, soft cosmetic brush, and a stack of blank index cards. "Time to see what I can get off car door handles."

***

Say No to Heat Stroke!

South Florida is known for its bright sunshine and hot days, even in midwinter. Dehydration and heat stroke can sneak up on you, so be sure to drink plenty of water all day long, especially if you've been playing tennis, walking, swimming or taking part in any other sport.

Riverside Acres Health Team

Chapter 27

Saturday was another warm, sunny winter day in Fort Lauderdale. The dew sparkled on the grass when Nancy took Oscar and Rupert for their morning walk. She still marveled at the fresh tropical breeze outside, gently rustling the palm leaves. She could smell the ocean. *I'm not going to want to go home.* Not till April, anyway, she amended.

Nancy pulled the dogs into the apartment and unleashed them. They ran into the kitchen to check their food bowls.

Louise threw them a couple of bacon scraps. "Let's bring Carla over."

"I brought back donuts. Maybe she'd like to have tea with us." Nancy set the donuts on the kitchen table while Louise went next door.

She returned with Carla, who pet the dogs as she sat at the table. "How's Quint," asked Nancy.

"A lot of aches and pains," Carla grimaced, "but otherwise getting better."

"I guess he's really upset about his truck," said Louise, "and Mr. Connolly, of course."

"I suppose so," Carla took a donut. "Quint isn't taking any calls and not saying much about it to anyone, even that nice Mr. Johnston—and he's Quint's boss." She glanced up at Nancy. "He really hated losing his own truck, but he thinks Mr. Johnston will buy him a new one." She sighed. "He could have been killed!"

"Thank goodness he was spared," said Nancy, not daring to look at Louise.

Carla nodded. "He's a good driver. I can't imagine what happened and where he was going. Thank goodness Quint doesn't drink like Mr. Connolly, bless his soul. That Connolly, you just couldn't trust him." Carla sighed and mumbled to herself. She seemed to be pondering thoughts far away.

"Cup of tea?" Louise asked, breaking into Carla's reverie by setting down a mug in front of her and pouring tea into it

Carla raised her head, startled, like a surprised deer. "What?" Her eyes darted from Louise to Nancy. "Thank you. Don't mind me, I was just wool-gathering, you know. Thinking about Quint 'n all." She smiled. "A mother always worries, doesn't she?" Carla tried to chuckle.

"We happened to see Quint's truck," said Nancy, "taking George sightseeing. All of us like to wander the back roads. His truck was a wreck, all right. He was very lucky."

"Was it still there? By the side of the road?" Carla frowned. "Should have been towed away before you got there." She stopped talking and listened.

Nancy heard pots banging in the next apartment. "Sounds like Quint's up and about," she said.

Carla nodded. "He'll be wanting his breakfast, I suppose. Thank you for the tea." She hesitated, "I really hate to leave." She walked to the door. "See you later."

Nancy and Louise looked at each other.

"She seems okay," muttered Louise to herself, then she glanced at Nancy. "I thought Quint was out of commission. Recovered fast."

"It's odd that Johnston would give Quint a new truck."

"Maybe he needs a vehicle in his job." Louise picked up her cane and Carla's mug and hobbled toward the kitchen. "So what's going on today, Nancy?"

Nancy opened the newspaper and pointed to a long box on the front page. "Riverwalk Festival. All weekend."

"Sounds like fun."

"We'll go down there later this morning." Nancy read through the schedule of events.

"We don't have to take Susan along, do we?" Louise said, leaning on her cane as she hobbled out of the kitchen. She raised an eyebrow at Nancy.

"She comes in handy." Nancy shrugged. "But I can get to the city docks on my own. Susan took me down there when we were looking for the *Bonny Scot*."

"I'll give George a call." Louise picked up the phone.

Later that morning, Nancy, Louise, and George drove downtown, parked the car, and walked toward the river. The soft breezes and fragrance of mown grass made the walk relaxing and pleasant. Nancy smiled at Louise whose eyes followed a luxury powerboat passing by on the river. Tied up alongside the Riverwalk in front of them floated a sleek blue sailboat. A woman sat on deck hand-sewing a piece of canvas.

Vendors were still setting up their booths along the land side of the walk, and platforms were in place for the bands, although none had started playing yet. Nancy watched the passers-by, hoping to spot Jessica, knowing the chance to actually find her was nearly impossible. Louise and George stopped at each booth to chat, but most of the booth staff were busy setting up.

"I think Jessica is hiding from someone. She has probably disguised herself, but this festival should draw hordes of people, and there's a slim chance she'll be among them." Nancy could smell popcorn. "She has to get money from somewhere, so I suppose she might find a job at one of these booths."

"Unless she's been kidnapped." Louise flicked her braid. "Or murdered and dumped somewhere."

"True." Nancy watched a vendor lay hot dogs on a grill.

"She may not even know she's supposed to be missing," added Louise, "and is lying on the beach or traveling somewhere else."

They stopped to gawk at a young man whose every visible body part and the confederate uniform he wore were painted or dyed a steel color as if cast in metal. He stood motionless on a similarly painted garbage can as if he were a statue. A small can for donations was placed in front of him. Nancy found some quarters in her purse and tossed them into the can.

Louise couldn't take her eyes off him. "He's very good, isn't he," she whispered to Nancy. "I'd never believe he was a real human being under all that. How can he stay so still?"

Just then, the statue saluted a small boy who ran behind his mother and peeked out at the living statue as they passed.

Nancy grinned at Louise. They strolled down the walk. George stepped aside to let a family pass them. "Getting crowded," he said.

One by one, the vendors finished setting up. Nancy smelled the barbequed pork.

"I'm getting hungry," Louise said, tugging Nancy over to a food booth.

Nancy held back. "Too early for me," she said. She spied a young woman painting her arms and face white. Her hair was already covered in a stiff, white material that appeared to be plaster. A flowing, white toga covered her body from her neck to her toes. As she dusted white powder over the paint, she turned and her eyes met Nancy's. A spark of recognition passed between them. Then the young woman stepped onto an overturned white garbage pail.

She assumed the pose of a Grecian goddess, sculpted in marble and resting on a pedestal. The effect stunned Nancy.

As Louise and George stopped to peruse the pamphlets at a community service booth, Nancy approached the statue and saw its faint nod. The nod confirmed her suspicion. She pulled a twenty dollar bill out of her purse and dug out one of the business cards she'd printed with her name, local address, and cell phone number. She wrote a brief message on the back and slipped the card into the donation can along with the bill.

The statue bent down to Nancy in a theatrical pose and whispered, "I've seen you at Whisperwood when I visited Grandma. I need your help."

Nancy felt profound relief. She wanted to embrace the young figure and take her home immediately, but that would draw too much attention. Better to wait for Jessica to come to her. She was alive and well and had even devised a clever way to earn a living.

Nancy grinned at the statue. "I know, my dear." She nodded slightly toward the can. "Come see me."

The statue returned to its pose. Nancy walked on with Louise tugging George, who dragged back, sniffing the air and scrutinizing wistfully the food booths as they passed them.

"How about a hot dog?" he asked, pausing to watch hot dogs and hamburger patties sizzle on a grill.

Louise sniffed the delicious aromas. "Sure. I could use one."

Nancy stopped. She felt almost giddy. "I'll sit here while you get them." She needed time to tame her own feelings before she faced Louise and George with the news.

Louise hobbled off with George, while Nancy sat on a bench and observed the people passing by the white statue. The surge of relief she'd felt had turned to concern. Nancy wanted to wall Jessica off, protect her. Was anyone unduly interested in Jessica? Didn't seem to be—only the usual gawkers. A few threw coins into the can as they passed. How much would a person make in a day dressed as a statue? Was she living on that? Nancy hoped Jessica had more money, but if not, why hadn't she gone home? What was she looking for here? Was she really in danger? Why hadn't she told anyone where she was?

Louise and George returned and sat next to Nancy on the bench. Louise dabbed at a dribble of mustard on her shirt, smearing it into a pale yellow blot. She shook her head. "Always have to make a mess, don't I?"

Nancy laughed. "We can sit here till you finish eating. I'm watching for anything unusual." She nodded at the straggling passersby. Families, teenagers, old, young, people of all sorts, all dressed casually in shorts, T-shirts, even bathing suits. None of them seemed menacing, although a few were odd, this being Fort Lauderdale.

George wiped the excess mustard off his chin. "So what do we do now?"

"Let's just sit here and watch for awhile." Nancy gazed down the sidewalk behind them and sat up. The two men who had eaten lunch with Connolly and Johnston were sauntering her way, eyeing all the young women they passed. Glazer and Carrera. Both men carried backpacks. At the statue, they stopped and nudged each other, grinning, but Jessica's face was turned away from them. Deliberately? Nancy watched more carefully. The men walked on. Jessica turned her head, saw Nancy, and inclined her head towards the two men. Nancy nodded and leaned toward Louise.

"I'm going to follow those two guys and see who they talk to." Nancy rose.

"Wait for us. I'm finished with the dog." Louise picked up her cane and saw Nancy glance at it. "It's okay. I don't need it right now. I can keep up."

"Yeah," grumbled George. "Just because we use canes doesn't mean we're handicapped."

Nancy laughed. "Those two guys are ogling all the women, so they aren't going too fast anyway."

Together they strolled down the Riverwalk, following Glazer and Carrera who seemed to have nothing on their minds but casual entertainment. Sergio took a call on his cell phone, then said a few words to Glazer. At one point, Glazer boarded a boat alongside the Riverwalk at the owner's invitation. They went below for a few moments, then Glazer returned, still holding the backpack.

Nancy pulled out her cell phone and took a photograph. The two men continued their way down the river, boarding a boat here and there. Nancy photographed their activities and noted the names of the boats while Louise covered Nancy's activity in case one of the men spotted them. Both men had met Nancy. They probably wouldn't remember her. Probably to them one old lady looked like another.

The walk came to an end at a street where a black car with tinted windows waited. Nancy walked toward it, bent over and emphasizing a limp. As she approached, the two men got into the car, but Mike Glazer noticed her and pointed her out to his friend Sergio. They had recognized her. Then the car sped away before she could memorize the license tag number.

***

Used Medical Equipment for Sale

From respiratory equipment to scooters and canes, you'll find what you need for the price you want to pay at Riverside Acres' annual sale of pre-owned medical equipment. All items are in good condition and were discarded when their former owners no longer needed them. The sale will take place at the pool area on Monday morning, 8 a.m. till noon.

Riverside Acres Medical Team

Chapter 28

Driving home from the festival, Nancy interrupted Louise's paeans to the festival food. "I've found Jessica."

Louise stopped talking abruptly. "You what?"

Nancy smiled at her. "She was the white Grecian statue."

Louise's mouth dropped open.

"I dropped my card into her donation can along with twenty dollars. I'm hoping she'll stop by tonight. We'll have to put her up here."

"You recognized her? Through all that gunk?"

Nancy kept her eyes on the road. "She recognized me. Said she met me at Whisperwood when she visited her grandma. She motioned to me to pay attention to those two men we followed. I'd met them last week or so when I watched them have lunch with Connolly and Johnston."

Louise whistled. "How do they fit in? Do they work with Johnston's driver service?"

"We'll have to wait until we see Jessica."

"So we hang out tonight and hope she shows up." George sat back and gazed out the window.

Nancy drove into Riverside Acres. The gate attendant stepped out of the guardhouse and motioned for Nancy to wind down the window. She did.

"Two cops came by, asking about you, ma'am. Thought you

should know." He raised an eyebrow and looked her over as if she might be harboring fugitives.

Police asking about her? Maybe Alleso had come to his senses. Nancy smiled at him. "Thank you. You're doing good work, and we really appreciate it. I have no idea what that's about, but I'll check on it."

"I'm sure you didn't break any laws, ma'am."

"Of course not. No parking tickets either."

The attendant smiled as he made a note on his clipboard. "Have a nice day." He waved them on.

George leaned forward. "Got the cops on your trail, Nancy?"

Louise laughed. "Too bad we missed them."

"It's got to be Alleso. Maybe he's found out something," said Nancy. "I'll give him a call."

Nancy parked next to Eveline, who was struggling with two large bags of groceries. Dashaune had run on ahead and was poking a stick in the roots of a royal palm.

"Wait. We'll help," Nancy said as Louise tottered toward the management office. She returned, pulling a wagon. Nancy helped Eveline settle the bags into it.

"Thank you." Eveline's face crumpled, and she started to cry.

Nancy folded her into her arms and held her. "There, there…"

"I've got the bags. Don't you worry," Louise stood by as Eveline tried to gain control of herself.

"Just got to me," she sniffed. "It's too hard, you know. There he goes, runnin' into the street again, and after I told him to stay with me."

"Tough being a single parent," said Nancy.

"I just can't watch him twenty-four hours a day, seven days a week. He's too much." Eveline gulped and tears flooded her eyes. "I am so depressed. It's not enough my daughter dying and all. . . ."

Nancy hugged her. "You don't have any family here that could give you a break?"

Eveline shook her head and stepped away. "Nobody is around during the day. Everyone works or goes to school. Nobody has the time." She took out a tissue and dabbed at her eyes. "I need help, I gotta pay for it. Day care costs a bundle, you know."

"Come on, Granma." Dashaune had run to the elevator and was stabbing at the buttons with his pudgy fingers.

She managed a weak smile. "Coming," she called to him and turned to Nancy. "Thank you. Don't know what came over me." She walked to the elevator with Louise pulling the wagon and Nancy and George trailing behind. They waited for the elevator to descend at its glacial pace.

At Peter's apartment, Nancy and Louise stopped and let Eveline take the wagon. She and Dashaune pulled it down the hall to their place.

Louise opened the door and walked in ahead of Nancy. "She's at the end of her tether and on the way to a breakdown."

Nancy nodded.

George followed them. "Seems to me we ought to sit down and discuss what we know," George said as he tapped along with his cane. "A lot of loose threads is what I'm thinking."

"You're right, George." Nancy said. "We need to sort them out."

"Come over to my apartment. Have some cake. I baked it myself, I'll have you know."

"He's a good cook," said Louise. A fond light shone in her eyes.

"Maybe so," George said, "even if I can't help much with all those threads." He added deadpan, "I don't sew."

Nancy laughed, envying Louise and George's easy intimacy, but the usual wistfulness was displaced by the relief she felt at finding

Jessica alive and well. So far, Peter's problem and the search for Jessica were resolving themselves. Nancy felt a tentative bubble of joy. Maybe she was still useful on the planet after all—even if she was ninety years old.

They walked down to George's unit. "Make yourselves to home," he said, hobbling into the kitchen. They followed him and took seats around the table.

"Here's what we've got," said Nancy. "Peter called me because someone here threatened him, and he asked me for help. Then Jessica's grandmother asked me to find Jessica who came down here on a boat with Ray Slocum. When we got here, Peter had been poisoned, then we learned that Ray had been murdered, and Jessica had disappeared."

"And we think," Louise added, "that someone here poisoned Peter because Peter might recognize him or her from the 'Most Wanted' posters on the wall."

"Okay," said George, hands on hips. "And I think that whoever poisoned Peter is keeping an eye on us here. And the only one who's doing that is. . . ?"

Louise grinned. "Susan. She clings to us like a slick on a sidewalk."

"Don't forget that we've had two other accidents here," said Nancy. "Abby Summers drowned in the river, and Bob Connolly was killed when Quint's car crashed. Only luck that Quint survived."

"Hard to see how Susan could do all that," said George as he rummaged in a drawer.

"Maybe Quint manufactured the crash," added Louise.

Nancy nodded. "Also, I keep running into Harv Johnston, and he's somehow connected to the two men pointed out by Jessica. Susan has drawn attention to herself, but I would think the real culprit would be more subtle."

"Susan might think she's being subtle," snorted Louise.

"Maybe we ought to tell the police what more we know," said George.

"Let's talk to Jessica first," said Nancy, considering all these facts. What was the connection between Johnston, Glazer, and Carrera? Jessica knew them, and Johnston lived at the pink house on the river. Johnston also ran the driver service and hung around Riverside Acres. Were Glazer and Carrera making deliveries at the River Fest? Deliveries of what? Drugs?

George placed a towering chocolate cake in front of them. "My prize recipe." He waited for their admiration, then sliced it. "Anyways, I think the real culprit feels pretty safe. The cops don't have a clue about Ray or Jessica or even Peter. Nobody's roaming this place looking for crooks. And the detective stories I read all say that crooks have huge egos and think they can outsmart everyone."

"I think you're at least partly right, George," said Nancy.

"We're just going to have to watch everybody here," said Louise.

"And don't trust 'em an inch," added George. "What about Peter? Surely he's come up with something by now."

"I talked to him yesterday," said Nancy. "He's safe there, and he's doing the grunt work of putting together information on the questionable residents here. Then we'll hand the files to the FBI and let them use their fingerprint database and other tools to zero in on the culprit." She reached for the phone. "I'll call him, though. Find out how he's doing."

Peter picked up on the first ring. "I'm working on it, Nancy," he said.

Sounded like he'd been waiting by the phone, hoping someone would call. Probably bored, all alone in that hotel room.

"I googled everyone in the directory. Came up with some surprising information. Did you know a famous actor lives there? Anyway, I've manipulated those photos you and Louise took every way I can, and only one begins to look like someone in the flyers."

"Which one?" asked Nancy. "We'll download a new flyer of him."

"Stealing the flyers I put on the wall there and replacing them with others shows I'm on the right track."

"Whoever did it had to be desperate."

"Don't talk about that to anyone." Peter sounded strong and confident and more like the Peter Nancy remembered.

"So tell me about what you've found."

"Hard to believe since he's got his own business and seems so well set-up."

"Who?" Nancy knew who he meant, but Peter was milking every bit of drama he could get out of this.

"He's alone. Unattached. But if he's who I think he is, he's actually one-half of a couple. Trouble is, where's the woman?"

"You think you've identified one half of the brother-sister pair?"

"Right. Thinks he's a tough guy. You know who I mean."

"You mean. . . ?"

"Yep. Harv Johnston."

***

Later, Nancy and Louise sat playing with the dogs and discussing Eveline's problem. Carla had come over to chat.

"Eveline's not getting any break," Carla said, "but I'd love to be in her shoes, having a young child around the house." She sighed and frowned at Nancy and Louise. "I need something more to do."

"I keep busy. So does Louise," said Nancy. "Really helps with depression."

"Eveline's real busy," Carla muttered. "And she's real depressed." She frowned and seemed to withdraw into herself. Nancy didn't say anything, feeling she'd already been too pushy with the "keeping busy" comment.

Carla stood. "Excuse me." She walked to the door, opened it, and peered out. She looked back at Nancy and winked. "See you later." She darted out the door.

"Well!" said Louise.

"Good for her," said Nancy, guessing what Carla meant to do.

"She's really come out of herself. Our fatal charm, I suppose." Louise stepped toward the kitchen. "So what now?"

"I'm waiting for Jessica to contact us." Nancy picked up the dog leashes. "She should have been here by now. I hope no one spotted her."

***

Volunteers Needed

Time on your hands? Whether you're here for a month or a lifetime, you'll feel good about the time you spend helping others. Drop by the Management Office for a list of volunteer opportunities and contacts. You can make a difference!

Riverside Acres Resident Coordinator

Chapter 29

How long would Jessica wait before she left the Riverwalk Fest and made her way over to Peter's apartment? Twenty dollars would be enough for the cab ride. Would Jessica wait until evening?

Louise hurried out for a swim while Nancy downloaded another copy of the FBI's "Most Wanted" flyer of the couple and studied it. The booking photo showed a thin, dark-haired man with average features. Harv Johnston was heavier and almost bald, but it was possible. If Johnston was the person wanted by the FBI, then where was his sister?

Was his sister the one who had poisoned Peter? Killed Abby? Could Susan be the sister? Carla? Anyone else here at Riverside around that age?

She squinted at the jaw line and the shape of the nose. The ears were covered by the woman's long, straight, blonde hair. Nancy tried to picture Susan or even Carla as the sister but gave up. Both of them bore a slight resemblance. Of course, just because the brother might be here didn't mean the sister was. The sister could be one of Susan's bridge buddies, or a friend of Carla's.

Louise returned, wrapped in a towel.

"Nice swim?" Nancy asked absently.

"Fine. Didn't want to stay too long," she rasped. "Not going to let you have all the fun."

Susan arrived with a plate of cookies. "So what are we going to do next?" she asked as she passed the cookies around.

Nancy thanked her. "Don't know what to do next. Let me think about it." Nancy glanced at Susan's trim figure and well-groomed blonde hair, not at all like the slightly overweight little sister in the "Most Wanted" flyer. Could a person change that much? She could. Nancy remembered the ways she had adjusted her appearance in cases long past.

"Let me know if you need me." Susan walked to the door, sounding miffed.

Nancy had forgotten Susan was there and looked up, startled. "Sorry I'm not feeling up for much right now."

She needed to talk to Jessica before she let anyone else but Louise and George know about her. Susan could be a plant, but no one who looked at Nancy and Louise and figured out their ages would consider them a threat despite their prowess at Whisperwood last summer. Nancy remembered the friend who'd lost her life then. Nancy and Louise had almost lost theirs, and Louise still had problems with her wrist, but no one outside of Whisperwood would know anything about that.

Nancy studied the flyers. A couple, brother and sister, not man and wife. Peter thought the man resembled Harv Johnston, and Eveline said that Susan buddied around with Johnston. Again, it was possible that Susan and the woman in the flyer were the same, but, like Harv, only if you used a lot of imagination.

Who else here might be his sister. Carla? But she had a son, and the flyers hadn't mentioned that. Nancy couldn't think of anyone else at Riverside who might be around the sister's age.

Louise showered and changed back to her slacks and T-shirt. She brought a large glass of iced water into the living room and sat down with Oscar and Rupert panting side by side on the couch. She raised an eyebrow at Nancy who shook her head.

"Jessica hasn't shown up yet." Nancy called the dogs and picked up their leashes. "Now I've got to take these guys out again."

Louise nodded. "I'll hold the fort."

"I hope she isn't in trouble," Nancy said to herself as she led the dogs out.

Later, when Nancy was rummaging in the kitchen looking for something to make for supper, she heard a soft knock. The dogs scrambled toward the door with excited barks. Nancy peeked out the kitchen window which opened onto the outside walkway. "At last," she said to Louise.

Nancy opened the door and pulled Jessica and her bags into the living room as she glanced both ways down the hall. *No one watching. Good.*

Jessica fell into Nancy's arms and hugged her. "I've been so scared." Her voice wobbled. "I knew I had to hide, and I wanted to get those guys who shot Ray. I just wasn't sure how." Jessica sniffed and ran a hand across her eyes. "Ray was a good man. He loved his little boy and now his little boy doesn't have a dad anymore." She stepped back. "I'm sorry. I know I'm babbling."

"You poor dear," Louise said.

Oscar and Rupert sniffed Jessica's sandals. Her shorts and T-shirt were torn and stained. She leaned down and petted Oscar. Rupert leapt up and licked her face.

"You've done a good job at disguise," said Nancy. Jessica had dyed her hair dark brown and cut it short. "Changing your hair and then working as a statue. I would have thought you'd pick up a job as a waitress or some such."

"I didn't want to use my name," Jessica said, rubbing off a smear of white paint on her arm, "and I'd have to show them my social security card so I couldn't just bop in there with a fake name. Then I met a girl doing the statue bit. She was taking a week off so she loaned me her stuff. I just took her place. Worked well because no one would recognize me in that get-up, and I could see a lot of people in a short time."

Louise's eyes swept over Jessica from head to toe. "But how did you get all that white stuff off?"

Jessica shook her head, wiped the slobber from her hands onto her shorts, and smiled. "Nice dogs."

Nancy gestured to the sofa and Jessica sank down on it. "I'm so glad I saw you today," Nancy said. "What a relief!"

"Totally awesome." Jessica turned wide eyes toward Nancy. "I've been terrified."

"Where were you?" Nancy sat in a chair facing her. "Your grandmother has been worried sick about you. Your family, too."

"And us," rasped Louise. She walked over to the phone.

Oscar and Rupert yapped.

Jessica laughed. "You're kidding. No one knows what's happened. They all think I'm on a trawler with Ray. Why would they worry?" She tossed her head. "And anyway, I sent them a post card telling them I was all right, and I called Grandma."

Nancy shook her head. Had she ever been that young? That thoughtless? Probably. She remembered all the misadventures and narrow escapes she'd experienced when she was young. No. All her life, including last summer, which was as narrow an escape as she ever wanted to have. She looked at Jessica.

"You certainly had your grandmother worried. She heard I was coming to Florida and asked me to look for you. Of course, none of us knew how big a task that would be."

"Poor Grandma. I totally had no idea." Jessica stared down at her feet, a frown on her face.

Nancy glanced at Louise. "Then we read the item in the paper."

"What item?" Jessica said.

"About Ray Slocum being found in the Everglades shot to death," Louise put in. "What happened?"

Jessica stared down at her hands, then tears rolled down her cheeks. She shook her head and hugged herself. "Sorry," she said.

Nancy moved over to sit next to her and patted her back. "It's all right," she said. She could feel Jessica trembling. After awhile, the tears subsided. Nancy handed Jessica a tissue, and she blew her nose.

"I'm so sorry," Jessica managed. "I'm like really tired. It was such a shock. One minute we were enjoying the awesome afternoon on top of the boat. The next minute Ray was dead, and I was scrambling to get out of there."

"On the boat?" Nancy asked. "The newspaper said he was found in the Everglades."

"They must have taken him there," Jessica sniffed, wiping the tissue across her eyes. "Muddy the waters."

Louise circled her hand at Jessica. "So what'd you do?"

"I ducked down, crawled below to grab my purse, and then I hid in the shrubbery." She gulped. "I heard them run over to our boat, and when they passed me, I ran the other way. Left all my stuff." She gestured toward the two plastic bags she'd brought with her. "Except my purse. Got that stuff at Goodwill. I don't think they paid much attention to me once they spotted Ray watching them. But they knew someone else was on that boat."

Louise picked up the phone. "I'm gonna call George." She glanced at Jessica. "Why didn't you go to the police?"

"I was afraid to." Jessica shuddered. "One of the men I saw wore a police uniform."

"What?" Nancy sat up startled. "A police officer?"

"Yes. No way would I go to the police after seeing that." Jessica drew her brows together. "They might think I shot Ray. Or trump it up so it appeared that way. So far they don't know what I look like."

Louise raised an eyebrow at Nancy and said, "Uh oh."

"I'm afraid you're wrong." Nancy took one of Jessica's hands and patted it. Nancy had been afraid of this.

"Why would I be wrong?"

Nancy sighed. "Your family sent your photo to the police, and we gave them one, too. They're looking all over for you."

Jessica groaned. "Of course." She covered her face with her hands. "I'm a missing person." She laughed grimly. "A person of interest."

"Why didn't you go home?" Louise watched Jessica with folded arms.

Jessica sat up and stuck out her jaw. "Because I liked Ray, and I'm angry. Do you know he called his little boy every single day? Every single day. He was kind and generous. He deserved a long life." She looked at Nancy and lifted her chin. "I totally want to get those killers. That's what I've been doing here. Searching for them."

"We know most of them," Nancy interrupted, "like those men in the park today."

"You did notice them?" Jessica leaned toward Nancy. "I tried to signal you."

Louise frowned as she took a chair. "I didn't see any signal from you or anybody."

"I saw your signal, and I recognized them," Nancy said.

"You did?" Jessica's eyes opened wide. "Awesome."

"I was told their names are Sergio Carrera and Mike Glazer." Nancy sat back as Jessica stared at her open-mouthed.

Jessica clasped her hands together. "Those two men were there that night. At the house across the inlet. The ones who killed Ray." She looked as if she were still holding back tears.

"How many people were there, anyway?" asked Louise.

"Sounds like a party."

"I don't know. Those two men, the policeman and one or two others. One of them seemed to be in charge, but really, I only got a glimpse and then the one who seemed in charge, like, stared straight at us and, like, the next minute Ray was dead, and I was getting out of there fast." Jessica hugged Oscar, fidgeting in her lap, and held him tight.

Louise hobbled over to the door and took another peek out to the hallway. She turned to Nancy. "I'll bet Quint was one of them. He worked for Harv Johnston, who lived there. Sure wish Carla would come back."

"I don't know who the policeman is," said Jessica. "When I find out, I'm going to the top to expose all of them."

Nancy smiled. Did Jessica really think it would be that easy? Nancy remembered how naive she'd been when she started out as a private detective. She might have done the same thing as Jessica, given similar circumstances. Nancy stood up. "All right, but first you need a good dinner and a night's sleep."

She picked up her purse and walked to the door. "I'm going to run out to pick up a few items for you. Meanwhile, take a shower and relax. We'll fix up some dinner, and you can bed down on the sofa tonight."

"Cool," Jessica breathed. "I've been staying in a fleabag el cheapo motel down on Broward Boulevard. Scary place. Totally. And I'm running out of money."

Nancy smiled. "I'll bet. See you later."

Louise followed Nancy to the door. "I'll keep a watch out. Nobody comes in while she's here." She stood at the door, looking down the outside corridor. "Except George." She waved at Nancy. "Coast is clear."

George joined them later for dinner, but didn't stay long afterwards. Nancy gave Jessica the bag of clothes she'd bought for her. "Just some shorts, T-shirts, and jeans, and," Nancy peered into the bag and pulled out a bathing suit, " you'll need this, too."

Jessica reached for it. "Cool. Thanks, Nancy. I appreciate all this, but I'm not going to spend time around the pool. I still need to find those murderers."

"Don't worry." Nancy turned on the computer. "Take a look at these photos we've taken of the people around here. Recognize anyone?" said Nancy, still intent on Jessica's story. Could you tell what those men were doing over there?"

Jessica shook her head. "They were all standing out on the deck behind the house. A guy in a bathing suit and T-shirt stood in one of the fast boats tied up there. He was pulling bags out of the boat and putting them on the dock. Boats were always going in and out of that dock. A real nuisance."

"Interesting." Nancy glanced at Louise. "Do you suppose all those bags on the deck came out of the boats?"

"In which case…" put in Louise.

"Drugs, I figured," said Jessica. "They were smuggling."

***

Unexpected Guests?

The Management Office rents or sells cots, bedding, towels, pillows, and other supplies you might need if unexpected visitors show up at your door. The office is open from nine to six, Monday through Saturday.

Riverside Acres Management Office

After dinner, Nancy heard a soft tap on the door. She opened it to find Carla standing outside beaming at her. "May I come in?" she asked.

Nancy stood aside and followed Carla into the living room where Louise read and Jessica sat on the floor, playing with the dogs.

Louise looked up. "Glad to see you. Everything okay?"

Carla hesitated. "I didn't know you had company," she said, staring down at Jessica.

Nancy threw a swift glance at Louise, then Jessica. "This is my niece, visiting for a few days." She needed a name. What were they going to call her? Fortunately, Carla didn't notice the omittance.

Carla nodded at Jessica. "Nice to meet you."

"We've been worried about you," said Nancy, leading Carla to the couch. Nancy sat beside her.

"I am fine, just fine." Carla grinned at them. "Just wait till you hear."

"Okay," said Louise.,"I'm ready."

"I'm going to help Eveline out for a while," Carla said. "Taking care of Dashaune."

"A great idea." Louise reached over to shake Carla's hand. "Eveline needs all the help she can get."

Nancy smiled at Carla's happiness. Carla had seemed so dependent and vulnerable. Maybe she was working out her own solutions.

"Help her out? She's helping me out. I don't like living alone in that apartment. Even with Quint, I'm still alone most of the time. So now I'll be watching Dashaune." Carla smiled at them. "Don't you see? I love kids. I'd like to watch Dashaune, and that'll free up Eveline. She has been so depressed." Carla stood. "But I want to thank all of you for just being there for me." She cast her eyes at the floor and mumbled, "I'm not used to that."

"We were happy to help," said Nancy. "And we're very happy for Eveline—and Dashaune too."

Carla nodded. "So now you don't have to worry about me at all."

"We were concerned." Nancy pursed her lips as she stood to put an arm around Carla. Louise walked over to Carla and patted her on the back. "You're doing a wonderful thing for Eveline."

Carla blew them a kiss. "Thank you."

Nancy watched Carla walk back to Eveline's apartment before returning to the living room. Then she turned to Louise. "Carla hasn't had many people in her life who cared about her."

"She looks so vulnerable. Just the kind to attract users and takers." Louise thumped her cane. "So what's our next step? Back to talk to the police? Tell them we've found Jessica?"

Jessica buried her face in Oscar's fur and shook her head.

Nancy saw the gesture. "I think not. At least not yet."

"Why not?" Louise's tone was belligerent. "Detective Alleso isn't the man Jessica saw," she said. "He doesn't wear a uniform."

Nancy nodded. "That's right, but I bet they all discuss their cases at police headquarters. Whoever that policeman is, he's got his ears open."

"He'd come after me if he knew where I was," said Jessica.

Then she added, her voice small. "Anyway, the police might think I had something to do with it."

"The dock master at the city docks had your name and home address, too," said Nancy. "The police picked up that information before I ever went to them."

Jessica nodded. "I thought of that—it's why I didn't go home."

Louise looked from Jessica to Nancy. "Okay," she drawled. "The bad guys would never recognize her now, so what's her name gonna be? Who is she? Where's she from?"

Nancy folded her arms and smiled at Jessica. "She's my niece, visiting from…"

"Virginia," put in Jessica. "Arlington. Outside of Washington, D.C. The way I speak would make that believable."

Nancy nodded in approval. "So why are you visiting me?"

Jessica sat up. "I work for the government, and I had, like, a week's leave. Wanted to visit my aunt in Fort Lauderdale."

"That sounds acceptable," Nancy said.

Jessica laughed. "It's close enough to the truth. Ought to make lying easier."

"We need a name for you. Any ideas?"

"Oh cool. I've always wanted an alter ego." She hesitated, then said, "Sierra."

"Sierra?" Nancy repeated.

"Sure. I've always liked that name. Sierra, uh, Bennett." She laughed. "I could be an actress with that name."

Nancy smiled at her. "Right now you are."

***

Day Care and Babysitting Services Available

The Riverside Acres Household Services Department maintains a registry of qualified and certified day care centers and baby sitters for children of all ages and for adults who need caretaker services. Contact Household Services at 954-555-4632.

Riverside Acres Household Services Dept.

Chapter 31

The next morning after breakfast, Nancy gave Jessica a pair of sunglasses. "Pool time. You did a good job with your hair, but wear the sunglasses, too. And I'll find a hat for you."

"Cool." Jessica hesitated as she took the sunglasses. "But I don't have time for that. I need to be searching for those guys. Besides," Jessica peered out the kitchen window, "I don't belong here."

Louise glanced at Nancy. "I think it's a good idea."

"But I'll look out of place. Totally. This is a retirement community."

Louise shrugged. "Yeah, but guests visit here all the time."

Nancy smiled at her. "You won't be wasting your time. You might recognize someone here, and I've got a cell phone with digital camera."

"I'm a good photographer," said Jessica grinning as she caught on.

Nancy handed the phone to Jessica. "Keep this near you. We're going out for a short while, but if you see someone suspicious, act like a tourist and take his photo. That'll hide your face and keep anyone from bothering you. If necessary, you can call 911 if you feel threatened or," she glanced at Louise, "need help."

Jessica nodded. "Of course."

"So our next step is…?" Louise waited expectantly.

"I think we need to find out how Stan is doing," said Nancy, pursing her lips, "and see if there is any action around the pink house next door."

"You're going to the dock?" asked Jessica, a doubtful look on her face.

Nancy glanced at Jessica. "We think the same people who killed Ray are terrorizing Stan."

"They're putting the screws to Stan, beating him up and trying to force him to sell his property to them," added Louise.

"That pink house next door is probably a central distribution point," said Nancy, "but not where they sell or deliver the drugs to customers."

Louise stopped pacing. "Why do you say that?"

"They don't want anyone to know about that house." Nancy grabbed at Rupert as he ran by, pulling him into her lap. "It's too important for unloading the drugs from the boats and hiding them until they can be divided into small packets for delivery to the pushers and users." She nodded to herself. "It's sheer bad luck that Jessica and Ray tied up at the next dock. Those men probably thought Ray was spying on them. Now I need just one more thing."

She walked into the bedroom, pulled out a small vial and a spray bottle and took them into the kitchen. She poured a cup of water and the contents of the vial into the bottle and shook it. "Good," she said, eyeing the contents. Then she wrapped the bottle in a plastic bag and put it in a tote bag with her lockpicking tools.

***

The three 90s club members sauntered down toward the Riverside Acres parking area. Louise adjusted her sunglasses as she frowned at George's outfit. "Gotta cut the glare."

George smiled proudly down at the bright red, flowered Hawaiian shirt he wore over periwinkle blue slacks. "I thought this was what you wore in Florida. Anyway, I beat you to the punch. Looked up Stan's number and called him to make sure he's okay."

"Has his door been fixed?" asked Nancy.

"His buddy came by and put bars on the doors and windows. Now Stan complains it's like a prison."

"Some people are never happy." Louise flicked her braid.

On the way to Stan's house, Nancy stopped at a liquor store and turned to Louise and George. "Supplies for Stan." She bought a large bottle of vodka as Louise looked on disapprovingly.

"I think he'll appreciate this," said Nancy. "He reminds me of a man from Poland I once knew. He loved vodka with a sprig of mint in it."

At the grocery store, she filled a cart with an assortment of vegetables, fruits, meats, and a large can of coffee. Louise and George followed her around the store and through the checkout lane.

"I want to make sure we're welcome," Nancy said, "and that he has enough to eat."

"Hope he invites us to lunch," grumbled George.

Nancy laughed.

They drove to Stan's house, and Nancy parked in the driveway.

"No sign of intruders. Seems quiet," said Louise as she climbed out of the car.

George insisted on lugging the cart to Stan's house.

"Hold it right there," a voice yelled at them.

"It's Nancy, Louise, and George," Nancy yelled back. "We've brought some gifts for you."

Behind the doorway, now barricaded with iron bars on a security door, Stan sat staring out, a shotgun across his knees. The windows also had bars across them.

"Whatta you want now?" Stan asked. He'd picked up the shotgun and aimed it at them.

Nancy gave him a friendly smile, but she saw that his hands

shook on the shotgun. "We've brought you some vodka and a few groceries. Your friend did a good job on the door."

Stan sat back. The bruises had yellowed and faded, but scabs persisted on his face and arms. "He did. That's a friend for you. Don't go around calling 9-1-1 before you can turn around." Stan peered out beyond them, and Nancy looked back to see the *Bonny Scot* still floating tranquilly alone at the dock. "What do you want?"

"May we come in?" Nancy asked.

"We have something real private to discuss," George said.

"I told you before," Stan said. "I don't know nothing." He laid aside the shotgun.

"We know that." Nancy folded her arms and stood back. "But we just want to talk with you for a few minutes."

Stan scratched his head, staring down at his dirty, worn sneakers. At last he said, "Come on in then." He opened the barred door.

Nancy and Louise entered, while George pulled the cart up the steps behind them. Stan peered into the cart and whistled. He and George followed the women into the kitchen. Stan helped Nancy unload the groceries, then, lovingly, the vodka.

"How do you feel?" Nancy asked, sitting at the table with George and Louise.

"How do you think I feel?" He pulled out a handkerchief and spit into it. "And nobody's taken away that boat." Stan frowned. "How am I supposed to rent dock space with that still here?"

Stan pulled out a chair, turned it around and straddled it, hands gripping the top of the chair back. "Now what do you want—and don't tell me you got a boat you wanna dock."

George grunted. "Not bloody likely."

"Who is trying to buy this place from you?" asked Nancy.

"Who do you think?" Stan pounded his fist on the table. "Those bastards at the next place. They want to own the whole damn river here, that's who. Those bastards." He glanced at Nancy. "Pardon me, ma'am."

"I mean do you know their names? Have you met them?" Nancy folded her arms on the table, keeping her eyes on Stan's face.

"I met one of 'em, yessir, Smooth-talker. I told him no way was I sellin' this property. No way." Stan pursed his lips and frowned, eyes down at the table as if remembering the scene.

"How do you know they were connected to the thugs who beat you up?"

Stan drew himself up. "Because I seen 'em all over there one time or another. They're all in cahoots. And they want my place, but they can't have it."

Louise leaned forward. "Would you recognize them if we showed you their photos?"

"Sure I would." He hesitated. "Leastways I think I would."

"What do you think is going on over there?" Nancy asked.

"Nothing I want to get involved in," Stan said, frowning. "Not healthy. And nothing since Slocum got killed and that young lady disappeared. Laying low, my guess."

"The bullet that killed Ray Slocum came from that pink house, and now you're saying the men who beat you came from there too."

"Don't you suppose the police been all over that house?" Stan snorted in derision. "And anyways, how do you know the bullet came from there?"

Nancy took a deep breath. "We've talked to Jessica, and she told us what happened."

Stan sat back. "Well, now. Is that a fact. So she's okay. That's good." He scratched his chin. "Ray was shot here, you say?"

Nancy nodded. "From that house next door." She watched him ponder this fact. "What have the police said to you?"

"Nothing. And that's what they think. There's nothing going on at the house over there."

"I see." Nancy walked over to a window and peered out. "You can't see it from here. Just the hedge. You can only see it from the *Bonny Scot*."

Stan snorted. "That's the way I like it, too."

"We think those are drug runners next door," said Nancy. "We'd like to board the *Bonny Scot* and look at the view in that direction."

Stan reared back. "Whoa. I don't need no more trouble."

Nancy held up her hand. "We'll be careful so they don't see us. The last thing we want is to draw any attention toward you—or the *Bonny Scot*. You don't need another beating."

Stan rubbed his chin. "No lights. No sign you're on board, okay?"

"Agreed," said Nancy. She followed George and Louise to the door but stopped as she heard Stan muttering behind her. She looked back at him.

"I'm a real patriotic American, you know," he said. "Fought in Nam. Them drug pushers are gonna ruin America. Makin' the terrorists rich."

"Pushers have buyers," added Nancy. "Without buyers they'd be out of business—and so would a lot of the terrorists. No money."

"You sound like Louise," George said.

Louise flicked her braid. "Makes me proud."

***

Make Your Day Easier

Many nearby stores deliver their goods for a small fee. These include Hal's Liquors, Publix Supermarket, Pic-A-Posy Florist, Jimbo's Subs and Pizza, and others. Drop by the Management Office for a list of these stores and their phone numbers.

Riverside Acres Management

While George and Louise watched dubiously, Nancy threw the tote bag into the cockpit, gripped the rail with one hand, stepped onto the trawler's gunwales and down into the cockpit. Then Louise stepped onto the gunwales herself, with Nancy steadying her in front and George in back.

George took one look at the tannin-stained water between the dock and the boat and backed away. "Not for me, thanks. I'll just stay out here on terra firma."

Louise held onto a stanchion to steady herself. "Don't blame you, but act like a tourist and walk way down toward the other end, so nobody thinks you belong to this boat." She teetered at the rail before stepping down into the cockpit. "And make sure no one sneaks up on us. Keep an eye out."

Nancy retrieved her lockmaster's tools to open the door into the trawler's wheelhouse. "I'm getting a lot of practice with this," she said, thinking back to her experience at Whisperwood.

Louise followed Nancy into the wheelhouse. It could hold four or five people if they sat on the settees along each side, but the floor space between was narrow. The cushioned settee on the left was short to make room for the tall captain's chair at the steering wheel. A varnished shelf behind the wheel held the binnacle with the engine controls on the right. The other settee left room for an opening and a ladder that led down to the galley and cabin below.

Nancy looked through the opening down into the cabin. "Maybe Jessica's things are still there." She cautiously stepped down the ladder and disappeared below. She carried the spray bottle and sprayed judiciously on the table and settees below with no result. In a minute she was back, carrying a navy blue duffel bag.

"This looks like some of her stuff. Nothing of Ray's." Nancy frowned. "I suppose the owner cleaned out his belongings. Returned them to the family, but he didn't know what to do with this."

"The police have probably been through that and taken anything interesting." Louise sat behind the captain's chair and put her cane aside.

Nancy stared out the front windows toward the pink house across the inlet. "Can't see much from this height. Mangroves get in the way, but this boat sits high in the water, so if you sat on top of this wheelhouse. . ."

"And it was high tide. . ." Louise glanced up at the ceiling.

Nancy nodded. "You'd have a good view over the mangroves and hedges to the dock and pink house. Jessica's story checks out."

Louise stared at her. "You doubted it?"

Amused, Nancy glanced at Louise. "I've met baby-faced liars before. Always good to check."

"All right. Probably most of the boats Stan gets here are small runabouts or low-lying sailboats. Nobody on them would see anything." Louise pulled out her cell phone and took a photo. "I don't think I could manage a climb up there."

"I could." Still carrying the spray bottle, Nancy stepped out of the wheelhouse and climbed up to the wheelhouse roof. She held onto the short mast for balance and studied the pink house from this angle. The view was perfect. This was what Jessica and Ray saw—minus the men, of course. She scanned the pink house and stopped at the window as she saw a curtain sway, then movement behind it. Someone over there was watching her. Harv Johnston? Tiffany? She steeled herself to stay where she was and shift her view to the river and then the opposite riverbank as if she were simply a tourist. She could almost feel the rifle sight trained on her back. She clamped her jaw and forced herself to act unconcerned, but Ray was up here when he was shot. She used her body to shield the luminal spray she aimed at the cabin roof. Bingo. A splatter of green showed up. Blood. Jessica's story confirmed. She slid down off the roof and stepped into the cockpit.

"We need to get out of here," she whispered as Louise tottered out of the wheelhouse. "Someone over there is watching us."

Louise flicked her braid. "Maybe they're waiting for the next shipment."

"Quiet. Voices carry over the water. Let's go." Nancy scanned both sides of the river. "I've seen enough."

They climbed onto the dock and motioned to George to follow them back to the car.

Nancy started the car immediately and drove away. "Someone in the pink house was watching us," she told George.

"So that's why the quick getaway." He sat back. "Did you spot the old RV parked across the river behind the mangroves?"

Louise turned around and looked at him. "An RV?"

"Hidden by the mangroves from where you were looking. I was down the dock and looking at it sideways."

Louise glanced at Nancy. "We oughta drive over there and check it out. Do you suppose it's occupied?"

"All we could see above the mangroves was the back of a building," Nancy said. Had that RV been there before? She didn't think so.

"Why is that side of the river so industrial?" Louise asked. "Waterfront property is supposed to be desirable."

"That property isn't." Nancy shook her head. "Looked more like a junkyard over there. Of course it's uninhabited—except maybe for the RV, that is."

"Where to now?" asked George from the back seat.

Nancy pulled to the side of the road, opened her map of Fort Lauderdale and studied it for a moment. "I want to see what that pink house looks like from across the river." She crossed the Seventh Avenue bridge and drove back down Broward Boulevard toward Stan's place.

George peered ahead. "The river's behind buildings on a back street."

"I'm hoping we'll recognize the area." Nancy made a left turn and drove down a side street of ramshackle white frame houses.

She slowed the car as they passed a building that could be the one they saw from the boat. Garage-type doors with smashed windows lined the front of a decrepit warehouse, and grass grew up in the concrete parking area in front of the doors. She turned into the alley beside the building and saw the *Bonny Scot* floating on the other side of the river.

They'd found the right place.

Nancy looked at Louise. Louise looked back. "Fine with me," she said. "I've got my swordstick ready."

"Let's take 'em on," said George from the back seat.

Nancy drove slowly down the alley, following it as it turned to the left to go behind the building. She studied the RV, a Winnebago, as they drove by. Streaks of mildew ran down the side of it.

"It must be abandoned," George said as they continued along the alley, which turned to go up the other side of the building. "Did you see the mildew?"

Nancy turned back onto the street. "Could be camouflage."

George raised an eyebrow. "Or all they could afford in this

year's budget. Probably use it in all their drug busts."

Nancy laughed and headed back to the condo. At the gate, the gatekeeper waved his clipboard and twirled his finger.

Nancy wound down the window.

He shook his head at her. "I gotta wonder what you've been up to."

Nancy glanced around. "What makes you say that?"

"The cops. They been here again, and now they're waiting for you." He inclined his head toward a bench on the walkway leading to the elevator.

Nancy recognized Detective Alleso in a dark navy suit and white shirt, leaning back against the bench, deep in conversation with another man Nancy didn't know. Both of them seemed hot and annoyed.

***

**Afternoon Excursion:
Mangroves and the Rivers in South Florida**

Join naturalist Bob Segert for a boat tour up both forks of Fort Lauderdale's New River. He'll point out the mangrove species and birds that thrive along the river in this fascinating three-hour excursion. Thursday, 1 to 4 p.m. Cost: $50. Includes snacks and soft drinks. Sign up at the Riverside Acres office.

Notice approved: Riverside Acres Advisory Council.

Chapter 33

As Nancy debated turning around and leaving, her eyes met the detective's. He signaled to Nancy to park the car and meet them at the elevator.

"We're in for it now," George muttered.

"What do they want?" Nancy asked as she parked the car. "George, get out of the car on the side away from them and keep low while you walk away from me. Louise and I will handle this. If we get arrested or taken to the police station, we'll have you to call for help."

"Good idea." George hid behind the cars and crept across the parking lot in the opposite direction while Nancy and Louise walked toward the detectives. Nancy spotted Jessica waving at her from the side of the pool. Before Nancy could signal her to stay away, Jessica tossed a towel over her shoulders and ran up to join Nancy at the elevator, ignoring the man at Nancy's side.

"How'd it go?" she asked, before Nancy could say a word.

Detective Alleso's eyes flew from Nancy to Jessica and back again. "Good afternoon," Alleso said, nodding to Nancy and Louise, "and to you, Ms. Cantwell, I believe?" He smiled with narrowed eyes.

Nancy clutched Jessica's hand. Too late to hide her. Detective Alleso had Jessica's photo, but then she was a long-haired blonde. Now she was a short-haired brunette wearing a hat and sunglasses.

No matter how well-trained he was, he couldn't assume that was Jessica. All he had was a photo. He was bluffing.

"Good afternoon," Nancy replied. "I'm glad to see you." She gestured toward Jessica. "And this is my niece, Sierra. Perhaps we can go up to my condo and talk?"

"Just what I was going to suggest." Alleso turned to the other man. "And this is Detective Hernandez."

"Pleased to meet you." His voice sounded faintly Hispanic. Brown eyes. Brown hair. Muscular body as if he worked out. Both men wore suits and ties.

Feeling like a child about to be punished, Nancy led the way to the elevator and then up to the third floor and down the corridor to their apartment. She could hear the dogs barking and turned to the detectives. "They're good watchdogs, but they're harmless."

Hernandez shrugged. "No worries. I like dogs."

Oscar and Rupert barked and circled in ecstasy at having Nancy home again. They sniffed at the detectives, but their tails wagged, and once they had greeted everyone, they settled down. Both detectives eyed the slobber on their pants.

"Won't you sit down, officers," said Nancy. "I'll get some paper towels." She walked into the kitchen, using the time to think of some way to protect Jessica.

They sat in the chairs. Nancy sat close to Jessica on the couch.

"We're glad that Ms. Cantwell has been found," began Alleso.

"I'm sorry, but this is my niece, visiting from up north."

"And I'm sorry," Alleso leaned forward, "but this is Jessica Cantwell."

Nancy stared at him, and he stared back. He was not going to back down.

After a long silence, she asked, "How did you recognize her?"

"If I were hiding, I'd change my hair too.

Hernandez pulled out a cell phone. "We'll call off the search now."

Nancy shook her head. "I don't think you should. Not yet."

Hernandez raised an inquiring eyebrow at her.

"She saw who shot Ray Slocum," said Nancy. She put an arm around Jessica and hugged her. "The reason we didn't come to you immediately," Nancy smiled rerassuringly at Jessica, "is because Ray was on the *Bonny Scot* when he was shot by a man at the pink house. Jessica was there, and she saw the men who shot Ray. One of them wore a policeman's uniform."

"And it wasn't Halloween," put in Jessica.

Alleso raised an eyebrow at Hernandez and then sat back. "Wouldn't be unheard of," he said. "Was it a Fort Lauderdale police officer or a county sheriff's officer?"

Jessica shrugged. "What's the difference?"

Hernandez laughed.

Alleso leaned forward. "Sheriff's officers wear green and white and a Stetson type hat. Fort Lauderdale police wear dark navy. Okay?"

"Dark navy," said Jessica without hesitation. "Regular police uniform."

Detective Alleso turned to Hernandez. "One of our guys."

"But he didn't shoot Ray," Jessica added. "He was just standing there."

Alleso nodded. "By the way, we've got the house staked, and," he stabbed a finger at Nancy, "we don't appreciate amateurs endangering themselves and others by meddling. You were spotted there, and they called us."

"We simply wanted to check Jessica's story for ourselves," said Nancy. "And see how Stan Jaworsky is doing."

"Excuse me," said Hernandez. "You're dealing with murderers

here. They see you, you're dead."

Jessica gulped and nodded. Nancy glanced at her. Jessica was trying hard not to cry.

Alleso stopped writing in his notebook. "So after Ray was shot, what happened?"

Jessica shook her head. "I don't know. I got out of there fast and have been hiding ever since." Jessica hesitated. "Except that maybe I can identify some of the men."

Nancy patted Jessica's hand as she watched the detectives. "Do you know anything about the consortium that owns the pink house?" asked Nancy. "Who owns the consortium?"

Alleso frowned. "We're looking into that. It's none of your concern. What is your concern and ours, is protecting our prime witness here, Ms. Jessica." He sat back and studied her. "And getting descriptions of the men who were on deck at that house when Slocum was shot."

Jessica sat up. "I want to help."

Hernandez brought out his own pad and pen. "How many were there?"

"Five." Jessica gulped. "Ray and I were sitting on top of the wheelhouse, and we were laughing and talking and, like, looking at the guys on the deck at the house down the river. Then the next thing I knew, Ray was dead." She hugged herself and bit her lips. Tears spilled down her cheeks.

Nancy set a box of tissues next to Jessica.

"Okay." Alleso waited a moment before asking the next question. "What can you tell us about the cop? Young? Old? Stout? Thin?"

Jessica blew her nose. "Youngish, I think. Thin. Seemed to be in good shape. Clean-shaven, short brown hair." She was silent a moment, staring down at her hands. "He was so," she hesitated, "standard issue, like. I'm not sure I could identify him. In a line-up, I mean."

"What about the man who shot your boyfriend?"

Jessica waved the tissue. "He wasn't my boyfriend." She was silent a moment, staring down at her hands. "It all happened so fast. A man wearing one of those Cuban shirts, like, a guayabera, blue, and smoking a cigar, looked like a con man, actually. Scam artist. Kind of slick. Almost bald, a bit of a paunch, not much, but he didn't look like he worried about keeping in shape." She took a deep breath. "Anyway, he pointed to us, like, then the guy next to him shot Ray."

Nancy sat up. That description sounded like Harv Johnston. And he lived at the pink house. Sergio and Mike Glazer must have been two of the other men there, and probably one of them shot Ray. Nancy snapped her fingers. Yes. Jessica recognized them at the River Fest. She realized the others were staring at her. "I think I can name most of the people on the dock," she said. "But let Jessica go on."

Alleso nodded. "All right. What about the others."

Jessica sat silently, eyes closed. "I'm trying to remember." She opened her eyes and looked at Alleso. "One of them seemed to be quite elegant—the way he held his glass. A wineglass, like. Also gray suit. Pink shirt. Open collar."

"I know who he was, too," said Nancy.

Jessica blew her nose. "And the policeman, of course. The other two I saw again later at the River Fest. I pointed them out to Nancy."

"And I had met those two men downtown." Nancy smiled as Alleso and Hernandez said simultaneously, "What?"

She arched an eyebrow. "At least I know how they were intro-duced to me. Might be fake names, though." She'd been every bit the doddering old lady. They would have thought she was harmless, and so, yes, they would tell her their real names. Especially since she knew Johnston and Connolly anyway.

Hernandez waited, his pen hovering above the notepad.

"So who are they?" Alleso barked at Nancy. "And who introduced them to you?"

"A few days ago, I was having lunch in a café on Las Olas Boulevard." Nancy explained the situation. "Johnston was with Bob Connolly. Connolly lived here and worked with some tourism group.

"Oh yeah. Him." Alleso was getting testy. "So then what happened?" Nancy watched Alleso and Hernandez with her bright birdlike eyes. She didn't miss the almost audible groan that passed between them at the mention of Connolly's name.

"Johnston lives in the pink house and runs a driver service company, and," Nancy said, "he fits Jessica's description, too."

Alleso raised an eyebrow. "Go on."

"Johnston and Connolly were having lunch with those two men Jessica pointed out," Nancy leaned forward, "so when they got up to leave, I. . ." she smiled modestly, "I, er, said how pleased I was to see them again and Johnston introduced me to the other gentlemen."

Hernandez scribbled something into his notepad. "And their names?"

"Mike Glazer and Sergio Carrera."

Hernandez wrote down the names. "We'll see if we can get a make on them."

Nancy nodded. "At least we know they have some connection to Connolly and Johnston." She stopped and glanced at Jessica. "And Jessica recognized them. In fact, I'll bet we know who everyone was on that deck." She paused, chin in hand, "except for the policeman, of course."

"We'll pursue that," Alleso said. "Connolly is dead now." He looked over at Hernandez.

Nancy saw an unspoken message pass between them. She threw them a question. "He was killed in an odd accident. Could the truck have been tampered with? And the driver also seems like a bad apple to me." She described Quint and watched for any clue to what the police might think.

"Sheriff's Department. Traffic detail." Hernandez said in an emotionless voice. Not giving anything away. "Not our concern."

Alleso sat back and eyed Jessica. "Not a bad job. I made a lucky guess about you—that you were Jessica, I mean. And that was only because I knew this lady here," he gestured toward Nancy, "was searching for you. And you were the right age."

Jessica dabbed at her eyes but managed a smile. "So my disguise was pretty good."

Alleso laughed. "Damn good. No one would recognize you as the young blonde girl on the boat."

"Cool." Jessica managed a teary smile. "I was worrying that I'd have to stay hidden till, like, you got those guys."

Alleso stood. "I want you to come down to police headquarters and hang around. See if you recognize any of the cops who come in. Go through some photos." He glanced at his watch. "Tomorrow afternoon work for you?"

Jessica nodded.

"There's something else you should know," said Nancy.

Alleso folded his arms. "What?"

Nancy reminded them about the attempts on Peter's life. "He's been trying to find criminals on the "Most Wanted" list. He put up flyers on them in the den," she said, "if you want to take a look at them."

"I'll get the names." Hernandez pulled out a pen and pad and stepped into the den.

"So far," Nancy added, "we've seen a resemblance between Harv Johnston and one of the flyers, but perhaps you could check some of the residents out, using your databases."

"We already have someone assigned to Peter Stamboul's case, but we'll fill him in. Anyone in particular?" asked Alleso.

"Johnston, of course. Susan Withers," said Nancy, "and what about Quint Sandstrom?"

"We'd sure like to get those guys on the dock." Alleso said. "Bad business there."

Hernandez headed for the door. "Right now," he threw a glance at Jessica, "she's our main witness. Keep her wrapped up, okay?"

"Of course." Nancy smiled at Jessica. "But I also want to give you this sheet of numbers we got from the Mandell Consortium. Maybe your people can make sense of it."

Nancy found the paper in the den, gave it to the detectives, and ushered them out. She was glad the police were on the job. They'd catch those guys yet. She glanced at Louise. "They made a lucky guess about Jessica, but we were right about the Winnebago. The police do have that pink house staked out."

Louise flicked her braid. "We probably looked pretty silly."

Nancy laughed. "They weren't pleased."

Louise snorted. "Yeah? And why haven't the police caught that scum already if they're so good?"

***

Special Program: Fraud Alert!

The Fort Lauderdale Police Department will present a special program for seniors on frauds and scams that target the elderly as victims. Don't miss this important meeting. It may save your money, your livelihood, and your security. Next Thursday, 10 a.m., the Club Room. For more information, contact the Management Office.

Riverside Acres Management Office

Leaving Jessica with the dogs, Nancy and Louise strolled over to George's apartment to report. George gaped at them from the door. "I've been waiting for a phone call. So what happened?"

Nancy laughed. "We got caught all right."

"Caught?" George put a hand on his hip. "So how come you aren't dead?"

"By the police, George," Louise said. She walked into George's apartment, followed by Nancy. "They've got the pink house staked out."

George pursed his lips. "Of course they've got the place staked out. I coulda told you that. "

Louise just looked at him. "So why didn't you?"

"You were having too much fun." George sank down onto the chaise longue next to the phone. "And then when I got back, I had some napping to do." He gestured to the phone. "But I was right here if you needed me."

Louise stood. "Come on, Nancy," she said in disgust, "let's leave ol' trustworthy George to his nap."

"Wait a minute." George stumbled over to block the door. "What happened?"

"We've got all the culprits identified but the policeman," Nancy said, "and with Jessica as the star witness, he'll be riding a tumbrel in a day or two."

Nancy and Louise returned to Peter's apartment, and Nancy changed into her bathing suit. She needed to work off the stress of the last few hours. She swam several laps, then as she climbed out of the pool, she heard someone call her name.

Eveline ran up to her, her face beaming. "I've got to tell you what's happened." She stopped to catch her breath.

Nancy led her to the poolside chairs under an umbrella. "Good news?" she said as she sat.

Eveline bounced into the other chair. Her face was radiant. "You know Carla, the woman who lives next to you?"

Nancy smiled. She knew what the good news was. "Of course. She's very nice."

"You know I've been so depressed." Eveline clasped her hands. "Dashaune likes her."

"I know you were finding things difficult," Nancy ventured.

"A nanny twenty-four hours a day, seven days a week," Eveline caught her breath, "that's all I was, but I couldn't see any way out. I mean, what else could I do?" She stopped and frowned to herself. "And live with myself, I mean."

"So what's happened?"

"I got me a job, and," Eveline paused dramatically, "Carla's going to watch Dashaune for me." She clasped her hands and raised them in victory.

"That's wonderful." Nancy smiled at Eveline's obvious happiness.

"I'll pay her, but okay. Important thing I get out of the house and can talk to grown-up people a couple of hours a day."

"And that helps both of you," said Nancy. She had been worried that Carla, karate or no, endured abuse because she depended on Quint for income. Now she was earning her own. Not very much but hopefully enough to shore up her self-esteem.

"I've got to run." Eveline bounced up and waved at Nancy. "I am so happy!"

Nancy joined her to walk to the elevator. Harv Johnston had one hand on the door, holding it open for them. "Hello, ladies," he greeted them, waving a cigar as if it were a baton.

Nancy hesitated, but Eveline walked in. She couldn't let Eveline go up alone with him. Nancy followed her and gripped the rail on the opposite side of the elevator from Johnston. He must have seen her on the boat staring over at the pink house. What was he thinking? She glanced at Eveline. He wouldn't try anything here with Eveline as a witness. Surely.

She couldn't help coughing at the cigar stench. She noticed Eveline was holding her breath. Johnston got off on the third floor when they did but strode rapidly down the hall ahead of them.

Eveline took a deep breath, waving her hand in front of her face. "Whew. Does he even smell that thing?" she whispered.

"We sure could," said Nancy.

Nancy watched him until he disappeared into Carla's apartment. To see Quint no doubt. Did Carla know how dangerous he was? She walked into her own apartment and smiled at Jessica, who sat reading with the dogs on each side of her.

"So what do we do now?" she asked. "I can't just sit here and do nothing while they may or may not find the murderers. I should be out trying to find those guys. I can identify them."

Nancy checked her watch. "Just relax tonight. I've got some ideas for tomorrow," she said.

***

Mind Those Allergies!

South Florida's humid, hot climate is a wonderful host to molds, mildew, and plants that can make life miserable for

allergy sufferers. They can also suffer from exposure to co-
lognes, perfumes, scented candles, and potpourri that the
rest of us might think delightful. Cigars and cigarettes also
trigger allergies. Please consider others when you use these
products. And if you do suffer from allergies, come visit the
Health Office for tips and medications.

The Riverside Acres Health Team

Chapter 35

The next morning, Nancy glanced at Jessica's T-shirt and shorts and said, "We're got to get you some more clothes."

"Cool. This is all I've got left," Jessica said. "Thanks for bringing my duffle bag, but the clothes in there are mildewed. I need a few other things too."

"Clothes," said Nancy. "And a short visit to the hardware store."

"Hardware store?" asked Louise, looking up from the newspaper.

Nancy didn't reply. The dogs clamored around her as she pulled treats out of a jar and threw them into the living room, sending the dogs after them in a mad scramble while she and Jessica exited the apartment. Nancy saw the questioning look on Jessica's face. "They always want to go with us," Nancy explained. "Makes me feel guilty."

"Me too," said Jessica as she donned the sunglasses and hat. "I'm ready."

Nancy hoped Jessica would see Harv Johnston as they walked down the corridor and out of the building, but he didn't appear. She pulled Jessica with her into the Management Office.

"Do you have any old newsletters?" she asked the receptionist. "Maybe an obituary for Mr. Connolly? He was such a nice man. . ."

The receptionist nodded. "He was, but we don't publish a newsletter for the residents. Depend on the bulletin board over there." She nodded toward the elevator. "We posted the notice about the memorial service. Next Saturday, 11 a.m. Episcopal Church on Las Olas." She walked back to her desk and sat down behind her computer monitor.

"Thank you," Nancy called over to her. "I'll be sure to attend." She nodded her way out of the office. She'd already looked through the photos she'd taken with her phone, but none of them had a clear photo of Connolly. She'd check the Web.

An hour later, shopping trip done, Nancy and Jessica, unrecognizable in hat and sunglasses, sat by the pool, chatting with Carla as she watched Dashaune in the wading pool.

"He's a good boy," Carla said, nodding toward Dashaune.

"You're a real treasure for Eveline," said Nancy, pleased that their intervention had helped. . .for once.

"I've been so busy that I haven't been home at all," said Carla. "Been staying over at Eveline's in the evenings, too. She's a lot of fun. . .now." Carla smiled at Nancy. "Poor Quint has had to fend for himself." Her eyes moved beyond Nancy to Jessica. "You oughta meet my son."

"Really?" said Jessica. "I'd sure like to." She glanced at Nancy.

Nancy pursed her lips. Meeting Quint might be fine if he were innocent but dangerous if he weren't. He was too much like a night club bouncer and other tough guys she'd run up against in the early days of her career.

"I used to worry about him," Carla continued. "But he's a grown man. He can take care of himself for awhile. I've got Dashaune to worry about now."

Nancy nodded and patted Carla's hand.

Carla threw down her towel and ran after the little boy. "Just a minute. Dashaune!" He had headed for the deep end of the pool.

She caught him and took him by the hand to her chair, picked up a towel, and began drying him.

"I think it's time for a nap," she said and waved at them as she headed for the elevator.

"So now what?" asked Jessica. "No one's around."

"I'm watching." Nancy scanned the building walkways. "I'm sure he'll come by any time now."

"And then what?"

"Nothing. I want to confirm that he was one of the men on the dock." Nancy glanced at Jessica. "Anyway, we don't have to do anything else right now."

"Sure is boring." Jessica laid her towel on the chair and walked over to the pool, then she jumped in. "Wonderful!" she called out to Nancy and began swimming a lap.

Nancy watched Jessica as she debated whether to put on her own bathing suit. She lay back in the chaise longue, feeling the warmth of the sun. The pool area was so bright, so colorful. Sparkling aquamarine water, red hibiscus, pink and white oleander, rustling palm trees. Whiffs of chlorine and mown grass in the breeze. Drowsiness crept over her.

She heard her name called and peered up at the balconies. Susan was shaking out a small rug and waved. "I'll be right down," she called.

A guilty feeling crept over Nancy. She had neglected Susan the last couple of days.

"Hi!" Susan scraped another chaise longue across the concrete and placed it next to Nancy. "Who's your friend?"

Nancy hesitated. Had Susan really guessed at Jessica's identity or was that a mistaken impression. "A niece," she said. "Sierra Bennett. Visiting from up north. Hadn't expected her but glad to see her."

Susan laughed. "How nice." She winked at Nancy and turned to watch Jessica lazily floating in the pool.

Nancy glanced over at Susan. She was sharp. Had she bought the story?

"So what happens now?" Susan asked.

"We're concerned about Stan Jaworsky. He was beaten up, you know. Could have been the same people who killed Ray."

Susan shaded her face with a hand. "I wouldn't think so. He lives in a bad neighborhood. That's all."

"Maybe so."

Susan frowned at her watch. "Oops. Got to get some groceries. Let me know what I can do." She walked toward the elevator, nodding at Jessica as she passed. She looked back at Nancy and smiled.

Jessica emerged from the pool, shook out her hair, and walked over to Nancy to pick up a towel. "Who was that?"

"Susan. She helped us find you." Nancy walked toward the elevator with Jessica following behind. Susan had guessed who Jessica was. Who would she tell? Most people here had no idea what Nancy and Louise were trying to do. Whether that was Jessica or not meant nothing to them, but Nancy didn't like the idea that she was dangling Jessica in front of everyone like. . .like bait.

***

Later that morning, Alleso called them. "Just reminding you. I've got some photos ready. Come down as soon as you can."

"We can be down after lunch." Nancy raised an eyebrow at Jessica, eating a sandwich in the kitchen.

Jessica nodded. "Totally."

Nancy and Jessica arrived at the police department at one and claimed seats in the lobby to wait for Alleso.

"Just sit there looking glum and don't call attention to yourself or appear interested in anything or anyone," Nancy cautioned her.

"If you see someone you recognize, squeeze my hand."

"Cool." Jessica nodded. She switched her sunglasses to the cheap, fake glasses she'd bought the day before, and they both watched the parade that came and went, speculating on whether they were visitors, police officers, lawyers, or what. Forty-five minutes passed. Nancy did not feel a squeeze on her hand.

Alleso at last appeared, out of breath and rushed. He apologized for the delay, led them to the small conference room and opened a loose-leaf binder he carried. "Just go through these and tell me if you recognize anyone." He placed the open binder in front of Jessica and stood by her side.

Jessica leafed through page after page of scruffy characters. Some looked pathetic, hopeless, addicted. Some looked mean. Nancy watched for any sign of recognition or hesitation, but Jessica's face was expressionless. The stack was half done when Jessica stopped and hovered over a photo that Nancy recognized. She glanced up at Alleso, but he was watching Jessica.

"You recognize him?" he asked.

Jessica nodded. "He's the man who ordered Ray to be killed."

Nancy saw Alleso press his lips together and nod.

"Are you sure?" he asked.

Jessica studied the photo. She nodded. "Yes, I'm sure. He stared right at us and then…and then," her voice broke, "the man next to him shot Ray."

"Why did he shoot him? What were you doing?" Alleso asked.

Jessica drew herself up. "Nothing. We were just sitting on top of the cabin to get out of the heat below, you know. Kind of, like, talking and looking down the river. We saw them, like, hauling sacks out of those speedboats—Ray called them cigarette boats—and the next thing I knew that man was aiming at me, but I ducked and Ray was hit." She shivered. "I got out of there fast."

Alleso looked at Nancy. "Harv Johnston."

She nodded. "Real estate developer, I'm told."

Jessica sat back in surprise. "You know him?"

Nancy winced. "I wouldn't say I know him, but I've met him. He lives in the pink house."

"Then I'm right," Jessica said, chewing her lip.

"I just wanted confirmation," Alleso said. "That's why I slipped his photo in there. We suspect he's involved in some crooked stuff, including drugs but haven't been able to pin anything on him." He grinned at them. "So far. A background check turned up nothing more than two years old. Blank. That alone was odd. But he's a scumbag, that's for sure."

"He also runs a driver service," added Nancy.

"We know about that, too, and we're looking into it. He ropes in innocent people to be drug mules, hiding drugs in the cars they drive north."

"I think you should go through the rest of the photos," Nancy said, pushing the stack towards Jessica.

"I don't recognize anyone else." Jessica continued her way through the photos.

"I've seen Johnston with Connolly, Glazer, Carrera, and Quint, who lives next door." said Nancy. "And Connolly lived in my co-op building too. I have their photos on my computer, and I've got fingerprints too." Nancy turned to Alleso. "What about the people behind the consortium that owns the pink house? And the stake-out—has anything come of that?"

"The consortium is apparently an association of several corpo-rations dealing in land speculation. We've talked with officers of the corporations, who claim no knowledge of the river property or how it's being used. They referred us to Harv Johnston, who," Alleso studied his fingernails. "supposedly manages some of the rental properties. That house is probably one of the rentals, they say."

Jessica closed the book. "Nope." She sighed.

"That's fine, Jessica." Nancy patted her on the back. "Recognizing Harv Johnston as the leader gives the police an excellent starting place." She turned to Alleso. "Seems to me if you shadow Johnston, he'll lead you to Glazer and Carrera. You must have something on them. Their backgrounds are pretty unsavory, I would bet."

Jessica balked. "I was scared before, but now I'm getting really scared. Whoever ordered Ray shot is a dangerous man. Totally. I only saw them for a few seconds, you know, and I was so shocked. But what if I'm wrong about Johnston? I'd hate to wreck his career and be mistaken." Tears came to her eyes. "I read enough articles in college about how unreliable eyewitnesses are."

"You're providing supporting evidence," said Alleso, folding his arms as he looked at her. "We're pulling together everything we need to get a conviction."

Nancy put an arm around Jessica. "Several people were involved. If you recognize the others, that will confirm your identification." She pushed her chair back.

"Wait a minute. You're not done yet," said Alleso. He pulled a thick file folder out of his brief case. "I had Human Resources give me the file photos they have of our police officers." He laid it out in front of Jessica. "See if you recognize the officer you saw on the dock."

Jessica leafed through the folder. "He was younger than most of these," she said, laying aside a number of personnel forms, each with a photo in the upper right corner. "Could have been one of these." She pointed to a pile of forms. "I don't think I can narrow it down any further. I only saw a glimpse and then mainly the uniform."

Alleso picked up the pile. "All right. Gives us a place to start.

Now I'd like you to dictate a statement and sign it." He hiked up his pants and turned to Nancy. "Keep her under wraps. A lot of people would like to do her harm, and they seem to hover around Riverside Acres."

Nancy agreed. No more poolside time for Jessica.

***

Social Living At Its Finest

The Management is pleased to announce that Riverside Acres Retirement Cooperative and its many congenial social amenities and highly esteemed residents will be featured in an upcoming article in *Southern Lifestyle*. Just one more reason to be proud of "your place in the sun."

Riverside Acres Management

Nancy and Peter sat on the balcony of his ocean-front hotel room. The ocean spread out in front of them, white caps kicking up here and there and a warm breeze sweeping in from the south.

Peter licked his finger and held it up in the breeze. "Nor'easter coming in, for sure," he said. He smiled at Nancy. "Wind's from the south; then it'll swing around to the west and then to the north. That's the wind pattern here."

"I'll get my sweater out," said Nancy, brushing aside this superfluous information. "We've made some progress."

Peter leaned toward her. "You found out something about the residents?"

"Harv Johnston and Bob Connolly were working together on a real estate deal," Nancy said, "and the police think they were involved in drug dealing, using the driver service as transport."

"The driver service! That means when I drove north, I might have been one of their mules." He leaned back. "Imagine that—me, a drug mule."

"That's not all." Nancy paused for effect. "Jessica has identified Harv as the man who ordered Ray Slocum's killing."

"Holy smokes! He's a drug dealer and a killer." Peter sat upright and whistled. "He's probably the man who was after me." He ran into the living room and shuffled through the folders on his desk. He lifted up one and waved it at Nancy. "Harv Johnston." He opened it and picked up the printout of the photo Nancy had e-mailed him. "I told you he was the man in the flyer. Are the police arresting him?"

"I think they're trying to pull together information on the whole operation first." Nancy handed him a packet of cardboard. "I also brought these. I lifted fingerprints off car handles and glasses." She flipped through the pieces of cardboard. "I gave Johnston's to the police, but we can add the other fingerprints along with the photos to the folders."

"I weeded the possibilities down to twenty-three. We can go through them one by one and compare them with the flyers." Peter brought the stack of folders to the dining room table. Nancy followed with the flyers and the cardboard stack. "We might need photos or fingerprints to fill out their file, though."

"All right," said Nancy. "First, Harv Johnston." She picked up the photo while Peter found the flyer. They laid them side by side.

"Look at his nose, jaw, and ears. He's almost bald—makes that easier." Peter shoved his chair back and reached for the magnifying glass on the nearby end table. He held the glass up to examine the faces on flyer and photo. "Looks like a match to me." He handed the glass to Nancy.

She took a couple of minutes, poring back and forth from photo to flyer. Finally she nodded. "A match. He's the brother in the brother-sister pair."

"So the question is, where's the sister?"

"And are these the criminals who tried to kill you?"

Peter pursed his lips. "Kind of a stretch to think there are several unrelated killers at Riverside."

"Let's go through all these folders." Nancy set to work, starting with Susan's file.

"Till they round up that gang, it's still dangerous for me to go back there and dangerous for Jessica too." Peter shook his head. "Maybe she should come over here and stay with me."

"I agree," Nancy said. "The killer would never expect Jessica to be at Riverside, but it's still too dangerous for her." An uncomfortable memory of how easily Alleso had identified Jessica crossed her mind. Susan had guessed correctly, too.

Nancy searched through the papers on the desk to find a blank sheet and a pen. "Now I need a little extra help from you."

Peter came over to the desk. "What?"

"Tell me how the wiring works for all those lights you've got around the apartment. I want to make some changes."

They spent an hour going over the wiring system before Nancy checked her watch. She leaned over and pecked Peter on the cheek. "Gotta go. Hang in there. You'll be home soon."

"I hope so," said Peter. "I sure hope so."

***

Use Caution With Electrical Appliances

Be careful with hair dryers, space heaters, toasters, and other small appliances. Be sure to turn them off when you leave your apartment, and don't use them near sinks, basins, or tubs.

Riverside Acres Management Office

Nancy returned to Riverside around three, eager to work on a new project. She spread the tools she'd bought on the shopping excursion with Jessica out across the kitchen table along with the wiring diagram Peter had drawn. This project reminded her of the days long ago when she and her dad had fought the school officials and finally acquired permission for her to take a shop course as well as physics. She'd endured a lot of flack from the boys in the course, but at least she had acquired a rudimentary knowledge of electricity, plumbing, carpentry, and tools. All girls should know this stuff was her opinion then and even more so now.

Louise looked up from the newspaper. "What are you planning to do with all that?"

"You'll see," Nancy said. "Here's my pride and joy." She pulled an odd gadget out of a box. Listen." She pressed a button and a loud alarm sounded. Oscar and Rupert ran behind the couch.

Louise snorted. "So what's that for, aside from scaring dogs?"

"I'm making a few adjustments to Peter's lighting system." Nancy stepped on a floor board and a string of lights lit up across the wall over the couch.

"I thought you had turned all that off," Louise flicked her braid. "I have to admit I was impressed at first. Especially after the kitchen lit up when I sat in the armchair."

"I did." Nancy hefted the alarm in one hand and pliers in the other. "Now I'm turning off all the power in this apartment. Won't be long."

Louise turned back to her newspaper. "Good luck."

A little while later, Nancy replaced a floor board, wiped her hands, and grimaced as she used a chair to pull herself up from the floor. "Done. Now for the test." She flicked the main switch for Peter's extra lighting system. Then she stepped on the third floor board, which triggered a shrill alarm that sent the dogs scurrying behind the sofa again before Nancy flicked it off. "It works." She smiled at Louise. "I disabled most of Peter's connections, only left the floor board and a chair. That's all we'll need to send up an alarm."

"Whew. And that's enough testing, I hope." Louise looked at Nancy over her reading glasses. "All our neighbors will complain." She picked up her cane and hobbled over to see Nancy's work. "So that's our burglar alarm system?"

"Yep." Nancy grinned at Louise. "I got to thinking about Peter's escapes from death and Jessica's identification of Harv Johnston. And Quint lives next door. He works for Johnston and is probably in on their dirty schemes somehow. They must think you and I know something too. We're dangerous to them."

"Don't forget George." Louise tottered back to the couch.

"We needed some kind of alarm system."

Louise pursed her lips. "We've got Oscar and Rupert." She smiled as the dogs barked at hearing their names.

"Our neighbors are too used to hearing them bark. They won't pay attention."

"True. Too true." Louise frowned. "We do try to control them though. It's not as if we let them bark incessantly." She stroked Oscar's back. "We pay attention to you, don't we, boys?"

The dogs wagged their tails and wiggled.

Nancy walked to the wall switch next to the kitchen door. "Our alarm is off right now, but if we flip this switch. . . ." She flipped the switch. "Then the alarm will sound if a person steps on the third floor board or sits in the armchair to the right of the sofa." She flipped the switch to turn off the system. "Just in case," she said.

Someone knocked on the door. Jessica. "I was down at the pool," she said.

"Tomorrow morning, first thing, I'm driving you to Peter's hotel in Pompano Beach. Safer there," Nancy explained. "You can take a room close to him and the two of you can protect each other." Nancy glanced over at Jessica. "You'll like Peter. He can fill you in on what we've been doing."

"Cool, but I hope I can go home soon." Jessica said, heading for the bathroom. "I'll shower and get dressed." A few minutes later, she returned wearing the new shorts and T-shirt Nancy had bought for her. She paused in the doorway to announce, "Someone's spilled the beans."

Nancy looked up. "What do you mean?"

"At the pool, that woman you were talking to yesterday—the blonde, well-dressed one—walked by and, like, said hello to me by name, and I don't mean Sierra Bennett. She, like, caught me by surprise."

Louise flicked her braid at Nancy. "I told you that Susan was a problem. I'll bet she's busy telling everyone in the building about Jessica and us. She's a born gossip if I ever saw one."

Nancy called Susan's number.

No one picked up after ten rings. Nancy hung up. She looked at Jessica. "Get your things. I'm taking you to Peter's right now."

The doorbell rang, and the dogs ran to the door, barking.

***

Permits Necessary for Home Improvements

Residents must submit written requests to make improvements to their units. This is necessary because we live in a community. Changes made to one unit impact other units. Changes also must conform to the standards and style of the building. The Residents Council, your friends and neighbors, are on the board that oversees building improvements, repairs, and other changes. They want to help.

Riverside Acres Management Office

Nancy shushed the dogs and opened the door. Susan stood on the threshold with a smile and a large tote bag hanging on her arm.

"May I come in?" Susan's smile did not match the menacing, almost angry, look in her eyes.

Nancy stared at her, frozen. Her eyes darted to Jessica. Susan's eyes followed Nancy's as she stepped in past Nancy who still gripped the doorknob.

"Hello, my dear," Susan said to Jessica. "We searched all over for you. I'm so glad you're safe." Oscar sniffed at Susan's shoes, and Rupert stood on his hind legs to sniff in her bag.

Susan walked into the living room, nodding to Louise, who sat on the sofa. Nancy let go of the doorknob and followed behind Susan, but her eyes were on the tote bag. What was in it? Nancy had never seen Susan carry such a thing before. Could Susan be the sister in the "Most Wanted" flyer? She was the only one at Riverside besides herself, Louise, and George who knew about Jessica.

Nancy studied Susan's face. No resemblance to Johnston that she could see, but Susan could have had plastic surgery, and she certainly bleached and curled her hair. Peter's folder on Susan had detailed the story Susan had told Nancy when they drove to the marinas. Peter had even found her husband's obituary. The photo didn't match the flyer picture of the missing sister either. But she and Peter could have missed telling details, made mistakes in collecting the information. Susan had an air of menace about her now. If she were the guilty sister, did she have a weapon in the tote bag? Nancy gave Louise a long look and a slight nod toward the tote.

Louise saw Nancy's look. She stretched, then stood, tottering on her cane. She lurched into Susan, bumping the tote. It hit the edge of the couch with a soft thud.

"Sorry," Louise muttered. "Cane slipped."

Nancy breathed again. The bag didn't clink as if a heavy metal object, like a gun, were inside.

It could be wrapped up, though. The tote bag didn't swing freely, so it held something heavy.

"Have a seat, Susan." Nancy gestured to the couch. She had to get Jessica out of there. Now. "Louise, put on some coffee. Jessica and I have a quick errand to run." She looked at Susan. "We'll be right back."

"Oh, but I have something for Jessica. . ." Susan waggled the tote bag.

Nancy didn't want to see what was in the bag for Jessica. "We have to leave right now. We'll be back."

Susan looked dismayed."Well, hurry right back then. I'll just wait here."

Louise shot Nancy an irritated look. "Yes, you hurry back, now, you hear?" Louise flipped the switch for the alarms as she stepped into the kitchen.

Jessica picked up her bag of possessions and followed Nancy out the door. "She seems like a nice person," Jessica said as they walked to the elevator. "Even if she is gossipy."

"Probably she is a nice person," Nancy glanced back toward the apartment, half expecting to see Susan running after them. "But we can't take chances with you."

Forty minutes later, Nancy returned to Riverside alone, having rejected Peter's offer to take them to dinner. She didn't want to leave Louise with Susan any longer than necessary. She felt relieved that Jessica was hidden away with Peter. Now to deal with whatever Susan had in mind.

She walked in to find Louise fuming and Susan frowning with the tote bag in her lap.

"Sorry. Took longer than I thought," said Nancy. "Hope you had a nice visit."

Louise flicked her braid and sat with arms folded, pushing her lips in and out. She didn't respond.

Susan looked up at Nancy. "Well! At last you're back. You were certainly gone a long time." She looked behind Nancy. "And where did you stash Jessica?"

"Had to drop her off . . .at the store." Nancy took the armchair.

"I thought we were friends, Nancy," said Susan, anger more than hurt in her tone. "I've certainly tried to help you."

Nancy glanced at Louise. "Of course we are. I don't know how we would have navigated Fort Lauderdale without you."

"So why am I shut out now?" Susan asked. "Why didn't you tell me you'd found Jessica?" Susan waited for an answer, frowning with arms folded.

She certainly was angry, Nancy thought, hesitating. "We've appreciated your help, but more is involved than we knew. Please, it's critical that you keep Jessica's whereabouts to yourself."

"She's all right, isn't she?" Susan asked. "How did you find her?"

"Nancy's got brains and know-how," Louise said from the armchair.

"Of course," said Susan coldly. She picked up the tote bag.

Nancy moved her foot closer to the floor board with the alarm attached. She tensed and held her cup ready to throw.

Susan saw the two of them staring at her and put her hands on her hips. "Am I making you nervous?" She laughed. "You seem to think I have a dangerous weapon in here." She flapped the bag. "Must be all the recent goings on. I just thought Jessica might need more Florida clothes. Nicer ones."

She reached into the bag and pulled out a frilly white blouse and a flouncy skirt. She held up the blouse. "Hope she likes it. Guessed at her size." She reached back into the bag. "Also, a box of coconut patties. Florida stuff." She held up the box. "She's been through a lot. Just wanted to give her something to feel good about."

"That's really nice of you," Nancy stammered, a huge wave of relief sweeping over her. Susan was okay. Of course she was, but of all the people Nancy had met at Riverside, Susan seemed the most logical villain. She spent way too much time ingratiating herself with them, and she was on friendly terms with Harv Johnston.

But if Susan wasn't the sister in the "Most Wanted" flyers, then the next logical person, a person Nancy fervently hoped it was not, was. . . .

***

Florida Souvenir Sale!
Next Thursday and Friday, poolside, Florida Treasures Co. will hold a sale of their fine Florida products from artwork to designer clothing. This is your opportunity to pick up gifts, souvenirs, and items for your own use at discount prices. Don't forget. Poolside from 10 a.m. until noon, next Thursday and Friday.

Riverside Acres Management

Chapter 39

Nancy watched Susan walk to the elevator, feeling both relieved and worried. She turned off the alarm switch and Louise called George. "Come on over here. We gotta meet." She put down the phone. "He's coming."

Nancy leaned back in the armchair and fanned herself with her hand. "Whew! I thought she had a gun in that bag. Didn't think I'd get Jessica out of here alive."

"Me too," said Louise. "Sure acted suspicious. I had my cane ready when she took out that box. Floored me when it turned out to be coconut patties. She's just a busybody with too much time on her hands." She turned to Nancy. "Don't you ever leave me alone with her again."

"She has been very helpful," added Nancy with a smile.

"Too helpful." Louise hit her cane on the floor.

Nancy heard a rap on the door and let George in. Louise glanced at him and yelped. "I'm blinded! Blinded!"

"You like my outfit? It's pure Florida." George grinned, looking down at the pink and yellow striped polo shirt and pink slacks. "What's going on?" he added.

Louise filled him in. George frowned. "The way Susan's been tagging around with us, I coulda sworn she was one of those 'Most Wanted.'" He sat down in an armchair. "Guess that means I have to give back her GPS."

"The police are closing in on Harv Johnston." Nancy tapped her lips with a finger thoughtfully, looking over at Louise. "Susan's personality seemed to fit with someone like Johnston. Carla seems so cowed, so intimidated by life."

"Can't believe it could be Carla. She needs a lot of help, for sure." Louise pulled on her vest. "Maybe his sister is one of Susan's friends. That way she can keep tabs on us through Susan. Maybe it's someone we don't even know. Or maybe the sister isn't involved. Let's go out to dinner." She eyed George's outfit. "Maybe we'll get a free dinner since we're bringing the entertainment."

George swanned out the door. "Jealousy. Pure jealousy."

Several hours later, after dinner and a stroll down Las Olas Boulevard, they walked back to Riverside Acres. George glanced at his watch. "Can I join you gals for a cup of decaf before I head back to my apartment?"

"Sure," said Nancy, greeting the dogs. Louise stepped into the kitchen while George took an armchair.

A knock on the door sent the dogs barking. Nancy opened the door to Carla, who held a measuring cup in one hand and a purse in the other.

"Can I borrow a cup of sugar?" she asked, her eyes sweeping across the living room. "Hello, Louise, Mr. Burroughs."

Nancy looked at her in surprise. Where was the shyness Carla usually exhibited? Carla seemed different.

Carla glanced down the hall toward the bedrooms before turning to Nancy. "Where's your, uh, niece?"

"Come in," said Nancy, stepping aside.

Carla entered but remained standing near the door. She set the cup down on a nearby end table.

"My niece is away for a few days." Nancy gestured toward the couch. "Have a seat. How's Dashaune?"

"Dashaune is fine. I think I won't sit," said Carla with a grim smile. The nervous, fluttery Carla was gone. Nancy felt a quiver of fear. She was afraid her suspicion would now be confirmed.

It was. Carla reached into her purse and pulled out a gun. "But I invite you to sit." She pointed the gun at Nancy.

A chill ran down Nancy's back. She saw Louise's surprise, but George's face had turned blank.

"Louise, you too." Carla nodded at Louise, standing in the kitchen doorway. "Out of the kitchen. Sit down on the couch next to Nancy. In fact, I want all three of you to sit right there." She waved the gun at the couch. George moved to the couch.

"Sit down!" Carla pulled out a cell phone and used her thumb on one hand to tap in the number. She waved the gun at them. "When will your niece be back?"

"I don't know," mumbled Nancy.

Carla spoke into the phone. "I've got them here," she said. "Now what?" She listened a moment, folded the phone, and put it back into her pocket. "We'll wait for the other guests." She walked over to the window and closed the blinds, then unlocked the front door.

The dogs, sensing something wrong, began barking at Carla. She kicked at Oscar, which brought Rupert to the defense. He tugged at Carla's slacks, distracting her. Nancy saw her chance, grabbed Louise's cane, and swung it down hard on Carla's gun hand. The gun spun out and fired into the wall as it slid across the floor. The dogs barked and ran around joyously, tripping Carla who was gripping her wrist where Nancy struck it.

Nancy grabbed Carla's wounded arm and yelled, "George, get the duct tape in the kitchen drawer!"

Carla twisted around to bite Nancy's hand.

"Watch it!" Louise warned. She retrieved the gun and waved it at Carla. "Stop that right now." She pushed the dogs aside with her foot. "Quiet down, you two." She pointed the gun menacingly at Carla. "Now!"

George brought in the duct tape just as the front door opened. He stopped. Nancy and Louise stared at the man who stalked in. Mike Glazer. The dogs sensed the menace and growled at him.

The gun wavered in Louise's hand from Carla to Glazer. Nancy froze as Glazer used Louise's indecision to grab her gun hand and wrestle the gun away from her.

"Get up," he said, nodding at Carla. Carla pushed Nancy aside and scrambled to her feet. The dogs retreated toward the bedrooms, then stood facing the strangers and growling. Their stance showed they meant business, but their diminutive size took away the threat. Carla shooed the dogs into a bedroom and closed the door. Nancy could hear them whining.

"Enough of them," Glazer said, still holding the gun on the three friends.

"Give me the tape," he said to George. "Roll it to me." George set the tape on the floor and pushed it toward Glazer who threw it to Carla. "We're gonna take a little ride." He leaned against the wall, pointing the gun at them. "While we're waiting, sit down on the couch." He waved the gun back and forth at them.

Nancy joined Louise and George back to sitting on the couch.

"See if anyone's in the hall," Glazer said to Carla. He turned back to Nancy. "Hands out front on your knees."

Nancy obeyed but focused her mind on how to flip the electric switch to activate the alarm. She nudged Louise who looked at her and nodded as Nancy's eyes moved from a direct stare at Louise to the light switch on the wall. Louise understood at once, then nudged George and repeated the eye movements. He stared back, a puzzled look in his eyes, but of course he had never seen Peter's light show so he just shrugged.

Nancy glared at Carla. Not the shy, timorous, abused little woman after all. Anger boiled up inside Nancy. She and Louise had trusted this woman and tried to help her. Now their misjudgment could cost all of them their lives. Even Jessica's.

At least Jessica was tucked away up in Pompano. She liked Jessica. Imaginative. Intelligent. Tough. Look at the way she'd stuck around after the murder of her friend instead of running back home to her parents. Nancy could hear the dogs whining. More innocent victims. They'd tried their best, but their best was a joke.

"Harv's on his way," Carla said.

Nancy's hope rose. Surely the police were watching him.

Carla nodded at the three huddled on the couch. "Does Carrera have the van ready?"

"Sure," said Glazer. He winked at Nancy watching him from the couch. "First class accommodations for the three of them. Where's the other one?"

"Away for a few days." Carla nodded toward Nancy. "She says."

Glazer grunted. "We'll get her to talk and grab the girl when she comes back."

Carla kicked Nancy's leg and grinned as Nancy winced. "You couldn't leave well enough alone, could you? You had to keep prying. I'd finally found a place where I could make friends and help out, be useful, but you had to come along and ruin it." Her voice was tearful. "I loved that little boy. I could have been happy here." She wiped her eyes and kicked Nancy again.

Nancy closed her eyes, willing herself not to moan. Those kicks hurt like hell. She didn't think anything was broken, though.

Carla continued to rant. "It's all your fault." Then she looked at Louise. "Louise would have helped me. Now it's too late."

Nancy kept her mouth shut, but she recognized Carla's self-pity.

Nancy had never been a social worker, but she'd heard the same stuff from other criminals. Nothing was ever their fault.

The door opened and Johnston walked in. Maybe the police were giving him a lot of rope to get the whole gang. Nancy studied Carla's face. Surely Carla must be the sister, but Nancy couldn't see any resemblance either to Harv Johnston or to the sister in the flyer. Carla had gained weight, changed her hair style and color and affected a diffident attitude that had thrown all of them off.

Johnston closed the door and was now leaning against it, arms folded. He frowned at Carla. "We'll get rid of these losers, and then we'll still be okay here," he said. "This set-up is too sweet to give up because of a bunch of meddlers."

Carla stared down at her hands. "First it was Peter. He got too close, but he's gone. Now we've got these three to get rid of, and we have to find that girl. I didn't bargain for this. You said I'd be safe here. I like this place. I don't want to move."

"We're not going to move. We'll be just fine here. Nobody suspects us. I'm planning a big accident for these three."

Carla glared at him. "It better be a good one. You sure didn't impress anyone with the way you got rid of Peter. Four tries at him and you failed at all of them." She laughed, then spied Nancy's purse. "Good thing I took care of Abby." She rummaged through the purse, pulling out Peter's keys. "I'll drive their car out of here. Maybe a big accident in the Everglades."

"A boat accident," Johnston said, "is what I had in mind."

Nancy closed her eyes, as if unconscious or asleep, but her ears were open. None of this gang realized the police were closing in on them.

"We need to find out what they know first," said Johnston. "They've been talking to the police."

Glazer shook his head. "This ain't the place for that."

"Are the police still watching the house?"

Glazer laughed. "The Winnebago's gone from across the river. They don't have nothing to go on, nothing connects us to that place, and we scared that old man at the other dock shitless. He's afraid to come out of his house. A few more treatments and he'll sell us his property all right."

"That's good then." Johnston nodded and stroked his chin. "We can bring the boat around to that dock." He narrowed his eyes as he glanced at Nancy. "We'll make sure we don't have witnesses this time."

There was a long silence. Nancy opened her eyes slightly to see Johnston frowning down at his shoes and Carla chewing her fingernails. Glazer remained standing, leaning against the wall, pointing the gun at them. Nancy edged her way down the couch toward the switch.

"Call Carrera," Carla said to Johnston. "Tell him to take the van to the back of the parking area away from the gate and the lights and wait for us."

Johnston checked his watch. "Ten o'clock. They go to bed early here. Nobody will be around." He tapped in numbers on his cell phone and delivered the message.

Carla frowned at the captives. "I'll get Peter's car after we haul them out of here." She glanced around the room. "One more thing." She sat down at the end of the couch and lifted up the lamp and fiddled with the base. "I thought they'd found the bug." She looked at Nancy and laughed as she walked into the den. She ripped the flyers off the bulletin board and tore them up. "You won't need these any more," she said. Johnston sat in a chair, staring at the floor and chewing his lip.

Nancy shifted her body an inch closer to the switch. Carla peeked through the window blinds and nodded to Glazer.

"Get up. No false moves now," Glazer warned, motioning toward the door. "I'm ready to shoot the lot of you." He pulled Nancy up and pushed her toward the door.

Nancy resisted, but she was now too far away from the light switch.

Louise stood and lurched against the wall, attempting to fall against the switch, but Johnston grabbed her arm and pushed her towards Nancy. Glazer pulled George up so roughly that George fell against the wall, hitting the alarm switch and then putting his foot down on the now-activated floorboard. The alarm emitted a loud piercing siren. George jumped. Glazer pointed the gun at him while his eyes searched the room. The dogs howled and scratched at the bedroom door.

Carla fumbled with the switch to turn the alarm off. She kicked Nancy again. "Peter showed all of us his lights. I know what you did."

The kicks hurt. Nancy bit back the tears as she heard a knock on the door. She felt a thin sliver of hope. Some neighbor had heard the alarm and was checking on them. She took a deep breath, ready to scream for help, but Glazer saw her intention and brought the gun close to her head. She heard Carla open the door and step out into the hall, closing the door behind her.

Glazer's menacing closeness stymied Nancy's hope to signal for help. She couldn't see the door past Glazer, which meant that the neighbor probably didn't see what was happening in the apartment. Glazer waved the gun back and forth across the three of them as they listened.

Nancy heard Carla laugh and a mumble from someone else. Then Carla said, "Only a false alarm. Nancy's cooking something in the kitchen. It turned on the smoke alarm. Everything's okay."

Nancy couldn't hear the neighbor's reply. Carla returned. She frowned at Nancy. "You think you're so smart, but look at you." She stalked into the kitchen.

Nancy watched her. She could see the light glistening from the thick puddles of dog slobber on the kitchen tile. That stuff was slippery. Carla's foot skidded on the slime. She fell down hard. Nancy winced at the thud.

Johnston growled to Glazer, "Don't let them move," as he ran to Carla.

"My hip. It hurts. And my ankle." Carla began crying. "Are they broken?"

Nancy craned her neck to see Carla. Something was wrong with her leg, all right. Oddly crooked.

Johnston sat in a kitchen chair and held his head in his hands. "No, no, no," he muttered. He lifted his head and took Carla's hand. "Baby, we got to take care of this problem here," he nodded at Nancy, "as soon as we get them out of here, I'll carry you back to your apartment and call for an ambulance to take you to the hospital. Say you fell on the sidewalk. I'll come by later and pick you up from the hospital."

Carla tried to get up but collapsed. "I don't think I can walk."

Johnston patted her back. "Don't you worry. We'll take care of you."

Carla closed her eyes and lay back on the floor. "Those damn dogs," she muttered.

One down, Nancy thought as she watched Carla moaning on the floor. Nancy winced at Carla's pain but could do nothing to help. That left the three of them against Johnston, Glazer, Carrera at the van, and maybe Quint. Three against four. But where was Quint now? Was he really Carla's son or just another member of the gang?

Johnston turned to Glazer who used the gun to gesture at

George. Johnston pushed George out the door and turned to Nancy. "You too," he said.

Glazer and Johnston escorted their victims to the van. Nancy hoped to meet someone in the hall or elevator, but Johnston was right. The residents here usually went to bed early. No one was about. At least Jessica was safe. She glanced at Louise. Her face was white, and she held her wrist, the same one that had been broken in the last adventure of the 90s Club. Nancy herself felt stiff and sore. The three of them were in this fix because of her. She had no right to endanger all of them, just to prove she could still succeed as a private detective. So far, she hadn't proven anything of the sort. Somehow she had to get them out of this situation.

Louise glanced at Nancy. "It's all right," she whispered. "All those kicks from Carla probably hurt you worse."

George looked at Nancy and winked.

They reached the van, which was parked under the farthest reaches of the parking lot lights. Nancy recognized Carrera, leaning against the van, smoking. Johnston duct-taped the captives' wrists together behind their backs and stuck strips across their mouths, then pushed them one by one into the back of the van. He threw a heavy rug over them. Someone started the engine and moved the van forward, halted for the gate to open, then drove out onto the streets of Fort Lauderdale.

***

Parking Lot Rules

Delivery and moving vans are not permitted in the parking area after 6 p.m. Please be considerate of your friends and neighbors and help keep Riverside Acres safe and pleasant. Schedule your van visits from 9 a.m. to 6 p.m. only.

Riverside Acres Management.

Chapter 40

In the back of the van, the captives wriggled out from under the rug. The fresh air swept across Nancy's face, and she inhaled it through her nose with relief. She could tell that George was having a difficult time with a taped mouth and his allergies. His sneezing and dribbling nose stretched the tape covering his mouth enough so that he could bite into it. Nancy watched his suffering, wishing she could help, but then she saw him chewing and understood. Good old George.

The van arrived somewhere, probably the gate of the house on the inlet. This suspicion was confirmed when Nancy heard someone unlock the gate and then drive the van through. The van stopped, and they were pulled out, the tape around their ankles was cut, then they were marched into the house. Johnston turned on a light.

Glazer ignored all of them, tossing the gun on the dining room table as he stepped into the kitchen. "Any beer in this place?"

Nancy shielded George with her body, so the others wouldn't see the frayed piece of tape covering his mouth.

Johnston pointed to the couch and pushed Louise toward it. Nancy and George followed, but Johnston held Nancy back. "We have plans for you," he said. He pushed Nancy ahead of him to a chair next to the dining room table and pushed her onto it. He yelled to Carrera, "Tape their ankles." He nodded toward Louise and George. Carrera took care of that and then joined Glazer in pulling tabs on beer cans in the kitchen.

Johnston ripped the tape from Nancy's mouth. She gasped. He leaned over her. His voice menacing and ugly, he asked, "What did you tell the cops?"

She shook her head and tensed up, waiting for the blow. Looking past Johnston, she could see George using his teeth to tear at the tape on Louise's wrists behind her back. Nancy began babbling incoherent nonsense phrases to keep Johnston's attention on her, but behind his back, she saw Louise freeing herself in a few seconds, then ripping the tape off her mouth and turning to free George's hands. They tore the tape off their ankles with their fingernails. Nancy struggled and babbled even louder in the chair, making as much noise as she could to keep Johnston's attention on her while Louise and George raced for the front door.

But before they could reach the door, it was thrown open. Johnston turned around. Louise and George froze.

"Here you are!" A brute of a man stood in the doorway. Quint. "You owe me. Where's my pay?" The deferential tone Nancy had seen him use when talking to Johnston before was gone. Now he was terrifying.

And he blocked the door.

Quint surveyed the scene. "What's going on here? I think you rats are about to run out on me."

"We have business to take care of," said Johnston, casually picking the gun up from the table. "Why don't you just go in and get a beer."

"I want out. Now. I did the job. Give me my money." Quint's hands were balled into fists.

"We'll get it to you," said Johnston smoothly, walking into the living room, gun in hand. "We don't have it here, though." His eyes went from Quint to Louise who stood staring at him, a stunned look on her face, and behind her to George.

Johnston trained the gun on her as he confronted Quint.

Glazer walked out of the kitchen, beer in hand. "Hey, Quint, come on in here. Grab a brew."

Quint stood his ground. "Where's the money?"

Nancy watched in horror as she saw Johnston aim the gun at Quint. He meant to shoot. Quint must have seen that too, because he knocked Johnston's wrist to the side, sending the bullet into Quint's shoulder.

Quint stared at Johnston, then he roared and used his good arm to smash his fist into Johnston's face. The force sent Johnston's head into the wall and he fell to the floor, head bleeding. Carrera rushed toward Johnston, but Quint stopped him with a kick to the kidneys. Glazer stood open-mouthed in the kitchen doorway.

Quint turned toward Glazer as if to attack him but slumped instead to the floor. Blood had splattered everywhere and still dripped from the wound.

While George gaped, Louise ran to Nancy and tore at the duct tape binding her. They turned to the door, but Glazer had picked up the gun and now blocked the door. "Where do you think you're going?"

Carrera sat on the floor against the wall. He pulled out a cell phone. "Guess we need the police, doncha think?" He tapped in numbers and waited.

Nancy felt a fleeting sense of relief quickly dispelled as she remembered the policeman Jessica had seen on the dock. The police. Just which police was he calling?

"Dylan? Carrera here. Got some pigeons we need to boil. River place. Yeah. Okay. I'll wait."

Quint lay still on the floor. The pool of blood grew larger.

"Quint needs an ambulance," Nancy said, forgetting her own pain.

Harv Johnston moaned.

"And so does Johnston."

"Don't forget Carla," Louise added.

Carrera walked over to stand next to Glazer, giving Quint a fierce kick to the kidneys as he passed. Then Glazer sank onto an armchair, still pointing the gun at the captives. "Flesh wound, that's all." He prodded Quint's shoulder with his foot and watched the blood flow from it. "Alligator bait," he said.

***

Chapter 41

Glazer motioned to Nancy, George, and Louise to move back against the living room wall. Johnston groaned as he struggled to sit up. He seemed dazed. "My sister," he mumbled. "My sister needs an ambulance."

Glazer glanced at Carrera. "Get some chairs from the kitchen," Glazer said. He waved the gun at the prisoners. "I'm thinking they need a long rest."

Carrera brought out the chairs. Nancy watched. The three 90s Club members now faced only two men—Glazer and Carrera. She smiled at the thought; she had to take hope somewhere. Three against two. She had thought Johnston was the boss, but now it seemed Glazer had taken control, and Johnston and Quint were captives too.

"Sit," said Carrera to the captives. He turned to Johnston. "You too. Get over there." He looked back at Glazer. "We need another chair."

"What are you going to do?" asked Glazer.

"What does it look like?" Carrera sneered. "I don't think we need this baggage any more," he snickered, nodding at Johnston and Quint, "do you?"

"Never did." Glazer threw the duct tape to Carrera who began winding it around Johnston's wrists.

"What do you think you're doing?" Johnston's voice sounded

high and shrill. "You don't have the connections for this business."

Carrera pasted a strip across Johnston's mouth. "I think we can make some. Our own connections."

"Don't need to hear any more from him," Glazer said while Johnston twisted and bounced in his chair.

Nancy watched Carrera once more wind the tape around Louise and George's wrists and ankles. She looked for any weakness in their captors. Anything. But in only a few moments, Louise and George were both again bound and helpless.

The faint stirring of hope Nancy had felt a moment ago dissipated. In all her years as a detective, even last summer when they'd almost been killed at Whisperwood, she had never felt so desolate, so hopeless. There would be no rescue. Her alarm hadn't worked, and their escape attempt didn't succeed. She didn't think they'd be given another chance. She'd lived a long life, probably much longer than she deserved. She could die now. But she'd had no right to bring Louise and George into it. Then she thought about Jessica. So vibrantly alive. At least Jessica was safe. And Peter. The murderers would not get away. So perhaps she had succeeded to some extent. And at her age. She almost smiled.

Carrera pasted tape across George's mouth, then moved on to Louise.

"Okay, tape that one's mouth," said Carrera, "but not that one." He nodded at Nancy. "We need to find out what they told the police."

Glazer taped Louise's mouth, then stepped back.

Nancy suddenly realized that they had not bound her. Her hands and ankles were free. This was a miracle. A small one, but a miracle, nonetheless.

Another miracle happened. Glazer set the gun down on the table within her easy reach. Two miracles. Glazer felt very sure of himself. Nancy willed herself to stare at Glazer and not the gun.

Carrera had sunk into the armchair in the living room. "Wonder where Dylan's at?" he said.

Glazer walked up to Nancy and slapped her face hard. "What'd you tell the police," he said, his fist next to her mouth.

The slap hurt worse than Carla's kicks, but it brought Glazer so close to Nancy that his legs almost straddled hers. She lifted one of her legs quick and hard.

Glazer shrieked and fell moaning to the floor. Nancy got the gun.

"What the...?" Carrera sprang out of the chair.

"Get back in the chair," Nancy ordered. "And stay there."

She held the gun on Carrera as she stepped over to Louise.

"I don't have a knife. Lift your wrists up," she said to Louise.

Louise lifted her wrists, and Nancy bit into the tape to cut it. Once she had the beginning of a tear, she ripped it apart with her hand and pulled the tape off. Duct tape might be tough, but it was easy to tear once you got the tear started.

"Get the rest of the tape off and free George." Nancy saw that Glazer had sat up. "Lay face down on the floor," she said to him, motioning with the gun. She turned to Carrera. "You too." Carrera stood up and walked towards her.

"You're not gonna shoot me now, are you?" Carrera grinned at her. "You been brought up nice. Now you just be a nice girl and give me the gun." He walked closer.

Nancy shot him in the knee. Carrera screamed and collapsed. *Good.* She glanced at Glazer whose face had turned white. *Glazer won't try anything now either.* She kept an eye on both of them as she studied the gun. A nine millimeter Beretta Nano. She'd practiced at the range with similar handguns, but this one had a better feel to it. They'd probably loaded it before showing up at the apartment, and so far three shots had been fired.

"Louise, George, are you okay?" she asked. She could hear Louise and George behind her but didn't want to take her eyes off Glazer and Carrera.

"Fine. Good move, Nancy," said Louise.

"George, go over to Stan's house and call the police. Hide in the shrubbery if you hear anyone coming. Louise, you call them from here. Use the land line. Try to get Alleso. Tell them we need an ambulance too."

"Will do." George hobbled out the door. Splitting George and Louise up would give them an advantage over any more surprises.

Louise made the call and then tottered over to stand by Nancy, taking a wide berth around Carrera, whose eyes were shut and teeth were chattering. "He might be going into shock," she said. "I'll throw a blanket over him."

"He looks bad," agreed Nancy, "but I had to shoot him just to take him out of operation, not to kill."

"Don't take that gun off Glazer," Louise said as she hobbled into a back bedroom and returned with a blanket. She threw it over Carrera. "That oughta hold him."

Nancy frowned at this cast of crooks. "I told the police all about you and your gang of murderers and drug dealers," Nancy said. "They know how you shot and killed Ray. And how you're using this house. The police have all the details." Nancy crossed her arms, letting the gun dangle from one hand. "And a signed statement from a witness. They're just waiting while they put together the case."

Behind her, she heard Johnston struggling with the tape, but it was wound as tightly around his wrists as it had been around hers.

"She's signed a statement to that effect," Nancy added. "They're onto all of you."

Nancy waited. She could hear a clock ticking, then she caught the sound of a car driving up to the house. It stopped. Nancy heard the crunch, crunch, crunch of footsteps on dead leaves.

"Had to act like it was a routine call," a voice said as the door opened..

A young man in police uniform stepped into the living room. He put his hands on his hips and frowned as he surveyed the bloody scene. "Well, well, well. What have we here?"

Was he a good cop or the bad one? Nancy kept the gun in her hand, waiting for his next move. She could shoot him before he got his gun out of the holster. She watched him survey the scene and click through possible reactions to it. The name badge on his uniform said he was Dylan Smith. Bad cop, then, but ol' Dylan wasn't too swift.

"Looks like you did a good job overpowering these criminals," Dylan said at last. "Now why don't you hand me that gun, and I'll take over."

"Stay right there," said Nancy. "We have a call in for the police and an ambulance. Let's just wait till they get here."

"But I took the call. You can see I'm the officer in charge of this scene. Now just hand me that gun."

He saw the blood around Carrera and knows I'm willing to shoot. "Stay right there!" Nancy said again, gesturing with the gun.

Surely Alleso and his men were still watching this place. Surely they were suspicious of Dylan anyway. But they may have ruled out this house, and Dylan was only one of many cops. Why would they suspect him necessarily? Maybe they were watching someone else.

The police knew all about this gang. At least that's what Alleso had told her, but if Dylan answered the call, Alleso might never hear about it.

She hoped George had reached Alleso. She sighed, then stopped to listen. She heard more rustling outside that sounded like footsteps. Surely there weren't any other gang members around. Hope again sprang into Nancy's heart. Alleso?

"Police. Open up!" The voice was loud and authoritative. Nancy glanced at Louise.

"What the hell?" Nancy heard Dylan curse, his eyes darting back and forth as if seeking escape.

"Police. Open up!" The voice said again. Then with a loud crash, the front door flew open and four police officers entered, guns drawn. The lead officer yelled, "This house is surrounded."

Dylan turned to greet the police. "I was answering a call and found this set-up," he said. "I was just going to call for back-up."

Detective Alleso took Dylan's gun and patted him down. "Sure you were." He handed him over to another police officer. "Take him." He looked at the two groaning bodies on the floor and then at Nancy.

"You did this?" he said with grudging admiration.

"I only shot one—in self defense.

Quint opened his eyes.

Alleso stood up. "Ambulance on the way."

Quint nodded and closed his eyes again.

Alleso nodded toward Johnston.

"Glad to get this one under wraps," Alleso said.

"And his sister." Nancy rubbed her wrists. "She's either back in her apartment or in the emergency room." Nancy told him the situation.

"You've had a busy night. I'll check on her," Alleso said, making the call. "My people will be happy to meet her at the hospital."

"He's one of them too," Nancy nodded at Quint.

Alleso shook his head. "Yeah. We been after this piece of. . ."

Nancy opened her mouth but, looking around her, she had

nothing to say. Her hands trembled and legs wobbled from the tape restraints and the terror. Her face stung, and she felt bruised and achy from the kicks. Leaning with one hand on the wall, she walked down the hall and examined each room. This house made such a suitable depot. And the car delivery service, how convenient. Using innocent travelers to carry drugs from place to place. The legitimate money they made with the car deliveries must seem like meter change. No wonder they wanted Stan's place too. She returned to the living room where Alleso sat, writing notes in a small pad he'd taken out of his pocket.

"Quint was a mechanic," Nancy said. "He worked for Johnston fixing up the cars."

"Sure." Alleso glanced down at Quint. "Mainly he rigged the cars with drug caches hidden in the doors and other places. We've been watching this gang and almost had the whole thing wrapped up, then you people got involved." He stepped aside as Glazer and Carrera, handcuffed, were pushed forward and out past Nancy and Louise.

The ambulance drove up, its red lights flashing on the walls and windows. Two paramedics entered, paused, then one went to Quint and the other to Johnston.

"What about Quint?" asked Nancy. "Wasn't he Carla's son?"

"They played it that way. It was a joke between the three of them. Johnston wanted to keep him handy, which was just fine with Quint."

Alleso stopped and stared at Nancy's face. "I guess we got here in the nick of time."

"You could have come sooner," Louise grumbled. "But at least I'm glad we didn't become alligator food," added Louise, "endangered or not."

"You can't imagine how glad we are to see you," Nancy said as she remembered how hopeless their situation had seemed just a few moments ago.

"Uh huh. Right. Now why don't we all sit down here, and you tell me what's been happening."

***

First Aid Classes Coming Up

Learn how to save a life. It might be someone you love. The Riverside Acres Health Team in cooperation with Broward County General Hospital will offer first aid classes, including CPR and the Heimlich Maneuver in the Club Room every Monday morning at 10 a.m. Classes start Feb. 1 and will last six weeks. Register now at the Riverside Acres Management Office. Everyone needs to know first aid.

Riverside Acres Management

Chapter 42

Late the next afternoon, Oscar and Rupert barked at the knock on the door. Nancy shushed the dogs. Susan stood outside, smiling.

"You've been busy," she said. "Thank goodness you're all right. Everybody here is talking about the excitement and wants to know what's been going on."

Nancy invited her in as Louise straggled out of the bedroom. "Just a few abductions, shootings, murder, and mayhem," said Louise, yawning. "Nothing to fuss about. Normal stuff living with Nancy."

"I don't think I could have been that brave," said Susan. "I know you hurt my feelings when you didn't let me in on what was happening, but now I'm glad. Duct tape and shootings." She shivered. "I wouldn't have liked that at all."

She turned with surprise as Peter, beaming with pleasure and dressed in a pink guayabera and white slacks, walked out of the kitchen carrying a tray of tall glasses. "My tropical rum punch," he said. "We ought to celebrate."

"Looks like I rescued you from Pompano just in time," laughed Nancy as she took one of the glasses.

Susan picked up the next glass with a smile at Peter. "You won't believe what's been going on here while you've been whooping it up in St. Thomas," she said.

The front door opened and Jessica appeared, her hair wet from a swim and bathing suit covered by a short terrycloth robe. "Look who I found," she said, dragging in Detective Alleso.

"Came by to check on all of you and wrap up the case," he said, smiling at Nancy.

"I'll call George." Louise stepped to the phone and tapped in the number. They waited. "George, come on over. You want to be part of this." She hung up and grinned at the rest of them. "He's coming."

Peter passed the drinks around and then brought out chairs from the kitchen. George walked in just in time to grab one. "Resting up from my vacation," he said. "Been fun, you know."

Nancy laughed at the irony, but then turned to Alleso. "How is Carla?"

"Broken hip and twisted ankle, like she said." He took a long sip of the drink. "She'll be laid up a long time, but she's not going anywhere else but prison."

"She pretended to be so helpful," Louise said, "but she fooled us all. Would never have pegged her for the villain."

"Sad story. Her older brother may have roped her into crime," said Nancy. "I think she really wanted to live a quiet, normal life. And she really did seem to love Dashaune."

Louise snorted as she looked at Susan. "My bets were on you," she said.

Susan sat up, surprised. "Me? I've always been a law-abiding citizen." She stopped. "Well, pretty much."

Peter shook his head. "I never realized. . . Carla seemed like a sweet little old lady. . .like so many others here."

"Never make assumptions," said Nancy. "Some people think I'm a sweet little old lady too."

Peter laughed. "I happen to know you use that image to find out what you want to know. Great for your business."

"Retired now," Nancy said, beaming. Maybe not retired, after all. She still had good years ahead of her. She had come to Fort Lauderdale with two assignments: To protect Peter and find out who was threatening him and to find Jessica. She had succeeded with both. The 90s Club had succeeded with both. Nancy couldn't help smiling at Louise and George, holding hands now. *And we still have almost a week before we have to go home. Fast work.*

Jessica turned to Detective Alleso. "I still don't get it. Those guys at the other dock were smuggling dope? They thought Ray and I were spying on them?"

"As you've guessed, Harv Johnston and Carla Sandstrom were a brother and sister act wanted for murder, mail fraud, drug dealing, and other crimes. They changed their appearance and their names, lived apart, and Carla took on Quint as further camouflage. Since he worked for them, he agreed to pose as her son."

"And all this time I thought he was abusing her," Peter said.

Louise laughed. "I was ready to take her to a shelter."

"All those thumps we heard were her practicing karate," said Nancy.

"What? That sweet little old lady?" Peter looked at Nancy in astonishment. "Karate?"

"I thought Harv and Carla knew each other," said Susan, "but only from meeting each other here."

"Johnston formed the consortium to buy the river house and use it as a base for his drug smuggling operation."

"We were glad to collar Dylan," put in Alleso. "He was a bad apple anyway. Discipline problems, and we suspected a habit."

"He's the reason I didn't want to go to the police," said Jessica. She clasped her hands together. "Poor Ray."

No one spoke. Oscar crept closer to Nancy's feet, and Rupert jumped up on the couch to sit next to Louise.

Finally, Peter raised his glass. "A toast," he said. "To the River-side Acres 90s Club," he nodded at Nancy, Louise, and George, "to Jessica," he lifted his glass to Jessica, "and to our hero, Detective Alleso, who got us all out of a hell of a fix."

***

Luxury Retirement Condos for Rent and Sale

Make your Florida dream come true. Riverside Acres on Fort Lauderdale's scenic New River offers a beautifully landscaped gated community for your retirement years. Minutes away from broad sandy beaches on the Atlantic Ocean, world-famous Las Olas Boulevard, and award-winning museums and library. We have several luxury condos available now!

Magazine Ad for Riverside Acres